No Ordinary Billionaire

THE SINCLAIRS

J.S. Scott

This is a work of fiction. Names, characters, organizations, places, events, and incidents are either products of the author's imagination or are used fictitiously.

Published by Montlake Romance, Seattle
www.apub.com

Amazon, the Amazon logo, and Montlake Romance are trademarks of Amazon.com, Inc., or its affiliates.

ISBN-13: 9781477849736
ISBN-10: 1477849734

Cover design by Laura Klynstra

Library of Congress Control Number: 2014916986

Printed in the United States of America

No Ordinary Billionaire

THE SINCLAIRS

CHAPTER 1

It was completely annoying that it had been sunny and bright on the day of Patrick's funeral. Not one single cloud in the sky as a sea of men in uniform, their badges all covered with a black horizontal stripe to mark the loss of one of their own, milled around a cemetery. Their expressions were solemn, and many of them were visibly sweating from wearing heavy uniforms in the Southern California heat.

Detective Dante Sinclair's eyes were riveted to the screen as he watched the video on his laptop computer, a huge lump in his throat as he listened to the customary last radio call go out for Detective Patrick Brogan, unanswered. Patrick was officially proclaimed to be 10-7, out of service, and the dispatcher declared how much he would be missed.

Dante gulped for air as he slammed the laptop closed, wishing like hell that it had been a shitty, rainy day during the funeral. Somehow it didn't seem fair that the services had been held on just the kind of day Patrick had loved, and he hadn't been there to enjoy it. It was the sort of weather that would have had Patrick itching to be out fishing. Instead, he'd been dead, entombed in a casket covered by a US flag, unable to enjoy one single thing he loved ever again.

Casting the laptop off the bed, not caring whether it shattered into pieces, he sat up, unconcerned with the pain it caused him to do so. Christ! He hadn't even been able to attend his own partner's funeral because he'd still been in the hospital. But he'd been compelled to watch it. Patrick had been his partner and a member of Dante's homicide team for years. He'd also been the closest friend Dante had ever had.

It should have been me who died. Patrick had a wife, a teenage son who was left behind without a father.

Hell, Karen and Ben, Patrick's wife and son, had practically adopted him, having him over for dinner almost every night when he and Patrick could actually manage to catch dinner—which wasn't often. Their jobs kept them out at all hours, especially in the evenings. Murder rarely happened during the daytime hours in his district.

Karen and Ben will never have to worry about money. It won't make up for the loss of Patrick, but it will help.

Dante had resolved any financial problems for Karen and Ben by donating several million dollars to a fund for the Brogan family anonymously, but it wouldn't bring back the man they loved, the husband, the father. It seemed like a pitifully small thing to do considering he had plenty of money and would never miss it.

Although he and Patrick had gotten promoted to detective at the same time, Dante's partner had been well over a decade older, and a hell of a lot wiser than Dante had been back then. Patrick had taught a hotheaded new detective patience when Dante had none, and he'd helped Dante become a better man in more ways than he could count.

Christ! It should have been me! Why wasn't I standing where Patrick was standing when the shooter opened up and fired?

He and Patrick had been so close—so damn close—to nailing a murderer who had raped and killed three women in their rough, gang-populated division. They had been tailing the suspect on the street, waiting for backup to arrive to arrest the subject. The murderer had gotten sloppy on his last victim, leaving behind enough DNA evidence to finally arrest the bastard.

Swinging his legs painfully over the side of the bed, Dante relived the last few moments of Patrick's life, flashing back to the instant when he'd lost his best friend.

He and Patrick staying close enough to keep the suspect in their sight.

The piercing sirens nearby screeching through the air.

The suspect suddenly panicking and pulling out a semiautomatic pistol and starting to shoot.

Why the suspect had suddenly cracked at that moment was still a mystery. The sirens had probably spooked a murderer who already knew the law was on his tail and closing in. Ironically, the sirens had had nothing to do with them taking down a murderer. They'd been wailing for a completely separate incident. Like the police were really going to announce they were coming for the asshole? Still, it had been enough to send the suspect over the edge, shooting at anyone or anything behind him without warning.

Patrick had been the first to fall, with one bullet through the head. Dante had pulled out his Glock as he took several bullets from the shooter at close range, shielding Patrick with his larger body until he'd managed to get a kill shot in on the asshole shooter. At the time, Dante hadn't realized it was already too late for Patrick. The bullet through the head had killed his partner instantly. Luckily, the few civilians who had been hanging around on the street during the early morning hours had scattered, leaving Dante the only one injured—Patrick and the suspect both dead.

He'd been wearing his vest, but the close-range shots had caused Dante some blunt-force trauma. However, it *had* saved his life, leaving him with only some cracked ribs instead of bullets through his chest. The shot to his face hadn't entered his skull, but he did have a nasty wound to his right cheek that extended up to his temple. The bullet to his right leg had passed through the flesh of his thigh, putting him in surgery after the incident, but it hadn't shattered the bone. The one to his left arm had just been a graze.

Lucky bastard!

Dante could almost hear his partner's voice saying those exact words to him jokingly, but he was feeling far from fortunate at the moment. He'd been injured badly enough to spend a week in the hospital, unable to attend Patrick's funeral, unable to say a final good-bye to his best friend. Karen and Ben had visited him after his surgery, Patrick's wife tearfully telling him how glad Patrick would have been that Dante had survived, and actually thanking him for trying to protect her husband. Neither one of them blamed Dante for what had happened to their beloved husband and father, yet Dante couldn't get past the fact that he wished it would have been him instead of his partner, that he had somehow let Patrick down by not being the one to die.

Survivor's guilt.

That's what the department psychologist was calling it, telling Dante it was common, considering the circumstances. That comment had made Dante want to send the little head-shrinking bastard across the room with his fist. What the hell was normal about wishing himself dead?

"You okay?" His brother Grady's low, concerned voice came from the doorway of the small bedroom. "Need anything? We're only about an hour out from landing. I thought I heard something crash in here."

It was ironic that Dante and his siblings had always wanted to protect Grady—too often unsuccessfully—from being the primary target of their alcoholic, abusive father. And now *Grady* was the brother who was trying to take care of *him*. Every single one of his siblings had been at the hospital in Los Angeles, flying in as soon as they had heard that he was injured. But he was going home with Grady to his vacation home in Maine, a house Dante owned but had only seen briefly a few times since it had been constructed. Every one of the Sinclair siblings had a home on the Amesport Peninsula, but only Grady had actually made his house a permanent home. Dante hoped he could escape there, stop reliving the last moments of Patrick's life in his nightmares. Right now the only thing he could see every time he closed his eyes was Patrick dying.

At the time, Dante hadn't realized that Patrick was taking his last breath as his friend hit the ground with a gasp, his eyes still open and his head covered in blood. Now that he *did* know, Dante couldn't stop seeing that horrifying vision over and over again in his mind.

They were currently in flight on Grady's private jet, making their way from Los Angeles to Amesport, Maine. They'd be landing in a small airport outside of the city limits.

"I could use a beer," Dante told Grady in a tortured voice, not looking at his brother as he buried his face in his hands. "Ouch! Shit!" Dante moved his hands away, the pain of the still-tender wound on his face irritated by his actions.

"Alcohol and painkillers don't mix," Grady mentioned calmly as he picked up the laptop from the floor. Miraculously, the computer was still working, and Grady frowned as he opened the top and saw what his brother had been viewing. "You were watching the funeral? We were all there, Dante. I know you feel like shit because you couldn't be there. Every one of us went for you because you couldn't."

They all had, and the fact that his brothers and sister had attended the funeral for him while he was laid up in the hospital, to pay their last respects to a man they never even knew, touched him deeper than they would ever know. They'd stood in his place, united in their support of him at Patrick's funeral. It had meant a hell of a lot, but . . .

"I had to see it myself." Dante looked up at his older brother, his expression stony. "And I'm not taking the painkillers." Maybe it was stupid, but feeling the pain of his injuries seemed to somehow make him feel less guilty that he was still alive. If he was fucking hurting, he was paying the price of still being alive while Patrick was buried six feet under.

The psychologist thought he was having self-destructive thoughts.

Dante didn't give a shit.

"Hold on," Grady answered gravely, leaving briefly and coming back with a bottle of beer. He screwed off the top and handed it to Dante. "It's not exactly the healthiest thing for you to have right now, but I doubt it will do much harm."

Tossing his head back, Dante took a gulp of the cold liquid, letting it slide down his throat, suddenly questioning the intelligence of doing so. The taste brought back a flood of memories, all of them about the many times over the years that he and Patrick had hung out together having a beer. He finished it quickly as Grady watched him pensively, handing the empty bottle back to his brother after he drained it. "Thanks."

Grady took the bottle from Dante's hand with an uneasy scowl. "Are you okay?" he asked again in a husky voice. "I know your wounds hurt like hell, but they'll heal. That's not what I'm asking. I need to know if *you're* okay."

Dante stared at his older brother, the concern on Grady's face nearly breaking him. Although the Sinclair siblings had all scattered to different areas of the country after they'd left their hellish childhood and adolescence behind, the affection they all had for each other had never died. They might only get together on rare occasions, but they all still cared. He had seen it in every one of his siblings' eyes at the hospital.

The anxiety and distress that was lodged deeply in Grady's gray eyes finally made Dante admit for the first time, "No. I don't think I am."

Patrick was dead. Dante wished he had died in his place. His body was racked with pain, and everything inside him was cold and dark.

Right at that moment, as his anguished eyes locked with his older brother's, Dante wasn't sure he would ever be okay again.

CHAPTER 2

"Did you read my column today?"

Dr. Sarah Baxter bit her lip to keep from smiling as she looked at her elderly female patient, still sitting on an exam table after a routine visit. Elsie Renfrew was eccentric, but she was also a member of the Amesport City Council, and the biggest gossip in town, so she was far from demented. Sarah had grown very fond of the older woman, but she knew just how wily she actually was, and that Elsie knew the personal business of almost every resident in Amesport. Most people in town called her Elsie the Informer, but Mrs. Renfrew had enough power and clout locally that nobody would dare mention that moniker to the venerable woman face-to-face. Sarah rather admired the older woman's spunk, but she found herself constantly and carefully monitoring anything she said to the chirpy, inquisitive woman. Even a casual comment about another Amesport resident was likely to end up in Elsie's What's Happening in Amesport column of the *Amesport Herald* if there was even a hint of juicy information. Sarah might admire the fact that her patient was over the age of eighty and still so active in the community, but she'd also readily admit that Mrs. Renfrew terrified the hell out of her sometimes. Just the slightest slip and the seemingly sweet woman would twist the information around and make it the subject of town gossip. Not that Elsie was mean-spirited. She just felt it was her duty to report any news in Amesport since her roots in the area went back to the time the town was founded.

"No, Mrs. Renfrew, I haven't had a chance to read the paper today." Sarah knew she was blatantly lying, but she quickly justified that fibbing was better than the possible alternative. She'd read the newspaper this morning at breakfast, including Elsie's article titled "Another Sinclair Hottie Returns to Amesport Wounded." If there was one thing Sarah definitely *didn't* want Mrs. Renfrew to know, it was that she knew way more about *that* situation than anyone else in town—except for the so-called rich hottie's family.

"Now, honey, I told you to call me Elsie ages ago." The tiny gray-haired woman patted Sarah on the arm and hopped nimbly to the ground, her sneakers absorbing most of the impact. Amazingly, Elsie still looked elegant, even though she was dressed in white sneakers and a red sweat suit.

Sarah sighed as she snaked a hand out to catch the woman around her upper arm to make sure she was steady. She still wasn't used to the informality around the friendly coastal town of Amesport. "You did tell me that. I'm sorry, Elsie." Even after nearly a year of practicing here, Sarah still had a hard time calling her patients by their first names if they requested it, and had realized that she actually got to know them well enough that every one of her patients preferred it.

She'd done her residency in internal medicine and first year of practice in Chicago, rarely seeing a patient for very long before moving on to the next one. Her focus had been on hospitalized patients, so she'd rarely had a chance to get to know any of them personally, except for a few who required extensive hospitalization.

Sarah shuddered, a reaction she had every time she thought about even entering a hospital now.

"I kind of thought you might end up being the doctor who is seeing to Dante Sinclair's injuries when he gets here." Elsie raised an eyebrow with a sly look on her face. "It's not like we have very many doctors here."

Sarah shook her head, focusing her attention on her patient. "Even if I was his doctor, Elsie, I couldn't tell you. Patient confidentiality." *And thank God for that.* Being a doctor gave Sarah a good excuse to clam up when Elsie asked any questions about other residents.

"So are you saying you are going to be this Dante Sinclair's doctor?" Elsie said shrewdly, shooting Sarah a calculating stare. "But you can't tell me because of medical ethics?"

"No. I didn't say that at all." Elsie wasn't trapping her into admitting anything. "I was just reminding you that no physician can gossip about any of their patients," Sarah said firmly, knowing if she gave Elsie an inch, she was likely to take way more than a mile. The determined elderly woman would drag her across the whole country to get an answer.

"He's very rich, you know. Single and a hero. He threw himself in front of his partner to try to save his life, and killed the shooter so no one else got hurt. He'd be a good one for you, honey," Elsie told her thoughtfully. "Beatrice and I were just talking about you two this morning."

Oh, God. Just the thought of Elsie talking to Beatrice Gardener about her destiny was a terrifying thought for Sarah. Beatrice was the second-biggest gossip in Amesport and considered herself the town matchmaker. Around the same age, the two women were absolutely lethal together. "I'm not looking for a man," she told the older woman hurriedly, her voice almost desperate.

Elsie opened her mouth to argue, but there was a tap on the door before she could say whatever it was she wanted to say.

"Come in," Sarah called eagerly. *Please, please come in.*

Kristin, her cheerful, redheaded office manager and medical assistant, popped her head in the door. "All ready to get your blood work,

Elsie." Kristin opened the door completely and motioned for Elsie to come with her.

"Thank you," Sarah mouthed silently to Kristin as Elsie's lips turned down in an irritated frown. Elsie was obviously unhappy that she hadn't achieved her objective but started heading reluctantly toward the door. Sarah called out to Elsie, "Have a good day. I'll see you again in a few weeks to go over your blood tests."

"Remember what I said," Elsie called over her dainty shoulder. "Beatrice and I are rarely wrong. You two are perfect for each other. Beatrice is having one of her hunches about you two."

"Okay," Sarah answered weakly, breathing a sigh of relief as Elsie exited. Kristin shot her a knowing wink as she closed the door, leaving Sarah blissfully alone.

Thank God.

It wasn't that Sarah didn't like her patients, and most of the time she could have a lively conversation with Elsie about other things that didn't revolve around the Amesport gossip. But her patient had definitely been on an information mission today, and Sarah had been afraid she'd inadvertently give away something in her expression because she was a lousy liar. In fact, she sucked at it.

Probably because I never really had any friends to lie to before I came here.

She'd never had any need or reason to lie. When one dealt with scientific data, lying was generally unnecessary.

Dante Sinclair *was* going to be her patient. She'd already studied all of his medical records, knew he was flying in today from Los Angeles. She'd spoken with his attending physician at length and his department psychologist as well. Last night she'd studied his injuries and read his history, poring over all of the notes on both his medical condition and the incident that had gotten him injured in the first place.

He lost his partner. It had to have been a horrific experience for him. Yet he was still able to kill a serial killer, even after he'd been hit several times. And he did it while shielding his partner, who had already taken a fatal hit.

Sarah couldn't deny that Dante Sinclair was a hero, but judging by some of the psychological records, he wasn't taking the death of his partner well and was exhibiting some self-destructive behavior.

Survivor's guilt.

Even though Sarah wasn't a psychologist, and honestly didn't completely understand emotional behavior herself, it made sense to her in a rather convoluted way.

Survivor's guilt is a mental condition that occurs when a person perceives themselves to have done wrong by surviving a traumatic event when others did not.

If Sarah hadn't had to deal with some psychological trauma of her own the year before, she might have said survivor's guilt was totally illogical. But she couldn't say that anymore. Mental reactions weren't logical, but they happened, and they could destroy the lives of those suffering through them.

Quickly leaving the exam room, Sarah ducked into her small office and changed out of her scrubs, pulling on a pair of jeans and a purple short-sleeved shirt. After grabbing her purse and slipping her feet into a pair of sandals, she walked quietly through the hallway, wanting to get out the door before she encountered Elsie again. Kristin was drawing routine labs, but it wouldn't take long.

I can't believe I'm sneaking around like a criminal in my own office.

Taking a deep breath as she left the building, she let the scent and feel of the coastal town soothe her soul. Amesport was just big enough to have everything she needed but small enough to still be quaint. Her office was in the center of town, and the area was alive with activity, as it always was during the tourist season in the early afternoon. The humidity made her shoulder-length blonde hair start to curl up at the ends, taking on a life of its own, but she ignored it. She wasn't about to go back into the office to look for a hair clip, and she was getting used to the Maine weather doing crazy things to her hair. As she headed for her compact four-wheel-drive vehicle, she wished she had the time to walk through the town square. She could desperately use a latte from Brew Magic, the local coffeehouse, and she liked strolling down Main Street. Most of the time she walked to work, but she'd driven today, knowing she was going to have to drive out to the peninsula.

Sarah drove slowly through town, mindful of the tourists and beachgoers, thinking about her new patient. She knew very well why she'd gotten Dante Sinclair as a patient. Her practice wasn't nearly as busy as the other physicians in town because she only saw patients on an outpatient basis, and she had only been here for a year. If she had a patient who needed to be admitted to the small local hospital, she turned their care over to one of the other doctors. She had more time than the other physicians to check in on Dante Sinclair at his home, something that was required due to his current condition. Besides, he was a Sinclair, and she'd heard about the wealthy Sinclair family from the first day she'd hit town. Grady Sinclair was looked at with awe because he actually used his wealth and power to help improve things in the town of Amesport. And everyone knew the story of how Grady had saved Christmas for the youth center. Now that he had married the director of the Youth Center of Amesport, he was considered a local hero.

It was hard to believe that Grady Sinclair had once been considered an antisocial beast. But that certainly wasn't true now, and Grady's wife, Emily, had actually become Sarah's patient and friend, initially switching to Sarah's services because she preferred a female doctor for routine exams. Sarah liked Grady, and he was very nice and down-to-earth, considering he was a billionaire and came from a family in Boston that had been obscenely wealthy for generations.

What kind of guy is a billionaire and becomes a cop, a homicide detective in Los Angeles?

Sarah's brain worked rather like a computer, trying to analyze data, but she came up empty every time for the answer to *that* question. She had a genius IQ, but what Dante Sinclair had done was just . . . irrational.

He's a patient just like any other. I certainly don't need to concern myself about his unusual career choice.

Sarah left the city limits, shaking her head, wondering why her brain was even curious about Dante Sinclair.

Maybe it's because I spent the entire weekend listening to messages and pleas from his colleagues, siblings, and friends.

The moment his partner's funeral had ended, her office phone had rung continually, forcing Kristin to allow the answering service to start picking up the calls. Sarah had surmised that his siblings had let his fellow officers in Los Angeles know where Dante Sinclair was going and who was going to be taking over his care. Call after call had come in to her office from the people of Los Angeles, everyone from his siblings to his poker buddies begging her to help Dante get back to normal again. Many of them had offered to do anything to help him. Certainly, Los Angeles had a lot of cops, but Sarah had never seen anything similar to the outpouring of concern for Dante Sinclair. Many of them had even offered money to help him if he needed it, mostly the individuals who probably didn't think about the fact that he was injured in the line of duty and all of his medical expenses were completely covered. But it was pretty clear that not one of the people who called—except his siblings—knew that Dante was, along with his four other siblings, probably one of the richest people on the planet. The sorrow of these callers had been genuine, leaving Sarah to think that Dante Sinclair must have been one hell of a guy before this incident.

Pulling her car up to the gated entrance to the peninsula, she waited as the automatic gate swung open, allowing her to enter the Sinclair domain. The entire projecting mass of land beyond this gate belonged to the Sinclair family, and it was one prime piece of real estate.

Sarah had always wanted to explore it but had never had a reason to enter the area . . . until now. Emily lived in a house near the end of the peninsula with Grady, but she'd always met up with her friend in town because it was easier.

A crack of thunder startled Sarah, and she looked dubiously at the dark clouds moving in as she pulled into the first driveway on the right. As she approached the house, she couldn't help but gape as she parked her car distractedly, barely registering the fact that the short, private road to Dante Sinclair's residence had opened up to a driveway large enough to park a whole fleet of vehicles.

The house was enormous, and built in the Cape Cod style, just like her small residence outside of town. But this home was no cozy cottage, the square footage probably at least ten times what she had in her own house.

"Who has a house this big and never uses it?" she mumbled to herself, her vision obscured as the rain began to fall, large droplets plopping onto her windshield faster and faster.

Grabbing her purse, Sarah opened the car door and made a mad dash for the front entrance. She knocked and then rang the doorbell, feeling a little anxious. While she was just fine in the office with patients, she was socially awkward in nonprofessional situations, probably a result of being accelerated so fast in school. She'd never had real friends until she'd made her move to Amesport, and most of the students she'd gone to school with had either thought she was a geek—which she actually was—or were too old to try to make friends with her because they didn't have much in common.

Socially, things just popped out of her mouth as she thought about them. Most of her comments were probably incredibly boring to the majority of people on the planet unless they really wanted to know every scientific detail of the universe. Or any of the other millions of facts that stuck in her head, no matter how long ago she'd studied or read about them. She seemed to retain information like a computer with an unlimited amount of storage space.

Maybe she *was* getting used to making small talk since she'd come to Amesport, but she struggled with everyday conversations with people she didn't know very well.

He's still a patient. I'm just seeing him in his own home. A patient is a patient, no matter where I'm seeing him. We'll talk about his medical condition, what he can do to speed up his recovery, and that's it. He's injured. He isn't going to expect or want social conversation.

Sarah ran her hands up and down her arms, wishing he would answer the door. The porch had an awning, but the wind was so brutal that she was still being drenched with a mist of rain.

He had to be home. She was here at exactly the time that had been requested to do her initial assessment, and Dante Sinclair wasn't exactly in any condition to be anywhere *except* home. She reached for the ornate latch on the door and pressed her thumb down, finding it unlocked. With a small exertion of pressure on the door, she found herself standing in the massive foyer of the house.

I can't just stroll into his home!

But apparently, she could—and just had. Maybe she shouldn't have, but what if he was hurt, what if he needed help?

"Mr. Sinclair," she called hesitantly but clearly. Her voice echoed through the cavernous great room in front of her. She called louder and firmer, shedding her wet sandals at the door and starting to move through the house. Her fear for his safety was beginning to overrule her misgivings about intruding into his home. A short while later, after searching the entire house, Sarah was still unable to find her patient.

Sarah was about to give up and call his brother Grady when she heard a loud crash near the kitchen. She found a closed door that she'd assumed was a closet and opened it, realizing that it was actually the basement. She flew down the stairs and stopped dead at the bottom of the steps, watching as a massive male figure lifted what looked like an extraordinarily heavy pair of dumbbells over his head again and again in shoulder presses.

There was no doubt in her mind that she was watching Dante Sinclair.

He hadn't heard her because he was wearing a pair of headphones, the heavy metal music blasting so loudly that she could hear it from the bottom of the stairs.

Further evidence that this was, in fact, Dante Sinclair were the visible cut on his face and the massive bruising to a sculpted chest and torso that would otherwise be absolutely perfect. He was dressed in only a pair of sweatpants, the elastic clinging low on his hips like a lover, the happy trail of dark hair beneath his belly button disappearing disappointingly into the waistband of his pants.

Her eyes flew back to his face, watching as the sweat beaded and dripped down his forehead and sculpted cheekbones, landing on his chest. His dark hair was almost military short, and it was saturated with perspiration. His face was contorted with pain, and Sarah knew it wasn't from his workout. Ordinarily, it would take a lot more effort to actually make a toned, ripped body like his sweat. But with his type of injuries, she'd seen grown men cry just from a few wrong movements, or simply by breathing. Broken ribs were excruciatingly painful, and the activities he was engaging in at the moment made absolutely no sense.

What the hell is he thinking?

Moving forward, she snatched one of the weights from his hand on a downward stroke and dropped it to the floor. Before he could react to her presence, she swiped the other one, letting it hit the ground with a very loud *clang*, recognizing the noise as exactly what she had heard from upstairs. He'd obviously dropped the weight.

"Who the hell are you?" he growled in a low, dangerous voice. He pulled the headphones off and the music ceased. After dropping them into a nearby chair, he turned and scowled at her.

Irritated now, Sarah ignored him. "Are you trying to make your injuries worse than they already are?" Putting her hands on her hips, she glared right back at him. She was tall for a woman, five foot eight, but she still had to tilt her head back to look up at him. He had to be at least six foot three. Honestly, she was surprised Dante Sinclair was even on his feet, much less lifting weights in his condition. "If it hurts, don't do it while you're recovering. Are you a masochist, or just completely ignorant?" It was a reasonable question after what she'd just seen. It was obvious that the notes about his self-destructive behavior were correct. Her question was . . . why was he doing this? He'd been lucky, considering how many shots he'd taken. Why in the world would he want to make an already painful medical situation worse?

Sarah watched his face, fascinated as his nostrils flared and his hazel eyes grew stormy and hostile. He didn't look like he was in pain anymore—not physical pain, anyway. The look he was giving her was like he wanted to throttle her, or anyone else who kept him from doing exactly what he wanted to do.

Is this the same guy everyone wants me to help because they care about him?

Somehow, she couldn't seem to reconcile the man standing in front of her with the guy everyone wanted to be healed. His jaw was scruffy, like he hadn't shaved in a few days, and he didn't look like he wanted a damn thing except to be left alone.

"Masochist *and* ignorant?" Sarah murmured aloud, wondering if he was ever going to say anything.

"You broke into my house. And I told Grady I didn't need a fucking babysitter," Dante finally replied, his voice rough and graveled. "Leave."

Sarah crossed her arms in front of her. "Grady didn't send me. And I didn't break into your house. The door wasn't locked."

"I don't care who sent you. Just get the hell out of my house."

"I can't. I'm not a babysitter," Sarah replied calmly. "I'm here to take care of you."

"In that case . . . strip and bend over," he replied, deadpan. "I haven't gotten off in a while, and that's the only kind of help I need from you."

He doesn't mean a word of what he's saying. He's trying to shock me to make me go away.

"Sex is another activity you shouldn't indulge in for at least a few weeks," Sarah answered, not letting him get any satisfaction from his salacious comments. "You need to move around, but nothing strenuous." She was used to lewd comments from male patients, but the men uttering them were usually over the age of eighty, with dementia. "Do you need help upstairs?"

Sarah waited as she watched his expression go from hostile and angry to confused and irritated. It wasn't much, but it was something, and it told her exactly what she needed to know. She was beginning to realize that this Dante, the angry man in front of her, was a facade. He'd lost his best friend—his partner—and almost his own life. Part of him wished he would have died in his partner's place, and he was going to make himself suffer because he didn't die, even though the incident wasn't his fault. It was part of her job to make sure he got through this stage of his recovery without hurting himself. He'd been through enough, and her indignation faded away as compassion took its place. She was still angry that he was doing something so stupid, but she sort of understood why.

"I don't need anybody's help," he denied in a surly voice, moving forward with a limp to climb slowly up the stairs.

Sarah followed in his wake, unable to entirely ignore a backside that was so incredibly tight any woman would have a hard time not wanting to cop a feel. Admonishing herself for staring at his incredible glutes, she watched his big body painfully make its way upstairs. He wobbled a few times, but he made it without incident.

He faced her in the kitchen. "You need to go. I don't want anybody here."

He wants to lick his wounds in private. Sarah got that, but it wasn't happening. She had a job to do, and he had injuries that needed to be checked.

She countered, "You need a shower. Not only do you stink, but you need to keep your wounds clean."

"Are you planning on assisting me with that?" he questioned flatly, no teasing in his tone.

"No. If you were able to make it up the stairs, I assume you can clean yourself up."

"You're already wet," Dante answered hoarsely, reaching out a hand to finger a lock of her damp hair. "You might as well make yourself useful and help me."

Batting his hand away, she retorted, "In case you haven't noticed, it's storming, which is why I went ahead and came in. Like I said, your door was unlocked. Look, if you really do need help, I'll help you. I can do my exam at the same time." It made sense. He might be a little unstable, and she was going to have to check out the surgical wound on his thigh.

I'm a doctor, for God's sake. It isn't like I haven't seen naked men before.

Although, she had to admit, she'd probably never seen a naked man formed quite as well as Dante Sinclair. But she could still manage to be professional. This whole home care thing was throwing her off-kilter. Her office was safer, a place where there were definite lines drawn as to what her duties were. Here, she felt out of place. With the money the Sinclair family had, she'd expected to see him have an aide of some kind. Obviously he'd refused.

"Exam?" Dante shot her a dubious look. "Who the hell sent you here?"

Sarah took a deep breath before replying. "Dr. Blair in Los Angeles. He turned your care over to me. I was selected to be your physician here in Amesport, and Dr. Blair's office sent me all of your medical records, and I've talked to him on the phone to get a report on your condition."

"Are you screwing with me? Are you even legal drinking age?" Dante scoffed. "Dr. Blair said he'd turn me over to a *doctor* here in Amesport. I'm going to need to be signed off to go back to work. Not that I want to deal with doctors anymore, but it's a requirement of my department."

"I'm twenty-seven years old, Detective Sinclair. My name is Sarah Baxter, *Dr.* Sarah Baxter, and I *am* your doctor."

His sharp hazel eyes assessed her, and Sarah cringed just a little. With her makeup gone and her hair drenched, she probably did look even younger than she really was, and she was still very young to be a physician.

Finally, Dante shook his head, a small smile forming on his lips. "Well, I'll be damned. You look more like a babysitter."

Without another word, he turned and limped toward the kitchen entrance, leaving Sarah to stare at his perfect ass once again as he retreated, wondering absently if he had even believed her as she followed him. "I'm an internist, and I don't treat kids. But taking care of you is certainly starting to feel more and more like babysitting," she muttered, disgruntled, as she escorted him upstairs.

CHAPTER 3

Dante sat at the kitchen table, watching the lithe, blonde woman with more than a little fascination as she moved around his kitchen with fluid, efficient movements. He hadn't had the heart to make her help him shower, even though he wouldn't have minded if she had joined him, since he hadn't gotten laid in a while. Instead, he'd had her wait in the bedroom until he was finished, and then let her look at his wounds with his dick completely covered. He smirked as he wondered if she'd noticed the tent under the towel, especially when she'd touched near the wound on his thigh. Hell, even her scent made him hard. She smelled like fresh rain and vanilla, a scent that suddenly made him feel fucking intoxicated.

"So are you really a doctor? Twenty-seven is awfully young to be a physician." Even fresh out of med school, she was too young.

But she's awfully bossy. She'd taken over his kitchen without even asking, letting him know she was making them both something to eat when she had discovered he hadn't had a meal that day.

"I am a doctor. I was a college freshman at the age of twelve. I finished two college majors, one in biology and another in music, by the time I was sixteen. I graduated med school when I was twenty-one, and I completed a residency in internal medicine in Chicago when I was twenty-four. I practiced for over a year in Chicago before I moved here, and I've been in Amesport for almost a year. I just turned twenty-seven last week."

"A child prodigy," Dante concluded, watching Sarah as she put the finishing touches on two sandwiches.

She shrugged her shoulders. "I hate that term. I just had accelerated studies."

Accelerated studies, my ass. She's a damn genius.

He'd pretty much already figured that out by listening to her speak, but he wasn't exactly concentrating on her superior brain right at the moment.

Dante's eyes scanned her perfectly rounded ass and her long legs, picturing them wrapped tightly around his waist as he buried his cock inside her wet heat. Beautiful and gifted would be a more appropriate description of Sarah Baxter, but he didn't tell her that. He'd made the mistake of mentioning her stunning eyes a few minutes ago, the irises appearing to be a violet shade. He'd then gotten almost a dissertation on how they were actually dark blue, and that violet eyes didn't exist on the Martin-something-or-other scale of eye color except in cases of albinism. She went on to talk about wearing certain colors, and the level of light making eyes look like a different color. He'd missed most of the details because he'd still been staring into those incredible eyes as she spoke, wondering exactly what color they'd be when they were glazed with desire as she came apart for him. Rather than being off-putting, her intelligence turned him on. She was unlike any other woman he'd ever met. Nothing seemed to really surprise or anger her—except for his moment of stupidity in the basement—so he'd given up trying to piss her off for now and started asking questions.

"Genius IQ?" he guessed, noticing that her hair was dry, and it was a lighter blonde than it had been when it was damp, the ends turning up in fat curls.

"One seventy the last time I was tested. That was a while ago," she admitted, sounding disgruntled.

"Einstein level," he commented casually.

Sarah set a ham sandwich in front of him and motioned for him to eat. "Actually, Einstein never took an IQ test. There's only a rough estimate that his IQ was between one sixty and one eighty. No one really knows for certain."

"Einstein level," he confirmed, amused by the data that just seemed to fly out of her mouth. Did she ever have a normal conversation? Dante picked up his sandwich and started to eat, surprised that he was actually feeling hungry for the first time since he'd been shot. Unfortunately, he lost his appetite as soon as she brought over his pain pills and a glass of juice a few minutes later. "I'm not taking the pills. I just took them a while ago." He figured it was easier to just let her think he'd already taken them. The last thing he wanted was another fucking lecture from someone about those stupid pills.

"No, you didn't." Sarah set the pills and juice next to his plate, brought her own sandwich and milk to the table, and sat down in the chair across from him.

Dante scowled as he looked at Sarah's unhappy expression. No, he hadn't taken the pills, but he was usually pretty good at bullshitting. He'd developed that talent pretty well in his job. "How do you know?"

Her eyes pierced him with a look that struck him straight in the gut, a look that said she knew he was lying, and she was disappointed. She took a bite of her sandwich, chewing thoughtfully before answering. "Evidence and reasoning, Detective Sinclair. You should understand that better than anyone. You were prescribed sixty pills, and there are still sixty pills in the bottle. I made the obvious conclusion. You haven't taken a single one of them."

Shit. Busted! Maybe I really don't like the fact that she's so damn smart! She actually counted every single pill. What doctor does that shit?

She took a sip of her milk before continuing. "You're breathing short and shallow. I'm sure your other doctor told you how important it is right now to be deep breathing and coughing to prevent pneumonia because of your broken ribs. You need to take the pain meds for a while so you can manage the pain of coughing and taking deep breaths. All of your other wounds are healing well."

"I want to feel the pain," Dante admitted testily.

"Why?"

Dante watched Sarah's eyes. She wasn't judging him right now, nor was she trying to pacify him like the department psychologist. She was simply . . . curious. What he was doing didn't make sense in her logical mind.

"Patrick's dead. I'm alive. He had a wife and son who adored him." Shit. How could he explain how he felt to Sarah when he didn't even get it himself? All he knew was that it should have been him. What did he have? His siblings cared about him. It wasn't like he didn't know that. But it wasn't the same as having the life that Patrick had been living with Karen and Ben. They'd been a family. Patrick had been a father. His son was now fatherless, and his wife was a widow.

Dante had never been that close to a woman. Sure, he got laid as often as possible, but mostly by women who wanted things as casual as he did. Being a detective in homicide was a job that pretty much existed twenty-four hours a day, seven days a week for him. He was the job. He ate, breathed, and slept the job. And he liked it that way.

"I understand that you lost your best friend and your partner, but what does that have to do with you taking care of yourself? How is it going to change anything if you just take your medication?" Sarah asked, confused.

"It should have been me who took that bullet. I wouldn't have left a fatherless son and grieving wife behind. Patrick had too much to live for. Hell, I knew the risks of my job when I took it, and I was okay with the fact that I could die on any given day trying to get murderers off the street."

"And you think Patrick didn't know that, too?"

He died doing exactly what he wanted to do. He loved being a detective, and your partner. This isn't your fault. Both of us knew the risks. I accepted them when I married him.

Dante's big body shuddered as Karen's words floated through his head. "He might have known intellectually, but I don't think he accepted that it could really happen to him," he finally answered grudgingly.

"People deal with risky jobs in different ways. I'm sure he knew, but he didn't dwell on it," Sarah answered reasonably. "And judging by the amount of phone messages I've had to listen to because of people's concern for you, I'd say you'd be leaving just as many grieving people behind. Take the pills, Detective Sinclair. And consider yourself lucky that so many people give a damn." Sarah gave him a pointed stare as she rose and carried her empty plate to the sink.

In a sudden surge of frustration, Dante swiped his hand across the left side of the table in an effort to make the pills fly off the surface. His palm missed the narcotics and slammed into the glass of juice, sending it flying in Sarah's direction. The glass shattered near the sink, right next to where she was standing. Stepping back in reaction to the noise, her bare foot came down right on top of the sharp glass fragments.

"Ouch!" She backed up in confusion, her other foot coming down on another piece of glass. This time she was less careful with her words. "Shit!" Stopping suddenly, she assessed the situation, her eyes scanning the floor before she backed out of the glass-and-juice mess, grabbing a handful of paper towels as she went. She sat back down in her chair and shot Dante an accusing look. "Were you actually trying to hit me? If you were, you have a lousy aim."

Horrified, Dante watched as the blood pooled and smeared on the floor where she'd stepped. As quickly as he could, he moved around the table and dropped to his knees, oblivious to any pain it caused him. He could have told her that he was an expert marksman, one of the best on the entire force, and if he was aiming at something, he didn't miss. "Fuck! I wasn't trying to hit you. It was an accident." He watched as she picked tiny pieces of glass from her feet, putting them carefully into a paper towel on the table, and tried to stem the flow of blood from her right foot, obviously the worst of the two, since it was the foot that was oozing blood. "What can I do? I'm taking you to the hospital."

"No!" Sarah exclaimed a little too forcefully. "I'm a doctor. It's superficial. I can deal with it myself." She pointed toward the kitchen entrance. "I need some of the bandages I used on your arm and leg."

Dante moved like his ass was on fire, even with his injuries, feeling helpless and more than a little guilty. He had the bags of bandages back to Sarah in moments. By the time he knelt in front of her again, she was examining the other foot.

"Superficial scratch," she murmured as she peered at her left foot, her blonde locks veiling her face as she lowered her head to look closely. She quickly slapped a large gauze bandage over the cut and switched to the right foot again.

Dante's breath seized as he saw the blood exiting the wound. Shit! He was a stupid bastard, and his heart sank as he realized his careless actions had caused Sarah injury. "Maybe it needs stitches." He might not be a doctor, but he was trained in basic emergency aid.

Sarah never looked at him as she answered. "It needs to be thoroughly cleaned. I'll take care of it." She wrapped a bandage around her foot after applying several layers of gauze directly to the cut.

Dante gaped as she stood and carefully started mopping up blood from the floor and picking up the large pieces of glass. "Leave it!" he ordered in a low, dangerous voice. He got up, wrapped his arm around her waist, and lifted her feet off the floor, unable to stop a low groan of pain from leaving his lips as he took her weight and her body collided against his chest when he swung her away from the glass. He was panting as he lowered her feet back to the ground, but he didn't loosen his hold around her waist. "I'm sorry. I didn't mean to hurt you, Sarah. I only wanted to get rid of the pills. I didn't mean to hit the glass. I didn't mean for it to break." Shit. He was babbling like an idiot, but for some reason it was important to him that she understood that hurting her wasn't intentional.

She moved away from him as she muttered, "I'm sure you didn't." But she didn't sound completely convinced.

Dante followed her as she grabbed her purse from the living room and slipped her bandaged feet into her sandals at the door. After pulling the door open, she looked back at him. "Look, I understand that you lost your partner, and I'm sorry for that. But think about Patrick, Detective Sinclair. Would he want you to be doing this to yourself, acting this way? If you had been the one who died, would you want him to behave the way you're behaving now? You're not helping your partner right now."

"I didn't mean for you to cut yourself," Dante grumbled, still concerned about the blood he'd seen on her foot.

Sarah shot him a stubborn look. "If you're really sorry, take the damn pills." Without another word, she left, pulling the door closed behind her.

Incredulous that Sarah had just walked out on her injured foot, Dante moved forward and yanked the door back open just in time to see her get into her car and head back down the driveway.

"Damn stubborn woman," Dante muttered irritably, unable to shake off the guilt of what he'd unintentionally done to her.

Would Patrick want him to act like an idiot? Hell no, he wouldn't. His partner would have chewed his ass about getting his temper under control and made him stop doing stupid shit that was self-destructive. In their early days as partners, Patrick had jerked Dante forcibly back more than once from acting on emotion, and Dante had learned the lesson quickly enough back then. Over the years, Dante had learned to keep a lid on his anger, knowing one stupid action could jeopardize an investigation.

Back in the kitchen, he slowly cleaned up the mess on the kitchen floor, cringing as he removed every droplet of blood from the tiles. He was panting by the time he finished.

You're breathing short and shallow.

Annoyed that Sarah Baxter's words kept haunting him, he took a deep breath and coughed hard, grabbing on to the edge of the cupboard to keep his balance as a pain so sharp and excruciating that he almost lost consciousness lanced through his chest. He was definitely seeing stars.

I'm an asshole. If I really wanted to torture myself, all I had to do was cough!

He could have saved himself the effort of going downstairs to the basement and lifting weights just by taking a deep breath or coughing. It sure as hell hurt just as badly—probably worse. Dante wasn't certain what the hell he'd been thinking when he'd done that. Truth was, he hadn't really been thinking. He'd been reacting. Maybe he'd been hoping the pain would keep him numb, stop him from thinking, reliving every moment of Patrick's death.

Would he want you to be doing this, acting this way?

Sarah's parting words were taunting him as Dante pulled a beer from the refrigerator, removed the cap, and sat down at the kitchen table. He and Patrick had had each other's backs for the last five years. When they were working on a hot case, they sometimes spent twelve to fifteen hours a day in each other's company. There wasn't much that Dante hadn't known about Patrick. They'd spent a lot of time giving each other shit, but he knew exactly how his partner would have reacted to Dante's behavior.

"You would have kicked my ass, buddy," Dante said quietly to himself before he took a swig of his beer and set it on the table. Scrubbing his hands over his face, he was careful not to irritate the healing laceration on his cheek. The way he was acting right now *wasn't* for Patrick, it was for himself. His partner would have wanted Dante to watch out for his family, make sure Ben and Karen were okay. He'd made sure they'd never have financial problems, but he hadn't been able to bring himself to call Karen or Ben since they'd visited him in the hospital. Just seeing them reminded him of Patrick, and the fact that he was alive when Patrick was gone. Karen and Ben had a lot of family in California, but it didn't matter. His wife and son had been the most important people in Patrick's life, and he would have counted on Dante to make sure that they were doing all right emotionally as well as physically.

Karen and Ben don't blame me. They cared enough to come to the hospital. I'm being a total asshole. I cut myself off from them because I felt guilty. Me. Me. Me. This has all been about me and not them.

Dante stood, grimacing as he reached for the pain pills, which were still on the table.

"Pity party time is over, Sinclair," Dante said in a disgusted whisper, using an expression that Patrick had used on him whenever Dante needed a kick in the ass.

He'd been acting like a jackass from the minute he woke up from surgery and realized Patrick was dead. He'd been distant with his siblings, even though every one of them had come running when he'd been injured, Evan flying in from across the damn world. And he hadn't even bothered to check in on Karen and Ben since he'd been in the hospital.

And he'd hurt Sarah Baxter, a woman who had only been there to help him, doing her own damn job.

All because I'm mourning my own loss. Sarah was right. What he was doing wasn't going to help his partner now.

Dante knew he needed to pull his head out of his ass. *That's* what Patrick would have wanted. He'd been numb after hearing about his best friend's death, burying his emotional agony deep inside himself, wanting to feel the physical pain because it was better than the guilt of knowing that he was still alive while Patrick was dead. Maybe he'd actually been numb because he was in denial. Strangely, as he finally stared grief directly in the face, the physical pain of his injuries came roaring to life without him even trying.

He grabbed the beer from the table, limped across the kitchen, and poured it down the sink. *No more of that shit until I'm healed.* Reaching into the cupboard, he grabbed a glass and filled it with water.

Christ! Even lifting his arm hurt. Every one of his injuries felt like it was on fire, the pain in his chest and ribs the worst.

If you're really sorry, you'll take the damn pills.

A small, genuine smile formed on Dante's lips. Sarah Baxter was probably one of the bluntest and most peculiar women he'd ever met, but he actually liked that about her. Honestly, she was a mystery, and the cop in him stood up and took notice—along with another part of his anatomy that he couldn't seem to control when he looked at her.

Dammit! He *was* sorry he hurt her. He was a cop, and his first instincts were always to protect. The police officer in him hated himself for failing to protect Sarah. In fact, he'd caused her injury, which made him even more pissed off at himself. He wouldn't deny that he wanted to fuck her, and those urges had roared through his body the moment he'd seen her. That was really saying something, considering he wasn't exactly in any kind of physical shape to even think about wanting to get laid. Yet he was thinking about it, about her. And there was something about Sarah Baxter that fascinated him on more than a physical level. Her mind seemed to process everything to find the logical answer, yet she still seemed to radiate innocence and compassion. It was an odd and intriguing combination.

Tossing his head back, he took the "damn pills" and swallowed them with the water in his hand, draining the glass before putting it in the sink.

Dante left the kitchen with a mission. He made several phone calls, the first and longest one to Karen and Ben.

CHAPTER 4

Sarah grimaced as she finished bandaging her foot. As soon as she'd arrived back home, she'd made sure all of the glass was out of the wounds on the bottom of her feet. Most of the cuts were superficial, and she'd soaked them and added some antibiotic ointment before wrapping her right foot in a bandage. The cut wasn't big or deep, but she had a nasty puncture wound that had caused a lot of bleeding. It might be tender to walk on for a while, but she'd live.

She got up from the sofa and started to put away her medical supplies, her small dog, Coco, right on her heels. Coco had belonged to an elderly patient who had passed away, and Sarah hadn't been able to resist adopting her. It had been one of the most impulsive things she'd ever done, but she'd never regretted it for a moment. Only six months old when Sarah had adopted her, Coco had been smart, easy to train, and alleviated some of the loneliness that had plagued Sarah for most of her life. Maybe it hadn't been sensible to get a dog, but knowing that she wasn't arriving at her cottage to an empty home every night helped to make Sarah's heart just a little lighter. Now Coco was her constant companion whenever she wasn't working, and the kids at the youth center absolutely adored her.

Grady Sinclair had supplied the Youth Center of Amesport with a variety of musical instruments, and Sarah donated her time to teach some of the kids the basics on piano. Although Sarah had thought the Steinway baby grand had been more than a little much for introducing kids to music, she couldn't help but appreciate the rich, beautiful sound of the instrument. She only held classes once a week, but Sarah found herself stopping by the YCOA just to practice and make use of the gorgeous piano every chance she got. Her cottage was too small for a piano. Maybe someday she'd get a bigger place and a piano of her own, but for now, going to the center served a dual purpose: it forced her to get better at socializing, and it allowed her to play the piano.

Thank you, Grady.

Beatrice and Elsie never stopped discussing how much things had changed since Grady Sinclair had married Emily. The YCOA certainly had everything imaginable for the population of Amesport and the outlying villages. Grady had changed the youth center from a gathering place for the local events that barely got by on a tiny budget into almost a free country club for everyone. Emily had been able to expand the programs for the children who utilized the center and make it the hub for any of the town's activities. It hosted everything from concerts and dances to weekly senior bingo now.

A small smile formed on Sarah's lips as she filled Coco's dog dish with fresh water and food, thinking about the obvious love and devotion Grady gave to Emily. The two of them were so in love and happy together. Emily claimed that her husband spoiled her rotten, but Sarah knew that Emily made Grady happy, too. Her friend had a huge heart, and as unlikely a match as they might've seemed on the surface, they were made to be together. The gruff billionaire and the bubbly blonde were a perfect pair.

Sarah absently wondered what it would be like to be loved the way that Grady loved Emily. Never having experienced that kind of love, she didn't have a clue whether she'd feel suffocated by it or if it would make her feel safe and comforted like it did for Emily and Grady. Sarah was used to being alone.

But I'm lonely and alone. I think I might want what Grady and Emily have, but I don't really understand it.

She was content here in Amesport, and she had friends for the first time in her life. She was learning to talk about small things that were important to the people in the community instead of constantly trying to analyze major scientific debates. Surprisingly, she found talking to normal people incredibly fascinating and satisfying. Sometimes talking about emotions was a lot more interesting than scientific theories. It was certainly more educational, because she knew next to nothing about mental states except for loneliness and the sorrow she saw every day as a doctor. Right now her lack of understanding was frustrating because it made it even harder to quite get a fix on what was happening with the handsome Detective Sinclair.

Somehow, she'd imagined that Dante Sinclair would share some similarities with Grady, but after their brief, tumultuous meeting, she couldn't find very many. They shared the same dark hair and some facial features, and they were both large, very well-built men. But while Grady was mostly a brilliant, quiet computer geek with a generous heart, Dante was surly and aggressive. Granted, the guy had just been through a horrific experience, but Dante nearly vibrated with a stubborn belligerence that Sarah was fairly positive was an inherent part of his personality. Maybe in better times he wasn't quite so surly, but she was willing to bet he could be obstinate and unyielding, even when he wasn't stressed.

He's a homicide detective in Los Angeles, in the district with the highest rate of annual murders. Maybe it's that bullheadedness that keeps him alive.

It made sense. Obviously, Dante and Grady had lived completely different adult lives. They were bound to have formed different personalities, different ways of dealing with things.

She'd believed Dante when he said he hadn't meant for her to get hurt. Remorse had flashed in those gorgeous hazel eyes of his for just a moment when she'd been ready to walk out the door. Dante Sinclair was angry at the world right now for taking away his partner and friend. She had just happened to be standing close to him when he snapped.

Sarah sighed, wishing there had been more she could have done to help Dante. He was her patient, Emily's brother-in-law, and Grady's brother. Hopefully, his family could help him emotionally more than she could.

She took a long bath, careful to protect her bandaged foot, and finished reading a romance novel Emily had recommended to her. Romance novels had recently become an obsession for her. So much emotion, and so much sex. She read the stories of love and desire with a fascination that she'd never experienced with any other books. Of course, they were fiction, but she wondered if it was even possible to feel that depth of emotion for a man. And the sex? Well, it certainly wasn't realistic in her experience, which she had to admit was so sparse it was almost nonexistent. But for some unknown reason, she was addicted to reading about relationships that she couldn't quite believe were even possible. As a doctor, she could admit that some parts of a sexual relationship could be pleasurable—probably more for a man than a woman because of anatomical differences. Still, women could definitely find some kind of pleasure with the right knowledgeable lover, she supposed.

I had sex with a med student. I would think he should have known how to do things properly. It wasn't pleasant in any way. Maybe I'm just not a sexual person.

The doorbell rang just as she'd walked out of the bedroom and was about to pop a dinner into the microwave. After shoving the low-calorie meal back into the freezer in case it was a medical emergency, she brushed her damp hands on her jeans and went to answer the door with Coco at her heels.

She gaped as she saw Dante Sinclair standing in front of her, a large white bag in his hand and a hesitant grin on his face. Dressed casually in jeans and a dark T-shirt, the man still looked big and dangerous.

"Peace offering," he informed her in a husky voice, jiggling the bag up in front of his face. "Lobster rolls."

It was twilight, and the rain was still falling in a light mist. He looked damp and so did the bag he was holding. Sarah grabbed the sack and pulled him through the door.

"You can't be out yet. Are you crazy?" Dante Sinclair needed to be resting, warm and snug in his own home. He was barely out of the hospital.

Dante shrugged. "I've been called worse. I wanted to see if you were okay. Those pills work. But they make me feel a little weird." He closed the door before asking with a scowl on his face, "Should you really be standing on those cut feet?"

Sarah blinked at him, still trying to figure out why he was even out of the house. "The cuts are fairly superficial. Detective Sinclair, you need to be resting. The pills make you feel strange because you're supposed to be home in bed sleeping after you take them."

"I was worried," he confessed hesitantly.

Sarah eyed him warily, happy that he'd finally taken the pills but wondering if he wasn't just a little high. "I think you're stoned, Detective Sinclair." She took the bag of lobster rolls to the kitchen, calling over her shoulder, "Sit down." Her house was small, and she could still see him over the breakfast bar as she set her precious cargo down on the countertop. "How did you know I liked lobster rolls?"

"Call me Dante. And finding out what you liked wasn't exactly difficult detective work. I called Grady and Emily." He moved up to the breakfast bar, took a seat on one of the stools, and propped his elbows on the counter, staring at her unnervingly.

Her dog trotted over to sit politely at his feet.

"Coco likes you." Sarah was starting to think she might like him, too, considering he came with a peace offering and had actually taken the time to find out what she liked. But the guy was way too intense, even if he was probably a little wasted on pain pills. "Please tell me you didn't drive."

"I didn't drive," he answered accommodatingly. "My brother Jared just got into town. He took me to get the lobster rolls and dropped me off."

Oh, God. Not another single Sinclair brother in Amesport. "Whatever you do, don't tell Elsie and Beatrice that there's another Sinclair brother in town." After grabbing two plates from the cupboard for the lobster rolls, she dropped two on one of the plates and pushed it across the tiled surface between them, along with a napkin.

Dante shook his head. "Those are for you. And who are Elsie and Beatrice?"

Sarah rolled her eyes. "I can't eat six lobster rolls. Eat."

"Elsie and Beatrice?" He looked at her curiously as he picked up one of the rolls from his plate.

Something about him seemed different now, and not nearly as sullen, morose, and angry.

Dante didn't live here permanently, so Sarah assumed he'd never met the dangerous duo. "Town matchmakers. Both over the age of eighty and very sweet ladies. But very scary when they start trying to happily marry off the entire town. I'm surprised they didn't know your other brother was coming into Amesport. They certainly knew you were on your way."

She watched as Dante took his first bite, his eyes closing for a moment as he chewed. Sarah wasn't certain, but she was pretty sure his expression was the same look of rapture that was on her face the first time she tasted the succulent Maine lobster in Amesport. Mixed with mayonnaise, lemon juice, and spices, it was incredible on the warm rolls, which were brushed with butter on each side. "You've never had lobster rolls? They're everywhere here." She went to the fridge, pulled out two cans of soda, and pushed one toward him.

Dante opened it and took a swig before replying. "I've only been here twice, and then I only stayed for a day or two. And had I known about these, I would have gotten some," he said before taking another bite.

Sarah started on her own roll, the two of them eating in silence for a while before she asked curiously, "Why have you only been here twice? All of the Sinclairs have had a house on the peninsula for years."

"That was Jared's idea. He decided we all needed to build a home here since we owned the property. Nobody argued, so he got them built. He did it after Grady put his house on the end of the peninsula. The only two times I even saw my house here was when Emily and Grady were first engaged, and for the wedding. I couldn't stay long either time." He stared at her, his expression concerned as he asked, "Should you be standing on that foot?"

Sarah's heart warmed just a little at the worried look on his face. "I went to med school, and I'm a doctor. I'm used to eating standing up. My feet aren't hurting. They aren't cut that badly."

After he refused another lobster roll, Sarah took both plates, rinsed them, and put them in the dishwasher. "Did you make the plans for the house yourself?" she called over her shoulder.

"Hell, no. The house is too damn big. I can't find anything there. I have a one-bedroom apartment in Los Angeles, and that's all I've ever needed. I told Jared I wanted an exercise room and a couple of other things. He took care of everything else." Dante finally looked down at the floor, where Coco still sat calmly at his feet. "Is that supposed to be a dog?"

Sarah took the last sip of her soda before tossing the can in the recycling container under her sink. She walked out to the living room, sat on the arm of her couch, and folded her arms in front of her. "Of course Coco is a dog. She's a Chipoo."

Dante turned on the bar stool to face her, a slight smirk on his lips. "What in the hell is a Chipoo? She looks more like a mop with eyes. But at least she's not a yappy jumper."

Affronted by his description of her precious canine, Sarah glared at him. "She's extremely well behaved and trained, so she waits for an invitation to snuggle. A Chipoo is a mixed-breed Chihuahua and poodle." Coco looked more like a dark brown small poodle, and her hair was long, but she looked like an adorable dog, not a mop. "And why in the world would you let your brother build your house? It doesn't make any sense."

Dante shrugged. "Does everything have to make sense to you? He wanted us all to have a house here, and I didn't give a shit. I didn't have the time to worry about the details. Since he wanted it more than I didn't want it, I let him do it."

Sarah shook her head, but she let the conversation go. It was obvious that the Sinclair brothers had more money than they knew what to do with. Maybe building a seven-figure home on a beautiful seaside peninsula and letting it sit empty made sense to Dante Sinclair, even though she still didn't see how it would. "If you had my mother, you'd always make sensible decisions," Sarah muttered to herself, slapping her thigh a few times to allow Coco to jump into her lap. She stroked the thick fur on her pet, and Coco settled comfortably into her lap.

"Lucky dog," Dante commented huskily before adding, "Your mother was a slave driver? You were already a prodigy. What the hell else did she want?"

Sarah sighed, stroking Coco's head absently as she replied. "My mother is a professor of mathematics in Chicago and a member of Mensa, along with a very long list of other scholastic achievements. The academic world is everything to her. She makes most tiger moms look like kitty cats. Having me move out of Chicago and to a small town to be a family doctor didn't exactly make her ecstatic. She was disappointed."

"And your father?"

"He died soon after I was born. But he was a genius, too. A real rocket scientist," she answered quietly. "What about you? Why did you become a cop? A billionaire cop doesn't seem very logical." It was a question she'd been dying to ask even before she'd met Dante Sinclair.

"It's the only thing I've ever wanted to do. My father was an abusive drunk, and luckily he was dead before I got out of high school. So I was free to pursue any career I wanted. And I wanted to be a cop. I went to college first, hoping I could advance through the ranks faster. I knew I wanted homicide, and I'd have to spend my time on patrol first. I got what I wanted when I turned twenty-six and got assigned to homicide."

"And you liked it?"

Dante shrugged. "I was satisfied. I think doing police work is kind of like a calling, the same as wanting to be a doctor. As a homicide detective, I was basically on the job twenty-four hours a day, seven days a week. Murders usually didn't happen in my district in broad daylight."

Sarah could understand that. "I never wanted to do anything else, either." She'd dreamed of being a doctor all her life, starting to fulfill her dreams at the same time most girls were just noticing that boys existed.

"Guess you didn't have much of a childhood, huh?" Dante mentioned casually, as though he had almost read her mind.

Sarah smiled wearily. "I don't ever remember being a child. When most girls were dreaming of being cheerleaders, I was studying college-level biology. I've always been . . . different. Amesport is the first place where I feel like I actually belong. I'm socially awkward, but nobody cares. They talk to me anyway. There's such a mixture of different personalities here that I guess I fit in."

"You're not different," Dante growled. "You're special. Gifted. There's nothing wrong with that."

"Alone is alone, right? For whatever reason it might be," she replied, giving Dante a questioning look. He was looking at her strangely, a gaze that she could almost swear was somewhat possessive and heated, and she started to squirm, feeling like a specimen under a microscope. Breaking contact with his fiery eyes, she set Coco on the floor and got up. "You need to be resting. I'll take you home."

Dante caught her upper arm as she walked past him, pulling her body close to his before he snaked an arm around her waist. Sarah's breath hitched as her hips slid between his jeans-clad thighs. With him sitting on the stool, they were nearly at the same height, and she was eye to eye with him, the fierce, stormy look he was giving her was even more frightening up close and personal.

"No boyfriend?" he asked gruffly.

Sarah shook her head slowly, unable to break away from his enthralling eyes and powerful grip around her waist. Honestly, she wasn't sure she wanted to. Even injured, Dante seemed to pulsate with raw power and dominance that drew her to get perilously close to him.

"Have you ever been with a man?" His question was low, and spoken in a tone that demanded an answer.

Sarah wasn't even going to pretend she didn't understand what he was asking. "Once. In med school. It was awkward and painful. I was dating another medical student, and I wanted to see what I might be missing. He broke up with me the next day. I guess neither of us really liked it. Or maybe I wasn't very good at it. I couldn't see what the big deal was all about. It's mating for the human species, and that's it. I've never really figured out what other reason there is to do it." She was speaking the truth, but she *had* been curious. So she'd tried it, only to find out that she was really missing out on nothing.

"Christ! Are you screwing with me? Is it possible to be a doctor and stay that innocent?" Dante rasped, his gaze sweeping over her face as though he were looking for something.

Her heart was thundering against her sternum as she watched his face, the healing scar on his cheek almost making him even more appealing, even more dangerous. "I'm not innocent and I'm not a virgin. I just don't like sexual intercourse. It's not very enjoyable."

Dante slid his hand through her hair and caressed the sensitive skin at the back of her neck as he smiled wickedly. "I think I just found one subject where you're completely misinformed. There's this little thing called sexual chemistry that you aren't going to read about in textbooks."

Okay. Yeah. Some people seemed to feel sexual chemistry and attraction, but she didn't. Obviously, she understood medically why sex might be enjoyable, but for her, it just wasn't. She'd never had the desire to try it again. "There isn't a thing that I can't tell you about the human anatomy. There's no basis to believe in sexual chemistry. Sexual attraction is just people assessing the reproductive potential of prospective mates," she argued, but she licked her lips nervously, wanting to lean into the intense heat that Dante seemed to be throwing off in waves from his ripped, hard body. Her nipples were beginning to get painfully hard, and she nearly moaned as the hand at her waist slipped beneath the hem of her shirt and started stroking over the bare skin at her waist and back. He made lazy little circles with his palm and fingers, sensitizing every area he touched.

"When I look at you, the last thing I'm thinking about is whether or not you can reproduce. I'm thinking about burying my cock inside you simply because it would feel so damn good," he answered seductively.

Sarah opened her mouth to say something, but she wasn't sure how to respond. Her body *was* reacting to his, and it certainly had nothing to do with his genetic potential as a prospective mate. Pure and simple . . . it was lust. "There's no such thing as true sexual chemistry," she answered weakly, even as her body said differently.

"You have no idea just how satisfying a great fuck can be," he told her in a harsh whisper, the hand at the back of her head spearing into her hair, holding her in a way that didn't hurt but definitely left him in control. "Kiss me," he commanded huskily, pulling her head to him, their lips close together.

Oh, God. Sarah couldn't catch her breath, and she was panting lightly with the need to breach the distance between their mouths. "Dante, no. You're injured and hurting." Confused, she tried to pull gently away from him, but he tightened his arm around her waist, and she didn't have the willpower or the desire to pull harder to get free. She felt ensnared and captured, and she felt strangely compelled to devour the man holding her captive. Sarah's core clenched as she felt his heated breath skitter along her lips, waiting.

"Kiss me, dammit," he ordered again, this time with a persuasive tone.

"I can't. I don't want to hurt you," she whimpered, desperate to be connected to him, feel his mouth against hers. "I'm your doctor." She completely gave up arguing the sexual chemistry issue. Whether this was lust or sexual chemistry didn't matter. It was something she'd never experienced before, and it had her dumbfounded.

"Screw your Hippocratic oath. I need this more than I need a doctor," Dante growled as he pulled her mouth to his with a needy groan.

Sarah tried to remember that he was injured and she couldn't grasp on to him. Instead, she curled her hands around the back of the chair and held on for dear life as Dante claimed her mouth with fervent possessiveness. The kiss swept every thought from her head except the delicious thrill of his tongue bursting through the seam of her lips to conquer and entwine them both in an embrace that rocked Sarah's whole world. Heat engulfed her entire body as Dante squeezed the cheek of her ass and pulled her core flush against his pulsating erection. She moaned as she pressed her pelvis against him, cursing the denim that separated her from his engorged cock.

She completely lost herself in his sultry, heated kiss, squirming against him as he nipped at her lower lip and then swept his tongue over it soothingly, teasingly.

"I want you, Sarah. I'll be the man to show you just how hot you can burn and how satisfying a hard, wild fuck can be." His low baritone was strained and insistent.

Yes. Yes. Yes.

Sarah's entire body was vibrating with need, clamoring to be possessed by this powerful male, the first man to ever make her feel this way. It was exhilarating and frightening both at the same time.

"I hate to break up this cozy little interlude, but it's time to go home, Dante." The male voice coming from the doorway sounded mischievous and nonchalant.

Flustered, Sarah nearly leaped from between Dante's legs, her face flushing as she turned to the incredibly handsome man who had just let himself into her house. She had no doubt that this was Jared, Dante's brother. "You could have knocked," she muttered, embarrassed.

"I did, actually. Several times. I guess you were both occupied," he replied casually. "The door was unlocked so I finally came in."

Oh, God. Sarah wanted to crawl under a rock somewhere and never come out. It was bad enough that she had been so involved in Dante's kiss that she hadn't heard the door, but he was her patient. Dante Sinclair had injuries that would have left any other man in bed crying for his mommy, even if he *was* taking something for pain. Yet she'd practically been mauling him and begging for more. "I'm sorry," she said, mortified. "He does need to be home in bed."

Jared lifted an eyebrow playfully.

"Alone," she added hurriedly. "Sleeping."

"Don't apologize to him," Dante told her in an irritated voice. "He just walked right into your house."

Jared smirked. "Didn't you hear me knock? You're the cop."

"I heard you. I just hoped you had enough sense to go away. Obviously I was wrong." Dante glared at his brother.

Sarah watched the two men, one irritated and the other looking highly amused. She'd never met Jared Sinclair, but he was another powerful and attractive man, just like his brothers. He and Dante shared some of the same physical features, but where Dante was a bit raw, this man was . . . polished. Jared's hair was more auburn than dark brown. Longer than Dante's, it was cut in a manner that looked professional, but she could see a few curls in the sleek style. Jared's eyes were almost a jade green, and the lashes surrounding those startling eyes were so thick that any woman would envy them. Maybe an inch or so shorter than Dante, Jared had the same muscular build as his brother's, covered by casual slacks, a collared button-down shirt that was probably silk, and what looked like very expensive leather casual shoes.

"Take Dante home, Mr. Sinclair. Give him his meds and don't let him leave the house for a week. He really should be resting so that he can heal faster. If anything hurts at all, he shouldn't be doing it," Sarah instructed almost breathlessly, ashamed that she'd let herself get so carried away.

"Call me Jared, please," the man insisted as he shot her a playful grin. "And I'm sorry I came in. I was getting worried. I waited in the car, but it's way past the time that Dante and I agreed on. I knew he shouldn't be out for long."

"I understand," Sarah assured him hurriedly. "I should have taken him home as soon as he got here. Can you keep him at home for a while? It will help him heal up faster."

"No."

"Yes."

Both men answered at the same time, Jared in the affirmative and Dante with a negative. She couldn't help but smile.

Jared opened the door and stepped through. "Let's go, Princess," he told Dante mockingly. "This is probably the one time in our entire lives that I can actually kick your ass. I'm taking advantage of it."

"Only in your dreams, little brother." Dante stressed the word "little" antagonistically as he glared at Jared's back, but he headed for the door. Before he followed Jared, he stopped and silently looked down at her.

Sarah's heart accelerated as he whispered in a husky voice, "We'll finish this later. And don't apologize for what happened. It didn't hurt a bit."

"It shouldn't have happened," she whispered back anxiously. "I'm your physician." Her ethics were screaming at her now.

"It did happen, and it will happen again. Count on it," Dante warned her ominously as he kissed her on the forehead and followed his brother. "Get off those feet," he called back over his shoulder as he slowly followed his brother out to the car.

Sarah closed the door and leaned back against it, wondering what the hell had just happened.

She tried for the rest of the evening to figure out the logic for her brief interlude with Dante Sinclair, and she failed miserably, thinking maybe she needed to research all the recent data on sexual chemistry.

CHAPTER 5

One week later, Dante was restless and irritated as hell. True to his word, his brother Jared—with Grady sometimes filling in as his jailer—kept him confined to the house. He'd only seen Sarah for very brief visits, and he could tell she felt awkward. She was professional and matter-of-fact, and Dante hated it. He was desperate for another taste of the warm, passionate woman he'd discovered at her house last week.

No such thing as sexual chemistry, my ass. We were both about to go up in flames, and I wasn't even fucking her.

His jaw clenched with impatience, and he was more than ready to give his adorable genius a few lessons on the subject of carnal pleasure. His time being idle in the hospital had been bad enough. Now being constantly inside was making him crazy. Granted, he'd liked catching up with Jared and Grady, since the brothers had seen each other so few times during their adulthood. But being stuck indoors was about to make him stir-crazy. He wasn't used to having a spare moment to do anything. His job had always consumed him, left him almost no time to think about doing anything else.

All I can think about now is making Sarah come. His need was almost an obsession, and it got worse every damn day.

Dante's body was healing, and he had stopped using the pain pills because he didn't need them anymore. It still hurt like hell when he coughed too hard, but he was regaining his strength, and he wanted to spend some time outdoors.

I'm bullshitting myself. What I really want is to get my cock inside my beautiful physician and give her a taste of doing something just for pleasure.

"The week is up. I don't need you two to babysit anymore, and I can go into the office to see a doctor when I need to be checked." Dante looked up at Jared, who was sitting in a chair in front of his desk, doing some kind of work on the computer. "What are you doing?"

"Looking at a possible project," Jared answered, sounding somewhat distracted.

Jared was a real estate developer and an architect. Dante knew that his brother had drafted the plans and personally helped build all of the houses on the peninsula except Grady's. However, he rarely got all that involved in any of his projects anymore unless they were personal, which none of them really were. Jared bought, built, and sold commercial real estate to make money, not that he needed it.

"I'm going to town," Dante informed him, getting up from the chair his ass had been warming for way too long. "You can go to your own house. Or stay here and finish. But you and Grady don't need to be my keepers anymore."

Jared looked up at him with a slightly wounded expression. "Look, I know you're pissed. But we wouldn't have been here if we weren't worried."

Dante knew that. "It isn't that I don't appreciate that you were concerned." He shoved his hands in the pockets of his jeans, having problems saying what he really wanted to say. His brothers might be a pain in the ass sometimes, but they'd been here when they thought he really needed them. "I'm just getting tense from sitting around for too long. I need to get out. I'm doing better now."

And I need to get laid! Unfortunately, only one woman will do.

Jared stared at him silently for a moment before releasing a masculine sigh. "I'll go to my house. You'll call me if you need anything?"

"Yep." *Only if I'm dying.* Dante needed a little space, a little time to think. He'd spent the last week in almost constant company with his brothers. It wasn't that he didn't want to spend more time with them, but not if it meant they were playing nursemaid . . . or jailer. He knew Jared planned on sticking around for a while this visit, probably until Dante was ready to go back to Los Angeles.

Jared stood up and shut down the computer. "It's senior bingo night at the youth center. I was thinking of stopping by."

Dante released a bark of startled laughter. "You? Since when do you play bingo?"

"I don't, and the bingo is for the seniors. But I heard Sarah was playing the piano tonight before the games start. Grady says she's better than most concert pianists. I thought I might stop by and check her out for myself."

Dante pulled his hands out of his pockets and stared at his brother, giving him a suspicious look. "What's your interest in her?" Jared was very rich, very successful, and very much in the public eye. He was known for never being seen with the same woman more than once. Dante didn't give a damn if Jared wanted to change women every day, but Sarah wasn't going to be one of his daily specials.

"My only interest is in hearing her play. She's a local doctor, Emily's friend, and a woman who's off-limits for me—just like she should be off-limits for you, Dante. She's not the type of woman you can play around with. You're going back to Los Angeles eventually. Don't start something that's going to leave her hurting. She's a nice woman."

Relieved that his brother wasn't going to hit on Sarah, he replied, "I don't want to play around with her. I actually like her. I can't stop thinking about her." He'd skip mentioning the sexual fantasies he had about her, and how desperately he wanted to fuck her.

"If you mess with her, Grady's going to kill you if you make Emily unhappy. You know how he is about Em," Jared warned ominously. "If she gets a hangnail, he about loses his mind."

Yeah. Dante knew how protective Grady was about Emily, but he knew even that knowledge wouldn't stop him from seeking Sarah out, trying to get closer to her. He felt like he was being lured by a feeling that was greater than lust. He wanted to fuck her, but there was something . . . more. "Maybe we could just be friends. I have several more weeks to recover. We could hang out." Okay, it was lame, and a complete lie. But he was attempting to be nonchalant in front of his brother.

Jared broke into a loud snort of laughter. "Who the hell are you trying to fool? Dante, I've seen the way you look at her. Every damn glance says you want her naked. And I catch her sending you the same signals."

"She is?" Dante looked at Jared hopefully. Honestly, he'd never really sensed, heard, or seen much from her in the last week except for her practical and logical side, which drove him completely insane after sampling the passion she was capable of feeling. He'd like to kill the man who'd initiated her into the world of physical pleasure. On the other hand, there was a primal part of him that reveled in the fact that she'd only been with one guy, and it hadn't been pleasant. He wanted to be the man who made her scream with pleasure, the only one who made her come until she shattered to pieces as she chanted his name like he was the only thing she could think about. The scar was healing on his face, but it would never be completely gone, and the rest of him wasn't particularly attractive at the moment. He knew he hadn't been the only one feeling the heat between him and Sarah, but he asked Jared anyway. "You think she's attracted to me?"

Jared shook his head. "You're really pathetic. Do you know that? Yeah. She's attracted. But the fact still remains that she isn't a woman to mess around with."

She's attracted. Dante ignored the rest of Jared's lecture. "I'm out of here. I'll catch you later." Dante wanted to get to the youth center before Sarah started playing.

"Dante," Jared called out to him.

"Yeah." Dante turned back to Jared impatiently.

"Here's the key to your truck."

Dante snatched the set of keys as they went sailing above his head. "Thanks," he muttered sincerely, happy to get his keys back again. Taking his keys once his truck had arrived in Amesport had been one of his brothers' many ploys to keep him grounded.

He stopped as he stepped outside, taking a moment to absorb the scent and sound of the ocean. He had his own small beach behind the house, and he loved the sound of the waves hitting the shore. Opening the window every night had become a routine, letting the sounds of the ocean lull him to sleep. Strangely, since his passionate encounter with Sarah, he hadn't had a single nightmare about Patrick.

He hopped into the driver's seat of his truck, a sense of peace washing over him just from doing something normal again. Evan had made sure his truck was transported to Amesport, an act that Dante had thought was unnecessary at the time. It wasn't like he wasn't going back to Los Angeles, and he could have rented a car. Now he was sending a silent thank-you to his eldest brother. The familiar feel of the big truck and the scent of the leather interior made him feel almost balanced again. "I owe you one, big brother," Dante whispered to himself, smiling as he felt the powerful engine jump to life.

Evan, at the age of thirty-three, was definitely the one who handled details like bringing Dante's truck to Amesport. He always knew what his younger siblings needed. Grady had just turned thirty-two. Dante was thirty-one, and Jared was the youngest male in the family, almost thirty. Their little sister, Hope, wasn't so little anymore, just having turned twenty-seven, and newly married to Jason Sutherland, a childhood friend of Grady's. Actually, Jason was a friend of the family because he'd grown up near their childhood home in Boston, but had come precariously close to getting the shit beat out of him by all the Sinclair brothers after the stunt he'd pulled to make Hope his wife. Luckily, it had ended well, because Jason handled both Dante's portfolio and Grady's, making sure both brothers continued to grow wealthier every day. Admittedly, Dante didn't care much about the money. He mostly lived on his salary as a detective and rarely touched the money his father had left him. He'd been pretty stunned when he'd drawn out money to give to Karen and Ben, finally glancing at his balance for the first time in years. He'd been incredibly wealthy when he'd turned his financial management over to Jason years ago, but now he was ridiculously rich.

Taking out the money for Karen and Ben hadn't even made a dent in his net worth. As much as the money might mean to the future of his deceased partner's wife and kid, Dante knew that his daily phone calls meant even more to them. The calls had helped him, too. Talking about Patrick, remembering everything good about his best friend, was helping all of them get through the process of grieving. Maybe none of them had gotten to the point of acceptance yet, but every day was getting a little less painful.

He accelerated the truck down his short driveway and swung a left turn to get to the gate leaving the peninsula. Dante had been to the youth center on his previous visits. Knowing Sarah would be there tonight filled him with an unfamiliar anticipation, and he pressed on the accelerator just a little bit harder.

"How were the lessons?" Emily Sinclair asked Sarah curiously, seating herself on the piano bench next to her.

"I think they're going well," Sarah answered, happy to see Emily. She'd just finished teaching piano basics to three grade school children, and although she loved doing it, she could use some adult conversation.

"The class started with ten kids, and it's finishing with only three, but they're dedicated." Sarah just taught the basics to get kids interested in music. "I think the three who are left are going to go on and take lessons, so that's something."

"It's fantastic," Emily replied enthusiastically. "You're amazing for volunteering to do this."

"I'm just trying to pay back for the use of this incredible piano." Sarah ran her hands lovingly over the keys of the baby grand.

"It's here for the public to use," Emily argued. "After Grady ordered it, I was thrilled that somebody could actually play it."

Sarah laughed, thinking about the illogical fact that Grady had ordered a piano like this and didn't even know if anyone in Amesport could play it. There were a few very good adult piano players in the town, but most of them had their own instruments.

"Jared told Grady that he saw you making out with Dante. Are you two an item?" Emily asked in a hushed, secretive voice.

Damn! The one thing I didn't want to get around town already has gotten around.

"Please don't say anything." Sarah looked at the vivacious blonde next to her, hoping the fact that she had been taking advantage of an injured guy on pain drugs hadn't gotten much further than the Sinclair family. She didn't understand how she had lost all reasoning that night, but she was still plagued by guilt over the incident.

"Nobody knows," Emily replied in a low voice, almost a whisper. "Jared and Grady would never tell anyone except family, but Grady's not crazy about the fact that Dante was getting hot and heavy with you. He's afraid Dante's taking advantage. What happened? I heard you got hurt at Dante's house, and Grady wanted to know what to give you to apologize. I've been dying to talk to you for days, but we've both been so busy this week."

Sarah sighed, wondering if she should tell Emily that she'd actually been ravaging her brother-in-law while he was under the influence of pain meds. "Our first meeting didn't go very well. He was being a self-destructive jackass, and he broke a glass by accident. The cut I got was no big deal, but I told him off. He showed up later that night at my house with lobster rolls and an apology. He was a little buzzed on pain meds. He kissed me. It was no big deal, Emily. He was stoned on legal medication. I'm sure it's something he wouldn't normally do. After that, we've been very professional. Everything's fine." *Well, everything except for the fact that I still lust over him every time I look at him.* Dante had started a flame that she couldn't seem to extinguish.

Emily shot Sarah a doubtful look. "I don't think a few pills motivated his behavior. There has to be sexual chemistry."

Oh, God. There were those words again. Lust? Sexual attraction? Sexual chemistry? Does it really matter? The fact is . . . I do feel something.

She couldn't deny it. "For me there was," Sarah admitted reluctantly. "But it can't happen again. He's my patient, and what happened wasn't professional."

Emily's delighted laugh floated through the music room of the youth center. "I went to Grady on business, seeking a donation from him. I ended up kissing him, too, even though I was there for a business transaction. Some attractions are impossible to deny. I know you. If you kissed him, you think he's incredibly hot."

More than hot. I think Dante is like a white flame, the hottest possible fire.

"I got caught up in the moment. That's all it was," Sarah said nervously, not wanting to admit to anyone that she found Dante Sinclair much more than just attractive. She had been drawn to him, craving him so desperately that her mind had let go of all rational thought, and she hadn't been able to concentrate on anything except the feel of his touch.

For just a few moments, she'd felt completely connected to him, and her loneliness had fled. Experiencing something like that had been a powerful aphrodisiac.

"The senior bingo crowd is coming. Meet me later this week for coffee?" Emily stood, giving Sarah a questioning look.

Sarah watched as the chairs in the room filled up. There were several rows available, and they were rapidly being occupied. Playing before the weekly senior bingo session had become a habit, and she didn't mind playing for anyone who loved music. She'd studied music since she was a child and had done more piano recitals than she could count. The ritual had started months ago by accident, when she had been playing for pleasure after her volunteer lesson for the kids. The seniors who had arrived early for bingo had started wandering in to listen before the bingo session started. After that, it happened every single week, seniors showing up in the music room a half hour before bingo to listen to her play before they went to the gymnasium where the bingo session was held.

"Brew Magic on Friday?" Sarah suggested. "After work?" She loved her girl chats with Emily, but she had a feeling this week she might be squirming. Emily could be as bad as Elsie when she wanted information.

"I'll be there. I want to hear the whole story," Emily warned her with a wink before she left the room to attend to her duties as director of the youth center.

"There's no story to tell," Sarah whispered softly to herself. It had all been a terrible mistake, an incident that should never have happened. She felt guilty, knowing she should have sent Dante home the moment he'd arrived, but she didn't. It wasn't just the lobster rolls or his attempt to say he was sorry. It was the man himself. Something about Dante Sinclair fascinated her, and she wanted to unravel him piece by piece to figure out exactly how his mind worked. Maybe it would give her some clue as to why she was so unnaturally drawn to him.

Needing a distraction, Sarah started to play. She didn't need to see sheet music. She could play almost anything by heart, having played most classical piano pieces hundreds of times.

She started with Rachmaninoff's Prelude in G Minor. It was one of her favorite classical pieces, the composer leaving so much of the arrangement open to the interpretation of the player. Losing herself in the melodic bass lines, she allowed herself to express her passion in the music, her fingers flying over the keyboard as she poured every emotion she'd been feeling throughout the week into her playing. *This* was her emotional outlet, the one activity where she felt safe letting go of intellect and reasoning to just . . . feel. Every emotion was woven into the music: sorrow, joy, confusion, disappointment, guilt, and pain. Finally finishing the piece to a round of applause from her small audience, Sarah started right in on another, Franz Liszt's "La Campanella." It was a livelier composition, and one that had never failed to make her heart a little lighter after performing it. She finished with gusto, panting as she struck the last chord. Standing to thank her elderly audience, she startled as she saw Dante and Jared Sinclair sitting in the crowd.

The two Sinclair brothers were hard to miss. They were the youngest listeners, their darker hair standing out among a sea of mostly silver-haired ladies. Her gaze locked with Dante's, his expression fierce and his eyes so hungry that he looked like a predator that had finally found some desirable prey. Dante's stare was so intense that Sarah couldn't pull her gaze away. She wasn't even entirely certain how long she stayed like that, frozen, her eyes captured by his, before the others in the room started making musical requests. Finally, Sarah jerked away from the fixed stare and nodded hesitantly when someone asked her to play a particular tune. She sat back down again and played for the next fifteen minutes, waiting for the next request before she started to play again, keeping her focus on the gleaming wood in front of her.

I can feel his eyes on me and the tension between us from here.

Sarah's hands were shaking when the last song was finally complete and the bingo crowd started filing out of the room, all of them smiling and telling her how beautifully she played before they left.

"You're incredible. I've never heard Rachmaninoff interpreted quite that way. It was very beautiful and incredibly eloquent," Jared Sinclair commented as he approached her. "That was the most pleasurable half hour I've spent anywhere in a long time."

Sarah smiled at him despite the fact that he'd spilled her secret. His tone was genuine and the praise obviously sincere. There was nothing more satisfying than knowing she'd made someone's day a little brighter with music. "Thanks. You like classical?"

"I do," Jared admitted. "I've heard some of the best pianists in the world, but your playing is outstanding. I'm surprised you never pursued a musical career."

Sarah stood and carefully pushed the bench in closer to the piano. "I don't think I'd enjoy it as much if it became an actual job." She couldn't imagine playing for a living, having her music become a duty that she had to do on a schedule. It wouldn't be the same.

"Thank you for sharing your talent," Jared replied, his tone genuine as he grinned at her before walking slowly out of the room.

"You're welcome," she called after him as she stepped down from the elevated platform where the piano was situated, grabbing her purse from the floor as she went.

Her head swung to the right as she noticed that the room wasn't entirely empty. Dante Sinclair hadn't moved from his chair, and his expression was still as focused as it had been earlier.

"I need to lock the room up," Sarah told him as calmly as possible, her heart beginning to race as he stood.

"We need to talk," Dante told her in a graveled, demanding voice.

He sounded like a man who wasn't going to take no for an answer.

CHAPTER 6

Mine!

Dante's entire body was wired up and tense, his instincts pounding at him to take Sarah away somewhere and satiate her until she couldn't think straight anymore. She was dressed in a pair of blue-and-yellow-striped shorts and a short-sleeved matching blue shirt. The shorts were long, almost to her knees, and weren't meant to be provocative, but on her, they were sexy as hell. Even the innocent, shiny pink polish on her toenails that peeked out from a pair of casual sandals made his dick hard.

He hadn't just listened to her play the piano; he had felt her. Underneath her logical, analytical exterior was a woman of fire and passion. Yeah. He'd already known that, but he hadn't realized just how raw those emotions really were. He'd watched her face the entire time he'd been listening to her pour her heart into her music, and it had leveled him, leaving him completely destroyed. He could feel her need just like it was his own, and the sensations hadn't stopped when the music had ceased. Dante could still feel that sense of longing, and he knew that he was exuding it just as much as Sarah was. Tension flowed in the space between them like an electric current, and his cock was so hard that he was barely able to suppress the need to touch her, to somehow claim her. Even watching her smile at Jared had nearly killed him. He didn't want another man near her, especially when she was vulnerable. Was it just him who could see that she wore every emotion close to the surface when she was playing?

"Let's go take a walk," Dante suggested, gritting his teeth to keep from suggesting what he really wanted: let's go home and fuck until neither one of us can move. He moved close to her and took her hand, guiding her out of the room.

"Wait. I need to lock up, and I have to go pick up Coco," she told him nervously.

He waited impatiently as she locked the door to the music room, following her as she dropped the key in a box near the front entrance, and then detoured to the gymnasium to peek into the bingo games. "Randi must have her," Sarah murmured, moving to another room and cracking the door to look inside.

Dante breathed a sigh of relief as Sarah opened the door wider and he saw the room contained only one petite, dark-haired woman and a couple of kids. Randy was Randi, and she was a female.

"Hey, Randi. I just wanted to get Coco out of your way," Sarah said, her eyes landing on the dog the woman was holding in her lap.

"She's never a bother. You know I love her. I'd steal her away from you if I thought I could get away with it." The woman rose from her seat and placed Coco on the floor. "And the kids love her. It took a while to get down to doing their homework." She leaned around Sarah's body. "Who's this?"

"Dante Sinclair, meet Miranda Tyler. She's a local teacher and a very good friend of Emily's," Sarah told him as she scooted from her place between them so he could see Randi.

Dante smiled at the brunette and held out his hand. "We've actually met. She was the maid of honor for Emily at her and Grady's wedding. It's good to see you again, Randi."

"Same here," Randi answered, taking his hand and shaking it before adding, "I'm sorry about your partner, Dante. And I'm sorry you were hurt. I was relieved to hear that you were doing better."

"Thanks," he responded quietly, uncomfortable because he wasn't quite used to talking about Patrick actually being dead. He didn't know Randi very well, but from what little he'd seen of her at Grady's wedding, she seemed like a nice enough woman.

Sarah pulled a leash from her purse and attached it to Coco's collar. "Emily and I are meeting at Brew Magic after work on Friday if you'd like to come."

Randi's face lit up. "I wouldn't miss it. It looks like I have a lot to catch up on." She glanced curiously at Sarah, and then at Dante. "I didn't realize you two were . . . together."

Dante watched as Sarah's face flushed, and she stammered, "Oh, no . . . we aren't . . . we don't . . . he's my patient."

Dante winked at Randi. "We actually are, and we do. And I just changed doctors so she isn't my physician anymore." *Because I want to fuck her too desperately to have her as my doctor.* Dante was damn tired of Sarah trying to ignore the attraction between the two of them.

"Difference of opinion?" Randi asked mischievously.

"Maybe for now. But I'll convince her," Dante told Randi adamantly as he grabbed Sarah's hand and pulled her out of the room, closing the door quietly behind him.

"I can't believe you just said that," Sarah whispered harshly as they walked toward the front entrance. "You lied. I'm your physician. I can't be seeing you in any other way."

"One of the things we need to talk about," Dante answered, squeezing her hand as she tried to pull away. "We're going to settle this now, Sarah."

"There's nothing to settle," she answered angrily. "I trust Randi, but if you don't let go of my hand, the whole town will think we're . . . together."

It was dark as they walked outside, and Dante headed for the boardwalk. There might still be people around, but it was a little more private. "I can't keep pretending that you're just my doctor, that I don't feel the need to rip your clothes off and fuck you until we're both satisfied."

"What happened at my house shouldn't ever have happened. You were under the influence of narcotics. I shouldn't have responded the way I did. I should have taken you home. I'm your doctor and I shouldn't have taken advantage of the whole situation. I'm sorry," she said breathlessly.

Dante halted underneath one of the lamps along the boardwalk to see her face clearly. Nope. She wasn't messing with him. He could see the remorse and regret on her face.

Shit. Was she really that innocent? She has to be. That guilty expression is real.

And damned if that didn't just make his cock that much harder.

"Are you under the impression that you somehow molested me? That I wasn't totally aware of every single thing that was happening?" Dante couldn't keep the amusement out of his voice.

"It's not funny." Sarah glared up at him. "Maybe I didn't exactly try to seduce you, but I contributed to what happened. I didn't stop it. I even encouraged it."

"That's what happens when two people get all hot and bothered, when they need to fuck so desperately that they can't even remember their own names," he told her gutturally, his mind focused on nothing except how badly he wanted to make her come. Really, he couldn't say he had a whole lot of experience with this particular situation. He'd never felt like this about a woman before.

"I don't get that way," Sarah protested.

That was a challenge if Dante had ever heard one. Maybe Sarah didn't mean it to be, but he'd certainly be willing to prove her wrong. "You wanted the same thing I did. Admit it." His need to hear her say the words wasn't something he could ignore. Possessive instincts were pounding at him, and he knew that the gnawing pain in his gut wasn't going away until she admitted that she wanted him just as damn desperately as he wanted her.

"It doesn't matter what I wanted. You weren't in your right mind, and I'm your doctor." She turned away from him to stare out at the ocean beyond the boardwalk.

Dante wanted desperately to laugh, but he didn't. Sarah was obviously upset and troubled, and no matter how strange her notions might be to him, they meant something to her. She really felt guilty for what had happened. It might be funny to him that she thought she'd somehow coerced him. Hell, he wished. He fucking fantasized about that.

He tried to tell her calmly, "I wasn't under the influence of the drugs. They had already worn off, and I didn't take any more of them until I got back home again. When I said they made me feel strange, I just meant I wouldn't drive while I was taking them, and I was speaking in past tense." He tugged on her hand, leading her down to a beach that was lit only by moonlight. Reaching down, he let Coco off her leash and dropped it into the sand. "I don't think she'll go far."

"She won't," Sarah agreed nervously.

Dante recaptured her hand and pulled it against his groin. "I've been like this since the moment I saw you. There isn't one damn second that my cock isn't hard when you're near me. This isn't drug induced, and I'll be damned if I even understand it myself. But I can't ignore it, and I'm past the point where I give a shit why." Dante wasn't in the mood to reason anything out. He needed her, and he wanted to do something about it. He was a take-action type of guy. He'd never been this obsessed over a woman. Not ever. And all he wanted to do right now was calm his ass down by satiating her.

Dante nearly groaned as her fingers hesitantly traced the outline of his engorged cock. Even over the denim of his jeans, the feel of her touching him made him hotter than any woman ever had, and his dick wasn't even out of his pants.

"I don't understand this." She kept tracing her fingers over the denim. "We hardly know each other. I don't know what your favorite color is or what kind of music you like. I have no idea what your favorite food is, or if you have a favorite book. You're a billionaire who has more money than just about anyone else on the planet, and I'm a doctor who went to school on scholarships and student loans. My father might have been a rocket scientist, but he wasn't good with money, and there wasn't much left for my mother when he died. We have almost nothing in common."

Dante could hear the uncertainty and confusion in her voice. Despite her brilliance, Sarah was still innocent. Her intelligent mind was still trying to make sense of the two of them wanting each other. In reality, it didn't make sense. It just . . . was. For Christ's sake, he was a homicide detective who got laid whenever possible, but he didn't get involved because of his job, and he didn't get territorial afterward. Ever. Now he was possessive, and all he'd really done was kiss Sarah. This wasn't his normal behavior, and he was more than a little unsettled by the whole damn situation. Problem was, he couldn't ignore his instincts. And the vulnerability he could hear in her voice made comforting her his first priority.

He grasped her hand that was cupping him through his jeans and pulled her body into his, wrapping his arms around her waist. He buried his face in her hair and inhaled, letting her fragrance fill his senses. "I love dark blue, a blue so dark that it looks almost violet. There aren't many types of music that I don't like, and it just depends on what mood I'm in. I think lobster rolls are my new favorite food, and I don't have much time to read because I'm never usually still enough to finish a book." His hands moved to her ass and pulled her pelvis up and against his aching cock. "And I don't give a shit about my money. I never have. I live in a one-bedroom apartment in Los Angeles, and my salary more than covers all of my needs unless I want something special. I use a family friend to manage and invest for me. My job has always consumed me, so I don't have time to even spend any money. I don't have a private jet, although I have to admit that I think Grady's is pretty nice. Most times, I forget that I'm even a billionaire. I live the same way you do: I live for my job."

Sarah squirmed, trying gently to move away from him. "Your ribs—"

"Would feel a whole lot better if you'd stop moving," Dante finished.

Sarah froze. "I'm sorry. Did I hurt you?"

Jesus. His dick was pulsating just from the heat of her covering him and the feel of her soft, fragrant body against him. "I'd give anything to have you naked right now," he rasped, his heart hammering against his chest wall.

"You'd be disappointed if I were," she told him warily.

No, he wouldn't, and he didn't understand why she'd think that. He'd taste every inch of her exposed, fragrant, soft skin until she was whimpering for him to take her. Unable to wait another moment, he moved his hands up her back and trapped her head between his palms. He figured she knew more than enough about him now. If she wanted details, she could have them later.

Fuck it.

He covered her mouth with his, savoring the sweetness of the connection as he devoured her. Spearing his hands into her soft curls, he lost himself in the feel of her body and the relief of finally being able to possess her in some way.

Mine. She's mine.

Dante didn't fight his needs anymore. He needed to brand her as his, he needed to dominate her and protect her, and he gave in to those entangled desires as his tongue explored her mouth, claiming every inch of it. When she wrapped her arms around his neck and pulled his mouth even harder against hers, Dante nearly lost his mind from the pleasure of her submission.

I need to touch her before I lose it.

Taking one hand from her hair, he let it slide between their bodies, yanking on the drawstring of her shorts.

One touch. There's nobody around. It's dark.

When his hand slid into her shorts and beneath a light pair of panties, he knew one touch wasn't going to be enough. His fingers met nothing but slick, velvety heat, and her pussy was saturated. Dante nearly groaned as he stroked through her sleek folds, his fingers searching and finding her clit.

He caught and swallowed a whimper coming from her throat, the sound of her arousal making him lose every thought except making her come. She needed, and he wanted to provide.

Pulling his mouth from hers, he rasped, "Come for me, Sarah. I need to make you come." His need to satiate her was unstoppable. As much as he wanted to bury himself inside of her heat, he couldn't. The beach was deserted at the moment, and there was only the moonlight to illuminate them, but he selfishly didn't want anyone to see her vulnerable except him.

"I can't," she panted. "I—"

"You can," he told her harshly, his breathing getting heavier as he grasped a lock of her hair and tilted her head back to taste the soft skin of her neck. He teased the small bundle of nerves relentlessly with his fingers, feeling her grow impossibly wetter as he stroked her over and over. "You're so hot, sweetheart."

"Dante, I can't stop—"

"Don't stop," he demanded, feeling her entire body start to tremble against him. "Come for me."

She moaned, making sweet sounds of pleasure that satisfied Dante in a way he'd never experienced before. He bit gently on the skin of her neck, and that seemed to make her even crazier. She squirmed, but he didn't give a shit about the pain it caused to his sore ribs. Her frenzy fed his, and he put more pressure on her clit, moving faster and faster.

"Dante, Dante," she moaned, her nails biting into his back through his light T-shirt.

"Come for me, Sarah," he growled, loving the sound of his name on her lips when she was on the verge of orgasm, needing to feel her release.

"Yes," she moaned, totally lost.

Dante covered her mouth again, this time to smother her scream as her body vibrated with the strength of her climax. He prolonged her bliss as long as possible, caressing her pussy until she sagged against him, spent.

Mine.

He wrapped an arm around her waist for support and laid her head against his shoulder, stroking her hair as he relished the feeling of exhilaration pumping through his body. The satisfaction vaulting through him right now was better than the best fuck he'd ever had.

"This is what we have in common, Sarah," he said huskily as he absently toyed with her hair.

"Lust?" she answered breathlessly. "I can't believe that just happened."

For some reason, Dante wasn't happy with her description of what was happening between them. He'd had lust. This was something entirely different. But he answered, "Yeah. What's wrong with lust?"

"I didn't think it would be like this," she admitted, her voice laced with uncertainty. "That was . . . overwhelming."

Dante felt like beating on his chest. Overwhelming was good. He wanted to shatter every illusion she had about sensible passion. She'd completely ruined him for ever having casual sex again. He knew that, and he wanted her to be as stunned as he was right now.

"Oh, God. I'm sorry. I'm all over you," Sarah exclaimed, sounding mortified. "You shouldn't be taking my weight right now. Damn! Why do you make me forget rational thought?"

Dante smirked into the darkness and tightened his hold on her. "It doesn't hurt, and you can't think straight because you just had a mind-blowing orgasm. And I wish you *were* all over me."

"This is not amusing." Sarah pulled away from him and picked up the dog leash on the sand. Coco was lying on the beach only a few feet away, and she snapped the leash onto the dog's collar before she turned back toward him. "We have to stop this, Dante."

"I can't," he told her gravely, knowing he couldn't. This was as new for him as it was for her, but he wasn't afraid of it. He was more afraid of losing the chance of having the intensity of the emotions Sarah made him feel. He'd been living in darkness since the day Patrick died. If he was honest, the emptiness had probably been there for quite a while on some level, even before Patrick's death. "You make me feel alive again," he confessed hoarsely.

Dante took her hand and led her safely to the boardwalk where there was more light. They started walking slowly back toward the youth center.

"I know these last few weeks have been difficult for you, Dante. Maybe you just need a distraction, but I can't do this," she said flatly as she walked along beside him.

"You think that's what this is? A distraction? A distraction is watching a movie or a football game. A distraction is going fishing or stopping for a beer. A distraction is not losing my fucking mind over a woman." Dante paused near his truck and grasped her upper arm to stop her from going any farther. "Have dinner with me."

She looked up at him, her eyes shining with uncertainty and damp with tears. Seeing her sadness and her eyes welled up with tears slammed him in the gut.

"What's wrong?" He was really worried now, and he was pretty certain this wasn't a side that Sarah showed to anyone often. He pushed her gently back against the truck and crowded her, putting a palm on each side of her on the truck. She wasn't getting away until she was smiling again.

"You make me feel alive, too," she told him solemnly, as though it were a horrible, life-changing event. "I don't know how to handle it. I don't know how to do . . . this." She motioned at herself and then at him.

Dante grinned down at her. "Sweetheart, I know how to do it. I'll be happy to teach you."

She frowned at him. "That's not what I mean. I know the anatomy part." She paused for a moment before confiding in a whisper, "I'm scared. I've never felt this way before, and my body doesn't react like this. I think, I reason, and when I'm with you, I just *feel* instead of trying to make sense of what's happening between us. My body is in control instead of my brain. That's never happened before, Dante."

Dante wondered if she had ever said those words in her entire life. Again, he was overcome with the desire to protect her when she was vulnerable. "Don't be afraid." He gathered her into his arms and held her, his heart racing as he tried to wrap her up inside him so she'd never feel afraid again. "Have dinner with me. We can go to Tony's Fish House. Jared said the food is good."

Sarah sniffled as she leaned back and looked up at him. "It's touristy and expensive. I've never eaten there."

"I think I can afford it. Go with me. We have to eat, right? I hate eating alone."

She eyed him warily, and Dante held his breath until she murmured, "I'm your doctor. I can't be seen out with you in public."

"You're not my doctor anymore," he told her irritably. "What I told Randi is true. I requested a change to Dr. Samuels. So no more bullshit. You'll see the request for my medical records on your fax in the morning." He knew if he didn't change doctors, she'd keep her distance. At least if he switched physicians, she wouldn't be able to use the excuse that she was his doctor. He was damn glad he'd done the switch now, after seeing how eaten up she was by guilt. The idea that she'd taken advantage of him was ridiculous, but she still had a deep sense of ethics. "So no more doctor-patient relationship."

"You really switched?" she asked him, looking astonished.

"Yes."

"Why?"

"Because I knew if I didn't, you'd keep treating me like a patient," he replied gruffly. "And that's the last damn thing I want from you."

"I'll think about it," she answered carefully. "Call me."

He would. Tomorrow. Or maybe later tonight. He'd wear her down until she gave in to him. He wanted to explore what was happening between them. And he'd make sure she caved in.

He let her go, waiting for her to walk to her car. She didn't. She started toward Main Street. "Where the hell did you park?"

"I didn't drive. I walked. I like to walk."

Dante calculated the distance to her house and some of the secluded areas she'd have to pass through to get there. "Get in the truck, woman." He broke out in a cold sweat just thinking about her walking home in the dark. "It's not safe for a woman to be walking home alone."

Sarah stopped and turned around. "This is Amesport, not Los Angeles or Chicago."

"I don't give a shit. There are too many places where something could happen. You have tourists in this town. Not everyone is a local." And even if they were all locals, there were crazy people everywhere. "Get in the truck."

Her brows drew together in irritation, leaving a tiny crinkle between her eyes. "I've been walking it for a year. I do need exercise."

"There are far more pleasurable ways to exercise," he told her ominously, unlocking and opening the passenger door of the truck. "In," he demanded. He'd be damned if he was going to let her walk one more step into the darkness.

She came toward him slowly, stopping in front of him. "Is that your police officer voice? It's pretty bossy."

"Sweetheart, you have no idea what an asshole I can be. Be happy you're not a criminal," he told her dangerously.

"It kind of makes me want to run out and commit a crime. That whole dictator thing is pretty hot," she mentioned matter-of-factly. "Not that I'd always obey your commands, but the whole caveman persona has its merits, sexually." She paused before adding, "I think I might like it."

Holy hell! She's going to make me crazy! I'd like to go caveman all over her ass right now.

Not that his erection had ever subsided, but his cock was twitching merrily right at the moment. He picked her up and set her gently in the passenger seat. After taking the leash from her hand, he picked up Coco and placed the dog in the backseat. As he fastened Sarah's seat belt, he replied, "You better get used to it, because I think you're going to throw me back into the Stone Age." He closed the door before she could reply. If she said one more word about the merits of being sexually dominated, his dick was going to explode.

Funny thing was, it was all an observation for her, and she was just starting to realize her own sexuality. Sarah wasn't coming on to him, but it didn't matter. The sexy, slightly bewildered, analytical voice just seemed to do it for him.

He jogged around the truck and jumped into the driver's seat. "No more walking alone at night. Your pint-sized mutt isn't exactly good protection."

"Yes, Detective Sinclair," she answered immediately, her lips forming into a smile.

Dante glared at her, wondering if she was being sarcastic. "What's amusing? Your safety is not a joke. It's dangerous for a woman to walk alone at night."

"Nothing is actually amusing. I guess I've just never had someone worry about whether or not I was safe," she answered carefully. "It's . . . strange."

"Then it's about time somebody did," he told her in a low, graveled voice, astounded that she'd never had anyone who looked out for her.

But she'd told him about her mother, a woman who seemed to only be interested in her daughter's scholastic achievements, and she had no siblings. It was highly possible that everyone assumed that because she was so gifted, so special, that she'd never needed any backup or support. How asinine was that? Because of her situation, what she'd really needed was a champion, a protector. Sarah dealt with things in black and white, logic and reason. Unfortunately, the crazies in the world didn't analyze things in their brains the same way Sarah did.

Mine!

He'd gladly be the man who watched out for her. She might be more intelligent than he was, scholastically, but he was street smart, which was exactly what she needed.

He started the engine, backed out of the parking lot, and headed toward her house. They didn't talk much, but every time he turned to look at her, she was still smiling.

CHAPTER 7

I just had an incredible orgasm on a dark beach like an overheated teenager!

She should probably be mortified, but she wasn't. For the first time, she felt . . . normal. Dante had just opened a portion of her soul that she hadn't known actually existed. She hadn't lied when she'd admitted to him that he made her feel alive. When he'd said that to her, it was like her body was echoing the same emotions, as if some part of her that had been dormant her entire life had finally awoken.

Sarah's entire world had revolved around study. The only enjoyable thing about her years with her mother had been her music, those moments when she could express her loneliness by playing the piano. Unfortunately, no one had ever wanted to actually protect her . . . until Dante. He treated her like she was special, but for the first time, it had nothing to do with her intelligence level.

He wants me.

Somehow, it was significant that he looked at her and liked the woman he saw in front of him, accepted her so easily. He didn't keep his distance from her because he was intimidated. In fact, he didn't seem the least bit daunted. He certainly had no problem trying to boss her around when he was trying to protect her, and her female hormones were standing up and taking notice. Maybe Dante did have a serious testosterone overload, but he was pushing her boundaries, making her aware of herself as a female. Yet she knew he had his own vulnerabilities, and that made for one hot male, a guy who was pretty much irresistible to her.

Brilliant deduction, Einstein. He's so irresistible that I lose all lucid thought every time he touches me.

The problem was, she really didn't want to resist him. She wanted him to touch her, teach her everything she'd missed. Her education was definitely lacking in the carnal pleasure department. If a simple kiss, a simple touch had rocked her world that much, she could only imagine what it would be like to get naked with him.

I can't do that. He'd probably be turned off completely if I actually did get naked.

"What happened?" Dante asked curiously from the driver's seat of the truck.

Sarah pulled herself out of her own thoughts. "Nothing. Why?"

"You're not smiling anymore. I don't like it," Dante replied gruffly.

Had she been smiling? Maybe she had. Basically, she had been focused on him and the afterglow of a stunning, eye-opening orgasm. She also liked the fact that he wanted to protect her. If that hadn't made her smile, nothing would. "Nothing happened."

Except I was thinking about getting naked with you, and how sad it is that I can't. Maybe in the dark . . . ?

"You didn't tell me your favorite food, or your favorite color," Dante said hoarsely. "Talk to me."

Dante's request to share something about herself with him hit her straight in the heart. No man had ever been curious about her as a person. Even the man who had taken her virginity had been using her, probably to help him get through a class that had been giving him problems. Either that or she'd been a lousy lay. She never really figured out why he'd dumped her after their first sexual encounter, but she hadn't really cared. The only thing they'd had in common was med school, and she'd been way ahead of him in class even though he'd been older. And she'd decided, after that uncomfortable experience, that she wasn't really missing anything. Now she was pretty certain she was wrong. She'd just been missing the right man to teach her.

"I don't know how to ride a bike, or dance. I never had a doll when I was a girl; I had a piano. I never had friends when I was young because it took time away from studying, and it wasn't essential in developing my potential. I've always felt odd because I was young in an adult world, but I don't ever remember actually being a child. And the only game I was ever allowed to play was chess because it was an intellectual game, but I was only allowed to play it with someone who could beat me because my mother wanted me to be challenged." Dante's desire to learn about her had opened up a flood of information that she'd never shared with anyone. "I never had real friends until I came to live in Amesport, and I've been lonely my whole life because I was different. I've never felt normal." Sarah took a shaky breath before adding, "My favorite color is red, although I never wear it because my mother felt it wasn't an appropriate color for an intellectual woman. Too flashy. You already know I love lobster rolls, and I love classical music, but I also like to listen to country. Honestly, I can find some musical merit in just about any type of music." She hesitated before adding, "I'm pretty certain that you're right: there's a lot more to sex than the mating of the human species."

Dante pulled his truck into her driveway and turned off the engine before turning to her, his expression astonished. "Who doesn't know how to ride a bike?"

Sarah shrugged uncomfortably. "Me."

"Christ! Don't you ever do anything just for the hell of it?"

"Not usually. But I've done a lot more things here than I did in Chicago. I walk just because I can. It makes no sense and it wastes time, but I do it because I like it, and I love all the little shops on Main Street. I get together with some of the friends I've made here, and I volunteer at the youth center. I love the classics, but lately I've been devouring every romance novel I can find." Sarah unbuckled her seat belt and hopped out of the truck. Maybe she shouldn't have said anything. Maybe now he thought she was a freak. Hastily, she dug for her house keys and pulled them from her purse, then grabbed Coco as she hopped into the seat that Sarah had just vacated. Once the dog was on the ground, she let Coco off the leash, allowing her to explore her own territory.

She hurried to the door, not realizing Dante was behind her until he took the keys from her hand and trapped her between his massive body and the wall beside the door. Looking up at his face, Sarah could see his volatile expression.

"What kind of mother never gets her kid a doll, teaches her to ride a bike, or lets her play any games as a kid? Shit! I thought I was screwed up because I had an abusive, alcoholic father, but even we had games. And because we were filthy rich, we had the best of everything, including bikes. If we didn't, it would have hurt the old man's image as one of the elite." His nostrils flared and his breathing grew ragged. "I think you'd be the most fuckable woman on the planet wearing anything or nothing, but red is sexy. Do you have a red dress?"

Sarah nodded hesitantly. She had one, but she'd never worn it, an impulse buy when she'd been shopping with Randi and Emily.

"Wear it when we go out for dinner," Dante instructed. "I'll teach you to ride a bike. I've seen some incredible bike trails here. Hell, I'll even let you kick my ass at chess. I play, but I have no doubt you're better."

Sarah looked up him warily. "Why?"

"Because it's about time you experienced life. I know what it's like to be wrapped up in your job, making it your entire world, so I can't say I'm not guilty of doing the same thing. But there have to be certain moments where you make time for other things. Pleasurable things. The best memories I have of Patrick were going out fishing for the day, or getting on our motorcycles just to get out of the city. I haven't balanced my life very well, but I plan on starting. Patrick used to tell me that life was too short not to take the time for guilty pleasures. I think he was right. And now I'm not just living my life for me; I'm living it for him. I'm going to do all of the things I've always talked about doing but never had the chance. I think he'd like that."

Sarah's eyes filled with tears as she watched Dante's expression turn from angry to regretful. He wasn't over his partner's death, but he was moving in the right direction. "I think he would, too," she told him solemnly, moving her hand up to cup his cheek.

"Are you ready to take a few chances?" A slow grin formed on Dante's face, growing steadily larger. "I'm a very willing teacher."

He was right. Her upbringing and history had kept her from doing a lot of things she'd wanted to do. Although she'd grown emotionally once she'd moved away from her mother, she was still a long way from really breaking out of the shell of isolation she'd surrounded herself with during her childhood and adolescence.

She wanted to spend more time with Dante, explore these new emotions and her sexuality. Her ethics would have eaten her alive if he was still her patient, but now that he'd solved that problem, she was free to explore this—whatever it was—thing with Dante. "Since you're not my patient anymore, I think I'd like that. Although Dr. Samuels isn't nearly as good a doctor as I am," Sarah teased. Honestly, Dr. Samuels was a fine doctor who'd been in practice for at least twenty years, but she couldn't resist giving Dante a hard time for dropping her services.

"I'd rather settle for a mediocre doctor than have you keep protesting and refusing to spend time with me," Dante rumbled impatiently.

Sarah opened her mouth to speak, but Dante swiftly captured her lips in a demanding assault that made her immediately forget whatever it was that she wanted to say. His embrace was brief, but rough and dominant. By the time he let her breathe again, her body was already clamoring for him to give her more.

"Go inside before I take you right here against the wall," Dante said rigidly as he unlocked the door and opened it before handing her back her keys.

"You're not well enough for that," Sarah argued, still gulping for air as she caught the grim expression on his face.

"You'd be surprised," Dante replied ominously.

Sarah stepped through the door, still dazed from Dante's kiss. But in less than a heartbeat, her mood went from hazy to horrified.

"Oh my God!" The first glance at her tiny, adorable cottage left her mouth hanging open in fear and revulsion, unable to say anything else. It literally looked like a bomb had exploded. Her cute little lamps and anything else made of glass was shattered, the shards of glass scattered on the floor. All of her furniture was shredded, every picture on the wall destroyed. In the place of the pictures that were now on the floor, only one thing remained . . . a message.

Her already racing heart skipped a beat as she read the message painted in red on the bare wall:

Die Bitch!!

"Fuck! What the hell?" Dante growled as he came in behind her. "Don't touch anything." He grasped her by the waist and physically hauled her out of the house. He deposited her on the porch. "Stay here and dial nine-one-one." His voice was graveled and angry.

Sarah watched as he darted to his truck and came back with a gun in his hand, and a look as coldly lethal as a killer on his face. He'd changed in an instant, and Sarah had to remind herself that Dante was actually the good guy. Panic seized her as she watched him enter the house while she fumbled for her phone. She watched as she explained what had happened to the dispatcher and was assured that help was on the way. She hung up the phone, gaping as Dante prowled through the house, holding the gun like it was an extension of himself, careful not to touch anything as he searched.

"Dante," she whispered softly as he moved out of sight and into the hallway where the two bedrooms and bathroom were located. Sirens sounded in the distance, but Sarah's entire focus was on Dante.

What if someone is still there? What if he gets hurt? He's not even healed yet.

She reminded herself that he was an experienced detective, a police officer, but it didn't matter. Cops died. He'd just lost a partner.

She held her breath as her whole body trembled with fear, waiting for any sound that would indicate that Dante was in trouble.

The sirens grew louder, and she released a sigh of relief as Dante moved carefully through the rubble, shoving his weapon into the waistband of his jeans at the small of his back. "The bastard is already gone," he rasped, gathering her shivering body into a comforting hug. "I'm sorry. Who the hell would do something like this? And why?"

Maybe he found me!

She tried to quiet the voice in her head, clinging to Dante as a lifeline, trying to make sense of what had happened. It was more likely that it had been destructive kids, maybe tourists out to make trouble, possibly while they were intoxicated on drugs or alcohol.

Die Bitch!!

Someone who knew her, or just a lucky guess that there was a female in the home? The phrase was eerily familiar.

"Were the other rooms okay?" she mumbled against his shoulder.

"No," Dante said simply.

"So the whole house is the same way?" It broke her heart to think of everything she owned in tatters.

"Yes. I'm so sorry, sweetheart." He tightened his grip around her waist, moving a soothing palm up and down her back. "I wish I could have caught whoever did this to you. Jesus. What if you had been home?"

Sarah was glad he hadn't found anyone. The thought of Dante having to go through any type of confrontation, especially when he was still recovering, made her nauseous.

A police SUV squealed into the driveway, followed by a few patrol cars. Sarah recognized the chief of police, Joe Landon, as he came running up to the door. Joe was generally a jovial man who could usually be seen around town talking and showing pictures of his newest grandchild, or his wife, Ruby. Sarah estimated him to be in his early sixties.

His dark hair was graying, but he had a stocky build and was in good shape for a man his age.

Dante quickly briefed the older man on what had happened, and that he had searched for the perpetrator but hadn't touched anything.

"The evidence team is right behind me," Joe remarked in a no-nonsense tone. "I don't recognize you." He glanced at the scar on Dante's face that was clearly visible in the bright porch light outside the door. "Are you that hero homicide detective that we've all been hearing about?"

Dante nodded sharply. "Dante Sinclair," he affirmed as he held his hand out to the police chief.

"Chief Landon, but everyone calls me Joe." He took Dante's hand and shook it hard before letting it go.

The evidence team traipsed up the driveway, and they all entered the house for an investigation after Joe briefed them, letting them know that they had almost no information except that the house had been ransacked.

"You answer your own calls here?" Dante asked, perplexed.

"Not usually. But my damn felony detective decided to move off to Boston. His wife got a job there. I'm filling in. There's nobody on the Amesport force with enough experience to do the job." He eyed Dante curiously. "I don't suppose you're looking for a job."

Alarmed, Sarah responded, "He needs to heal before he even thinks about doing anything physical."

"I'm a homicide detective. It's what I do," Dante replied emphatically.

"There's more variety here," the chief answered persuasively. "If you change your mind, come see me. You're probably overqualified, but I'm thinking of retiring in a year or two. Amesport will need a new chief of police."

"Thanks," Dante answered distractedly, watching from the door as the police collected evidence, keeping his arm around Sarah's waist for support.

Joe moved up beside him, supervising as his employees did the job they were trained to do. After a few moments of silence, Joe told Dante solemnly, "I'm sorry about your partner, son. It's never easy to lose a friend."

Dante shrugged. "It's a rough district. Lots of homicide, most of it gang or drug related."

"I did two tours in Vietnam, watched my buddies die one after another, sometimes right in front of my eyes," Joe replied. "Amesport doesn't see a lot of homicide, but I know what it's like to lose a friend in the line of duty."

Dante looked at Joe, astounded. "How the hell did you live through that?"

"One day at a time," Joe replied thoughtfully. "When I got back from my second tour, I met Ruby, and she changed my life. The love of a good woman can do a lot for a man. I never forgot the friends I lost, but I try to honor them by living a good life. Amesport has been good to me."

"Are you originally from here?" Dante asked curiously.

"Born and raised. Found Ruby here and she was all grown up when I came back home from Vietnam," Joe answered with a smile.

They continued to watch the team work silently for a few minutes before Joe looked at Sarah. "You have any idea who would do this, Doc? Considering the circumstances, I think we have to assume that it could have something to do with what happened to you in Chicago."

Sarah shuddered. "It could have been anyone. Maybe it was drug related, or troubled kids."

Joe knew all about her history because the case in Chicago was still open. She'd given him the basics about the situation when she'd moved to Amesport.

"Looks like there was plenty of stuff that could have been sold for drug money, but they broke it instead. Sarah, I know it's a scary possibility, but we need to be prepared. I need to put the force on alert for this guy. After the evidence is gathered, you can see if anything's missing. But we have to consider the possibility," Joe told her in a stern but kindly voice.

"What the hell are you talking about?" Dante demanded. "What happened in Chicago?"

"That's for Sarah to share with you, son. If she hasn't, then she doesn't want to."

Sarah shuddered, and her blood seemed to turn to ice. She didn't want to think about that possibility at all. Moving to Amesport had been her escape. She was supposed to be safe here. However, her rational brain kicked in, and she knew she had to face facts. "I guess it's possible."

"I'll get in touch with the Chicago police. See if they have anything new and let them know what happened here," Joe said, his voice emanating regret.

"Will I be able to get back into my house?" Sarah asked, knowing she would probably never sleep a wink after what had happened here.

"No. Not right now. And you shouldn't be alone," Joe answered firmly.

"She won't be. She'll be with me," Dante answered forcefully, the tone of his voice unyielding.

"I don't have anything. No clothing—"

"We'll get whatever you need. You can't go in there right now. I don't know exactly why your house was targeted, or what happened in Chicago, but somebody obviously wants you dead. This looks like something they did in a rage because they didn't find you here." Dante looked at Sarah with a pissed-off scowl. "You're going to fill me in on who wants you dead."

"You okay with that, Doc?" Joe questioned, looking at Sarah for confirmation.

"For tonight," Sarah agreed, knowing she couldn't get back into her house until the team was done collecting evidence and the mess was cleaned up.

Dante shot her a look that guaranteed they would argue later, but Sarah would worry about that once the trauma of seeing her house destroyed had passed. Right now she was still shaken, and she wasn't able to reason anything out. All she wanted was the comfort of knowing Dante was close.

"Are you carrying, Detective Sinclair?" Joe scanned Dante's body with his sharp brown eyes.

Dante reached behind him and slowly pulled the gun from his waistband. "In Los Angeles, I'm always carrying. I didn't think it was necessary here. But I had my Beretta in the truck." He handed the gun to Joe. "From now on, I'll always be carrying."

"So you're a Beretta man," Joe said, examining the weapon before handing it back to Dante.

"I have a Glock at home, too. Just so you know," Dante informed him.

"I have no problem with you carrying, especially now that you're looking after Sarah. Just watch yourselves and call me if anything out of the ordinary happens," Joe advised.

The two men exchanged phone numbers before Dante took Sarah's hand and started leading her to the truck.

"Coco!" Sarah exclaimed. "I have to take her with me."

The moment her pup heard her name, she was at Sarah's feet. Dante leaned down and scooped her up with one hand. "I've got her."

Sarah took Coco from Dante after she clambered into the passenger seat of his truck. The dog cuddled against her and laid her small head on Sarah's chest, as though the animal knew that Sarah was distressed. She tightened her hold on her pet, feeling like she needed every bit of comfort she could get.

CHAPTER 8

Dante's rage just kept rising to the surface as he looked through the police records of Sarah's case. Just a few phone calls had gotten the information delivered to his personal computer. He didn't give a shit if it was questionable that he was reviewing records while he wasn't on duty, studying a case that wasn't anywhere close to his own jurisdiction. He was a goddamn cop twenty-four hours a day, seven days a week, and this was personal.

Sarah had been silent on the drive home and had spoken to him only to ask for one of his T-shirts to sleep in. She'd showered and retreated to a guest room, barely saying a word. For the first time since he'd met her, she looked fragile and terrified. Dante didn't like it. He wanted to see her smiling again right fucking now.

Bastard!

Dante's fist slammed onto the desk in his den, right on top of the image of the suspect. It didn't help. He needed to hear the satisfying crack of facial bones breaking as he pummeled the bastard to death. After what he'd done to Sarah, he deserved it.

Gut instinct was telling Dante that this was the perpetrator behind the destruction of Sarah's house. It all fit: the rage behind the crime, the destruction of personal property, and the violent message left behind. The fucker who had nearly killed her still wanted her dead.

No wonder she avoids hospitals now.

She'd told him during one of her home visits that she was seeing outpatients only. He'd never really questioned why Sarah didn't admit patients to the hospital here in Amesport, why she turned their care over to another physician if they needed to be hospitalized. She was relatively new to the area, and he'd thought that maybe she just hadn't gotten her admitting privileges yet.

She doesn't want to go back into a hospital.

"Dante?" Sarah's hesitant voice sounded near the doorway of the den.

He looked up and saw Sarah standing there in just his white T-shirt. She looked exhausted, and her expression was troubled. He wanted to hold her on his lap and wrap himself around her until she felt safe again. Feral impulses made him clench his fists on the desk, and he had to suppress the need to reach for her immediately. She was approaching him, and he needed to let her talk. "I thought you were sleeping."

She shook her head slowly. "I couldn't. I think you need to know what happened. You're helping me. I don't want you to go into this blind. You need to know everything. I'm sorry. I guess I just didn't want to consider that this could be connected to something that happened in Chicago. But that's not rational. Chances are, it is connected. Things like this just don't happen in Amesport."

She's coming to me. She trusts me.

Even though she didn't want to talk about what happened, she was telling him about it to keep him from getting hurt because he didn't have all of the information. For Dante, that was so much more meaningful than him having to confront her and finagle the story from her. He wanted to hear it from her, but he hadn't wanted to push her. "Talk to me."

He watched as she came into the room and settled herself in the comfortable leather chair in front of his desk, tucking her feet beneath her body before she took a big breath. "I was just ending my first year of practice in Chicago when I got a new patient, a nineteen-year-old boy. He'd been involved in a car accident, hit head-on by a drunk driver while his mother was driving. His mom died immediately, but Trey lived through it. He broke both of his legs, and he had other injuries, but he was young, and he slowly improved. He was in his first year of college and wanted to go to medical school. I ended up spending a lot of time with him. We had an orthopedic specialist on the case, but I was his admitting physician. I started making a habit of seeing him last on my hospital rounds so I could help him stay caught up on college work and help him with some of his biology studies. We became very fond of each other."

"He developed a monstrous crush on you," Dante told her quietly.

Sarah shook her head. "No. It wasn't like that."

"Sweetheart, it might not have been that way for you. But believe me, I was a nineteen-year-old kid once, and I know what's primarily on the mind of a nineteen-year-old male." Dante paused for a minute before adding, "You're beautiful and kind, and were only a few years older than he was."

Sarah shrugged. "He never acted inappropriately. He mostly talked about his ambitions to be a doctor."

Dante could guarantee her the kid had his fantasies, but he prompted Sarah. "What happened?"

"I was helping him with some of his classwork one night about three weeks after the accident. His father was there, too. Trey wasn't close to his dad, and he said he had a bad temper. Trey was closer to his mom, and he was still coping with losing her. That night, while I was there helping him with his biology, Trey died." Sarah's voice started to quiver with raw emotion, but she continued. "We coded him for over an hour, but he was gone. The postmortem showed a very large pulmonary embolism, even though we took all precautions because he was such high risk. The case was reviewed and all of the physicians on the case were cleared of any wrongdoing. It just . . . happened." Her voice began to crack.

Dante looked at her tortured expression, his heart aching for her. How devastating must that experience have been when she knew the young patient so well, and was still in her first year of practice? She'd been so damn young. "His father blamed you," Dante stated flatly.

"I don't think he had anyone else to blame. His wife was dead, and the child who he thought was going to live after the accident ended up dying, too. I was there when it happened. I ran the whole code while we tried to resuscitate Trey and failed. The father had to be taken out of the room because he completely snapped. Telling him later that evening that his son was dead was one of the hardest things I've ever had to do. He was angry."

"Two days later, he tried to kill you. I saw the police reports, Sarah," Dante confessed.

Sarah squirmed in her chair and nodded sharply, repositioning her body in the other direction. "Trey's father knew I took the stairs to the ICU every single evening. He saw me coming in and out of the doorway to the stairs often enough. Two days later, he caught me in the stairwell, on the landing between the second and third floor. Everything else that happened is a blur. When he attacked me, he slammed my head against the stone wall in the stairwell. All I remember is him screaming that I killed all of his family and I needed to die. I tried to fight him off, but I didn't have much of a chance. He already had me on the ground, and as soon as he started stabbing me, I got even weaker from blood loss. The note he put on the wall of the cottage is the one thing I can remember him screaming over and over. 'Die, bitch.'"

"Twenty goddamn times. Holy fuck. It's a miracle that you're still alive," Dante rasped, trying to control his own homicidal urges at that moment. Granted, the man had lost his wife and son, but he'd taken his grief out on an innocent woman who had only tried to help his child. And the bastard had almost succeeded in killing her.

"Had one of the nurses not come down the stairwell at just the right time, I would have died that evening. John fled down the stairs and outside as soon as he heard somebody coming down the stairs. He hit an artery in my arm, and I would have bled to death very quickly from the wounds had I not already been in a hospital. The emergency crew there saved my life."

"The police never caught him." Dante met Sarah's gaze, seeing nothing but sadness in her dark blue eyes, tears trailing down her cheeks.

"No," she verified, swiping at her tears. "When I recovered, I couldn't bring myself to go back into the hospital. After Trey died, I was already nauseous just from walking in the door. And after all of the wounds healed from John's assault, I couldn't even make myself go into the hospital. I started having panic attacks."

Unable to control his instincts any longer, Dante got up and took Sarah's hand, pulling her up and wrapping her in his arms. "Who took care of you?" Dante asked in a low, comforting voice as he ran his hand up and down her back. Christ. He wished he had been there for her then.

"My mother. I had an apartment in Chicago close to the hospital, but I stayed with her for a while after the incident. I think it was hard for her, too, because she wanted her independent, successful doctor daughter back. But I couldn't seem to stop the panic attacks every time I tried to go back into the hospital, and I knew I needed a change. I started looking at smaller cities around the country that needed doctors, and I ended up here. I've always wanted to be on the coast, and when I found out how few doctors this town had, I thought it was perfect. I still haven't been able to go into the hospital here, but I've been happy in Amesport until tonight. It was like starting over for me. I never really thought he'd come after me. I thought he attacked me in a fit of post-traumatic rage and grief. If John did this, then he still wants me to die."

"It was him," Dante rumbled, holding her trembling body just a little bit tighter. Fuck! Who could try to hurt this woman? Every instinct Dante had was screaming at him to protect her. Sarah walked around in her own intellectual bubble, and that asshole had broken it in the most horrifying of ways. Now, instead of just feeling isolated and lonely, she felt alone and afraid when she'd never done anything but good for other people. He didn't know much about comforting a woman, but keeping her safe he could do. She was his to protect now—had been since he'd held her soft, responsive body earlier as she went to pieces in his arms.

"I know it's him," she sighed. "I can feel it in my gut. Nobody around here is crazy enough or hates me enough to have done what was done to my house. I knew as soon as I saw the message on the wall. It was the same thing he was screaming the night he stabbed me."

Dante tried like hell not to form that picture in his mind. If he conjured up an image of a crazy man stabbing away at Sarah, he was going to lose it. "You know I'm going to be your shadow until we catch him," Dante warned her.

"I need to go to work, take care of responsibilities—"

"Fine. Then that's where I'll be. Consider me your personal bodyguard. He's here somewhere, and he knows where you live. Obviously, he knows where you work. It's not a big city."

"Oh God, my office—"

"Your office is fine. I called Joe once you went to bed, and he'd already been by your office. Everything is fine there," Dante informed her calmly.

"Dante, I don't want to get you involved in this. You already have enough on your plate right now."

He was healing, and he didn't give a shit about the rest of his issues. He didn't have a single thing happening in his life that was more important than making sure Sarah didn't get hurt. "I'm already involved and I plan on staying that way until John Thompson is either in jail or dead," Dante growled, pulling his head back to give Sarah an obstinate look. "You don't do anything without me. You don't go anywhere without me. If you're stepping outside, I want to know. I'm not trying to make you paranoid, but we know he's in the area, and it won't take him long to find you. We need to nail this asshole, Sarah. You won't have a damn life until we do. I'd rather have you alive and pissed off at me than the alternative." Dante couldn't even bring himself to think about anything happening to Sarah. If she got hurt or worse, he'd lose what was left of his mind.

"This puts you in danger, too, and you still aren't healed. I don't like it," Sarah told him stubbornly as she pulled away from him and sat on the arm of the chair, her arms folded across her breasts.

"You don't have to like it," Dante agreed readily. "You just have to deal with it. You're a woman who deals mostly in reality. What's your alternative? You know you need protection, and you know we need to catch this bastard."

"I can leave. Move again. Go somewhere else and start over," Sarah cried desperately. "It has to be better than taking the risk of someone else getting hurt."

Dante looked down at her, noticing that her entire body was tense, and she seemed so exhausted that she wasn't thinking rationally—for a change. "For how long? Until he catches up to you again? Is that the way you want to live your life . . . running away? I can tell you for a fact that it doesn't work. Leaving Los Angeles didn't make things hurt less, and it didn't stop my grief over losing Patrick. I'm glad I came, but the only one who can resolve those issues is me. Location doesn't make a damn bit of difference."

"I have to do something," she told him desperately.

"Don't even try it," Dante told her irritably. Leaning down, he put a hand on each side of her hips, looking her straight in the eye. "Wherever you go, I'll find you. Wherever you move, I'll figure out where you are and follow you."

"Are you threatening me?" she asked defensively.

"Nope. Those aren't threats, those are promises. Trust me."

Jesus. She's a stubborn female.

Nevertheless, there was a part of her that was just so damn vulnerable, and Dante could see it. She could put on a brave face all she wanted to, but he understood the hell she'd been through, and he wanted her to finally live a life free of fear, a life that didn't make her feel different or odd.

"I do trust you. I just don't want to see you get hurt," Sarah said hesitantly.

Dante slowly shook his head, unable to understand this woman who cared more about his safety than her own. Did she forget that he was a cop? "I won't get hurt. This is what I do, Sarah. And I've done a hell of a lot more dangerous cases than this one." But right now, none of them seemed as important as keeping Sarah safe from somebody who wanted her dead.

I need to protect her. If something happens to her, I'll never forgive myself and I'll never get over it. She's mine to protect now.

"I want to resolve this. You're right. I can't run. I'd be putting other people in danger wherever I go. What can I do?" she asked, her voice resigned and determined now.

Obviously her rational mind is back. "Just don't run away. I'm not in any shape to go chasing after you, but I will if I have to."

Her face turned into an expression of concern. "Are you hurting?"

"No. But I will be if I have to come after your beautiful ass," he told her in a voice of warning.

"You're crazy. You know that, right? You hardly know me, yet you're willing to be my personal bodyguard." Her voice was bewildered.

"There's no body I'd rather be guarding right now than yours, sweetheart." He kissed her forehead before he stood up again. "I have future plans for it."

"I've already told you that you don't want to see me naked," Sarah reminded him warily.

"Oh yeah, I do," Dante contended, his hazel eyes narrowing into a challenging expression.

"Let's just get this issue over with and out of the way," she mumbled irritably.

Sarah stood up in front of him and stepped back. Dante watched in fascination as she crossed her arms, grabbed the hem of her makeshift nightgown, and lifted his T-shirt off of her body hastily, as though she might change her mind if she didn't. She wasn't wearing a stitch of clothing underneath the garment. She stood before him completely nude, and his cock was suddenly jerking in appreciation.

"This is the body you'll see," Sarah told him tremulously. "It's nothing but scars. The knife wasn't big, but the scars are numerous and not very pretty. I lived through the attack, but I see the reminders in the mirror every day."

Dante stood there gaping at her as his eyes ran up and down her body. Sure, she had scars, but that was to be expected after what had happened to her. Otherwise, she was absolutely perfect, from her beautifully formed breasts with pink, generous nipples to her long legs that seemed to stretch forever. He tried not to think about those slender legs wrapped around his waist as he pounded into her until they were both spent, and failed miserably. The blonde thatch of hair between her thighs was as light as the hair on her head, and Dante wanted to bury his face between her legs and feast on her. Touching her had been mind-blowing, but tasting her would be fucking perfect.

Mine.

The word radiated through his body until he could barely keep himself from taking what he already knew belonged to him.

"Put the T-shirt back on." His voice was coarse and graveled, his need to sweep her off to his bed nearly overpowering. But she'd been through too much today. Right now she needed a different kind of comfort, and he wanted to give her whatever she needed. "Go get some sleep."

Holy shit. I need her to cover that beautiful body now, before I do something I might regret. Not that I'll ever forget exactly what it looks like. It will be branded in my mind forever.

Fuck! He wanted her so badly he could hardly take a breath, but he didn't want Sarah like this. He wanted her hot and begging, giving herself to him because she was burning with need. This wasn't that kind of night, and he didn't want any regrets later. Painfully, he shoved his carnal instincts down, but he had a hell of a time doing it with her standing naked in his den. *Sex isn't what she needs. Down, boy!* What Sarah needed right now was a friend, and he'd be whatever she wanted him to be, even if it *was* nearly killing him.

"You can't say I didn't warn you about my body," she mumbled as she pulled the T-shirt back over her head.

Dante watched in confusion as she turned on her heel and hurried out of the room. He heard the padded sound of her footsteps on the carpet as she raced up the stairs before he really understood exactly what was happening.

She thinks I didn't want to look at her body because of her scars?

"Holy fuck!" Dante whispered fiercely, running a frustrated hand through his short hair. How could she *not* feel the sexual tension between them? Hell, *his* need was palpable, and thick enough that it was nearly choking him to death.

I see the reminders in the mirror every day.

Thinking back on their little discussion on sexual chemistry, Dante wondered if Sarah really bought into all that crap about the propagation of the species and being attracted to the ideal mate—one who, obviously, she was under the impression was minus any scars or imperfections. In his eyes, all of those hardly noticeable marks were part of her, symbols of the hell she'd been through and survived. For him, the whole package of Sarah *was* his ideal.

He shut down his computer and grabbed the pistol from the edge of the desk, checking the locks and setting the alarm system before he headed up to his bedroom. Once there, he set the Glock on the nightstand and shucked off his clothing, leaving it in a heap on the floor.

I was wrong. Sarah doesn't need just a friend, although I want to be the one she comes to whenever she needs someone to listen to her. She needs a lover, too, a man who will worship and pleasure her body, and it's going to be me. She needs to understand that physical desire goes a hell of a lot deeper than science.

He had to admit that what was happening between him and Sarah was somewhat out of his knowledge base. Truthfully, he'd never needed a woman as badly as he did Sarah. But he was willing to wing it, to listen to his instincts.

Dante stalked out to the hallway and nudged her bedroom door open with his foot, letting the hallway light flood over her bed. She was there, huddled in the very middle, curled almost into a fetal position. Not certain she'd grab on to him, he picked her up and tossed her over his shoulder, feeling the pain in his ribs as he grasped her ass to keep her steady, but he ignored it.

"Dante," Sarah squealed anxiously. "What are you doing? Put me down. You're going to hurt yourself, dammit."

He walked back to his bedroom with her over his shoulder, stroking her bare ass with his hand, and then smacking it hard. "Stay still. You're not my damn doctor anymore. You're a woman I desperately want to fuck. And from this moment on, I'm treating you that way."

He bit back a smile as she hushed entirely, her body completely still. He lowered her slowly to the floor once he entered his bedroom, nearly groaning as the T-shirt bunched up around her breasts. Her bare skin slid softly along his naked chest and abdomen as her toes searched for solid ground.

Tossing her hair back once she found the floor, she looked up at him, and then down. And then down some more, until her eyes landed on his engorged cock, and Dante couldn't keep from grinning evilly at the expression on her shocked face.

"You are crazy," she muttered softly, her eyes never leaving his groin.

Dante opened the top drawer of the nightstand and snatched his handcuffs and the key. He raised the hem of the T-shirt with his other hand, blocking her vision before yanking the garment over her head and letting it fall to the floor.

"Sarah Baxter, you're under arrest." He slapped the cuffs on her with her hands in front of her before she even knew what was happening. He made them tight enough so she couldn't slip her hands out of them, but not tight enough to hurt her wrists. Most of the time, he preferred to be the dominant in the bedroom, and from the quick flash of heat he'd seen in her eyes as he'd been cuffing her, Sarah liked it, too. Problem was, he'd never felt anywhere near this covetous and primal, and his feelings were already way beyond just a game of dominance.

Her confused eyes flew to his face. "For what?"

"Fleeing the scene of a crime," he told her, talking to her like she was one of his felons. He was pissed off, so he let his anger exit his body with his voice. "It was a crime to cover those amazing breasts."

"You told me—"

He shook his head. "Doesn't matter. It was still a crime. And then you fled."

Her body was trembling as she asked, "What's my punishment?"

She wasn't afraid; she was shaking with arousal, those needy violet eyes almost begging him not to stop. Dante picked her up and tossed her on the bed. Before she could get anywhere, he was on her. After opening one of the cuffs with the key, he threaded the cuff through one of the bars on the iron headboard, and then calmly reattached the cuff and tossed the key onto the nightstand.

"Punishment is learning the truth the pleasurable way," he answered her firmly. "Did you really think I even saw your scars?" he asked huskily.

She turned her anguished eyes to his face and nodded jerkily.

Dante's cock twitched as he knelt between her thighs and lowered his body onto hers, allowing him to finally be skin to skin with her. Seeing her shackled to his bed satisfied a little of his primitive caveman urgency, and now he was just enjoying the moment. He could tell that she was a little confused, but her body was heated and turned on, her nipples so hard he could feel them abrading his chest. "I saw the scars only because it nearly kills me to think of how much some bastard hurt you, and I'd like to kill the son of a bitch. But your body is perfect. I know you didn't miss the raging hard-on I have whenever I feel you or when I looked at you naked, right?" He brushed back a lock of hair from her face, and then gently ran the back of his hand down her soft cheek.

"No. I saw it," she whispered softly. "It was . . . confusing."

Dante knew he was now caught in a web of his own making, but he couldn't seem to make himself give a shit as he was captured by the look of raw need and vulnerability he saw in her eyes. He saw his own desire reflected in her eyes, and giving up any semblance of control, he lowered his head and kissed her.

CHAPTER 9

Sarah had never seen anything hotter than Dante, feral and untamed, towering above her while she was completely helpless beneath him. Her body was on fire, and seeing the possessive, desirous look on his face had made her come unraveled.

Dear God, I want him so badly I can hardly breathe.

She opened to him willingly, letting him have his way with her mouth as she gripped the bars on the headboard. It was the first time any man had ever wanted her this way, and it was heady and intoxicating to have Dante's ripped, muscular body holding her captive. He kissed her with a desperation she'd never experienced before, and she felt just as needy. Her tongue dueled with his, coming out on the bottom in their war for domination, which only made her body burn hotter.

She'd been right when she'd told Dante that she thought she'd like the whole bossy cop thing sexually. It definitely had . . . merit.

Sarah had been devastated when he'd told her downstairs to cover up, thinking he'd been repulsed by the scars left from the brutal attack in Chicago. But he hadn't been spurning her; he'd been protecting her from himself. Fortunately, she liked him just fine the way he was—thank you very much! She might be a smart female, but she was, in fact, a female, and he treated her like a desirable woman. Apparently, her brain liked to do its own independent thinking, but her body wanted to be manhandled in the bedroom. And the carnal part of her mind liked his dirty talk and dominant tendencies. Obviously, she had a thing for cops, or at least *this* particular cop. The more he became a bossy tyrant, the wetter she got for him. No doubt she'd fight him over being a dictator outside the bedroom. But here, she relished it.

Panting as he lifted his mouth from hers, she begged, "Please don't hurt yourself. You aren't ready for this." Her body wept from the comment, but her brain knew Dante wasn't yet healed.

"I'm ready to taste every inch of you, and bury my mouth between your thighs, sweetheart." He started to run his tongue over her old scars, starting with the one on her shoulder and moving down.

Her scars were everywhere, the majority of them on her belly and torso. Sarah shuddered as his mouth ran over her abdomen, his tongue leaving a trail of fire wherever it roamed. She whimpered as his hands came up to cup her breasts, his thumbs circling the hard points, making them even more sensitive. His mouth closed over one of the diamond-hard nipples, and her body arched beneath him as she lifted her hips against his muscular chest, needing . . . more.

She wanted to touch him, and the need swamped her as he nipped at her other breast, the pleasure-pain sensation almost unbearable. She clenched her fists harder around the iron bars above her head, gasping as his mouth slowly trailed down her stomach, his tongue still flicking over every single scar.

"Please," she moaned, feeling almost incoherent. The only thing she could recognize anymore was the feel of Dante's touch.

"I'm going to make you come with my tongue, Sarah. Is that what you want?" Dante forcefully commanded that she answer.

Is that what she wanted? She wanted—she actually desperately needed—something. "I haven't ever—" Her trembling voice broke into a groan as he parted her thighs and she felt the first touch of his mouth on her pussy. "Oh, God." The feel of his tongue delving between her saturated folds was exquisite. "Yes, yes." That *was* what she wanted.

Her hips lifted, begging for more, needing him to make her climax. The feel of his mouth on her clit sent a jolt of electricity through her entire body, the tiny bundle of nerves reacting to every stroke of his tongue.

"Dante. Please," she begged, not caring if she was pleading for mercy. He was in total control of her body, and it was evident that he knew exactly what he was doing: he was trying to drive her completely insane, and succeeding.

She squirmed, trying to get him to go faster, harder, but he took his time, exploring every inch of her exposed pussy, groaning into her flesh as he tasted her arousal. He thrust his tongue into her channel, pulled back, and then pushed into her again, making Sarah yank on the cuffs above her head, wanting nothing more than to grab on to his head and pull his face flush against her and ride his mouth into oblivion.

"I can't take any more. Please." Then she moaned as she felt his finger invading her channel, impaling her as he moved his tongue back to the tiny bud that desperately wanted his attention. He worked another finger beside the first one, stretching her open, filling her as he bit gently on her clit. Her body writhed on the bed as he worked his fingers like his cock, burying them deeply inside her, stroking a sensitive area that made her moan with every pump of his fingers.

"So. Fucking. Tight," Dante rasped against her flesh.

Finally, he put the pressure she needed on her clit with his tongue, matching the furious rhythm of his fingers, driving her over the edge.

Sarah felt herself flying to pieces, the spiraling in her belly snaking down to her pussy as she arched her back and climaxed so powerfully that her entire body quaked. Her channel tightened around his fingers, and she let herself go with an erotic cry of ecstasy.

The orgasm left her spent, panting, and gasping as Dante continued to lap at her juices like they were nectar.

He crawled slowly up her body until he was close enough to kiss her, and tasting her own essence mixed with Dante's in his fierce embrace was intoxicating.

Opening the eyes that she hadn't even realized she'd closed, she saw the carnal look on his face, but she could tell that he was hurting. Sweat was beading on his forehead, and his breathing was labored. "Open the cuffs," she requested firmly.

"I need to fuck you, but I don't have a damn condom," he grumbled, sounding frustrated.

Still trying to catch her breath, Sarah didn't think this was the time to tell him that she was on the pill to regulate her periods, and she'd seen all of his medical records. They were both clean. And oh, how she wanted to feel him inside her. But he wasn't ready for that kind of physical activity. "Undo me," she told him again. "My arms are going numb." Really, they weren't. But she knew Dante would let her go immediately if he thought she was uncomfortable.

She was right. He rolled over and snatched the key from the bedside table and released the cuffs so fast that her arms dropped limply to the bed before she could support them.

"I'm sorry." Dante rubbed her arms as though he were trying to return the circulation to her limbs.

"It's fine." She felt a little guilty because she had fibbed to him, but he really needed to stop pushing his body so hard. He'd thrown her over his shoulder like she was a featherweight, which she wasn't. Everything he'd done today was just too much. And she'd been the recipient of all of the pleasure while he was hurting.

She watched as he put the cuffs back into the drawer along with the key before he turned back to her and cuddled her against his side, his breathing starting to return to normal. She touched his chest, lightly tracing the bruises still visible there and on his upper abdomen. "You're hurting."

He turned his head and grinned at her, the gold flecks in his eyes almost shimmering. "It was worth every second. It's not that bad now."

Sarah rolled her eyes. "That's because you're at rest." She looked down at his raging erection. "Well, most of you is resting," she amended. Fascinated by the size and girth of him, she wrapped her hand around his cock, stroking the velvety head with her thumb. The tip was dotted with moisture, and she swiped at it with her finger and lifted it to her mouth, sucking his flavor from her finger with small strokes of her tongue.

Dante was watching her intently, his eyes turning to liquid flames.

"I want to taste you, Dante. Will you let me see if I can make you come with my mouth?" She'd never gone down on a man before, but she suddenly had a voracious appetite to sample Dante.

"I guarantee if you wrap those sweet lips around my cock, I'll come," Dante growled. "Probably in record time right now."

There was nothing Sarah wanted more than to give him some of the same pleasure he'd given her tonight. He gave so much and asked for very little. There was nothing she wanted more right now than to give him something of herself. She turned her body and grasped his cock again. "Help me do it right," she said hesitantly before licking over the tip.

She slowly moved her hand and wrapped her lips around the shaft, taking as much as she possibly could and applying suction as she pulled back.

"Sweetheart, I don't think I need to teach you much," Dante groaned, spearing his hand through her hair and guiding her head.

Sarah lost herself in the taste and smell of Dante, breathing him in as she kept taking him deeper and deeper with each downward stroke. His every groan of pleasure sent shivers through her body.

"That's good, Sarah. So damn good," he crooned to her. "Watching you go down on me is one of the hottest things I've ever seen."

Her eyes flew to his face. He had propped his head on the pillows, watching her as she pleasured him. Their eyes locked and held, but she didn't stop. His intense look of pure ecstasy made her belly flutter with heat, and she moved faster, took him even deeper, adding more suction as she tightened her lips around his cock.

His hand gripped her hair tighter, and his head fell back against the pillow, breaking their eye contact. Cupping his balls gently, she started swirling her tongue on the tip of his cock every time she pulled back, bringing a strangled groan from his mouth. He started controlling the pace, urging her head with his hand to go faster.

Sarah could feel his pleasure like it was her own, understanding why he found satisfaction in making her orgasm. Her possessive instincts kicked her right in the gut, and she took his cock into her mouth like it belonged to her, claiming it, owning it.

"Oh, Christ. I'm going to explode, Sarah," Dante told her in a harsh, graveled voice.

Come for me, Dante.

She needed to be the woman who satisfied him. After what he'd done to awaken her body, she was frenzied to do the same to him, desperate to taste his fulfillment.

Come for me.

He came with a low groan, his hand fisting in her hair, trying to pull her mouth from him. She ignored his nonverbal warning, wanting to taste his orgasm on her tongue. His hot release flooded her throat and she let it flow over her tongue before swallowing, moaning around him as his cock pulsated in her mouth. She ran her tongue up the shaft soothingly after he was spent, and then swiped it over the tip, wanting every drop he had to give. Dante tasted decadent and male, and he smelled like erotic bliss.

He leaned up, then hauled her back up beside him and kissed her.

"Now we taste like each other," she told him in an amused voice after he'd relinquished her mouth. Resting her head on his shoulder to avoid putting any pressure on his sore chest, she released a long sigh of contentment.

"Yeah. And I'm addicted to the taste of you now," Dante answered huskily. "All I'll think about is fucking you every time I hear your voice or see your face. Hell, I'll think it about it even if you're not in the same room."

Sarah flushed with pleasure. "You make me feel like a woman, Dante."

Actually, he made her feel like a sexual goddess. It was a strange feeling for a woman who had never felt . . . well . . . anything.

He turned his head and grinned wolfishly at her. "Last time I checked, you were a woman. And I examined you pretty carefully."

She punched him in his muscular upper arm playfully. "That's not what I meant."

"What, then?" he asked curiously.

"I've always felt like a geek, almost asexual." She'd never had a fierce attraction to any man except Dante, and her reaction to him was confounding her.

He rolled her beneath him and hovered over her, his expression troubled. "I guarantee you're not asexual, and you're beautiful and responsive. The most beautiful woman I've ever seen. I have no idea why you've never wanted to explore your sexuality before, but I'm greedy and selfish. I want you to do it with me. Only me."

I've never wanted to do it with anyone else.

After her one bad experience, she'd never met a man who moved her to explore the sensual side of herself. And after she'd become scarred, she'd put the thought out of her mind altogether.

Dante was definitely an inspiration, but he'd had no business doing the things he'd done in his condition. "No more fooling around until you're healed. I've waited this long, I can wait a little longer. You need to completely heal," she lectured, knowing that if he touched her again, she'd cave in. The man was like a highly addictive drug.

"I told you that you're not my doctor anymore," he reminded her ferociously.

"I'm still a doctor, and I know what you did tonight could have set back your recovery," she told him sternly.

"Baby, I guarantee it didn't hurt a bit." He shot her a shit-eating grin that nearly melted her.

Stay strong. You know he was hurting earlier. You could see it. He's trying to charm you into forgetting that you saw him in pain.

"No," she told him adamantly.

Flopping onto his back again, he groaned. "It will kill me."

Sarah bit back a smile. Honestly, his ferocious appetite for her delighted her as much as it concerned her. "You lived without my body for thirty-one years," she reminded him.

"Yeah. And it sucked," he told her sulkily.

Sarah had to bite her lower lip to keep from smiling. At the moment, he resembled a pouty boy. "I want to be with you, too. But not if I have to wonder every minute if you're hurting yourself." Really, he was the most stubborn man alive. He should still be down and resting with his injuries, and he was already trying to pretend they didn't exist anymore. "It has to stop." She was already afraid he was going to get hurt protecting her. She intentionally changed the subject. "Will I be able to get into my house for some of my personal belongings? My clothes and stuff like that?"

"No." His low voice was hesitant and reluctant. "Sarah, there's nothing there anymore. Even your clothing was hacked up. I'm sorry."

Sarah shuddered. "He really does want me dead."

"We'll catch him, sweetheart. I swear."

She didn't doubt Dante. She'd never seen a man who was more dedicated to righting a wrong, which made him an excellent detective. With his determined stubbornness, Sarah knew he'd do everything in his power to finally apprehend John Thompson.

"Seeing Trey die was hard. I was a new doctor, and I got too close. I guess learning how to lose a patient wasn't something I was really going to understand in medical school. It was like losing a friend. I guess John never came to terms with losing both his wife and only child, and really did go over the edge. I don't know if he was psychotic before this happened, or if it really was the accident that caused his radical behavior."

Dante wrapped his arm around her and pulled her flush against his side. "If a man or woman has the capability to murder, it's already there. What happened was just the excuse he needed to play out his rage. This isn't your fault, Sarah."

"I was hoping he'd just go away, find another life somewhere, and get over his grief, since he was never caught. Maybe somewhere in the back of my mind, I realized that he could end up coming after me. But I never really looked at it as a reality. I thought it was over." She'd wanted to start over again, forget the past. But the past had finally caught up to her with a vengeance.

"Once we find him, you can really start over again. You'll never have that niggling doubt or have to live with the fear that he'll find you. Judging by the brutal job he did on your personal possessions, his rage has just increased over the last year," Dante said soberly.

"It looks like it has," Sarah agreed, snuggling into the warmth of Dante's body.

"He's still here somewhere. Joe seems like a competent chief, and I'm sure he's making this a top priority."

"He's a good man," Sarah agreed. "He's really devoted to his family and his job."

"Do you still have the panic attacks?" Dante reached for her hand and rested their entwined fingers on his hip.

"No. Not unless I get near a hospital. I've tried to desensitize myself, but I can't seem to even get close to the entrance of a hospital without getting palpitations and dizziness." Sarah hated it. It was a weakness she couldn't overcome.

"You've managed to practice medicine anyway," he observed, his fingers tightening on hers. "You're a brave woman, sweetheart."

She didn't always feel very brave. She was just a survivor. "I'm an internal medicine doctor. Not being able to admit a patient to the hospital and follow their care doesn't feel right to me."

"I understand. It would be a little like me developing a fear of guns or something. I'd be screwed," he answered hoarsely. "But you've made the best out of it." He paused before asking, "How often do you talk to your mother? Did she take good care of you while you were injured?"

It seemed important to Dante that she'd been well cared for, that someone had been there to understand her mental state and comfort her. Sarah sighed. "She tried. I guess you have to know her. Her world revolves around education. When I was injured and anxious, she didn't really understand. I think she expected me to revert back to the same daughter I'd been before. But I couldn't please her anymore. She wanted to pick me the perfect man and see me married someday to another academic and have brilliant kids. She's still trying. We don't talk very often. She's usually too busy. When she does call, it's usually because she's found me a man with a similar gene pool."

Dante stretched his arm out and turned off the lamp on the bedside table, plunging the room into darkness except for the faint moonlight shining through his window. "You do realize the way you were raised wasn't normal."

"I do now. I don't think I ever really knew what normal was when I was younger. My mother was all I had, and I wasn't exactly a normal kid." She yawned, her body starting to feel relaxed and lethargic.

"You need sleep," Dante observed.

"Do you want me to go back to my own bedroom?" Maybe Dante liked his space when he slept, but she was hoping he didn't. She wanted to stay with him tonight.

"Hell, no. I wouldn't sleep all night, even if you were just next door. I want you to stay here with me."

He let go of her hand after a final squeeze, then turned on his side and wrapped his arms around her waist. She turned and let him spoon with her. "I'd feel better staying here. I guess I'm a little spooked after what happened."

"You have every right to be. And I want you in my bed."

Right at that moment, that was exactly where she wanted to be, too. She felt . . . safe. With Dante's arms wrapped protectively around her, she slept.

CHAPTER 10

"I've never owned this many clothes in my life." Sarah stared at the seemingly mile-high stack of clothing that occupied every inch of the bed in Dante's guest room. "What was he thinking?"

"Hey, I picked you out some very nice stuff," Emily Sinclair protested, picking up another hanger from a stack on the floor. She cut off the tags from a brand-new pair of jeans before she hung them in the closet. "I had a very large budget to work with," she told Sarah in an amused tone.

Randi sighed as she folded some sinfully soft lingerie and put it in the dresser drawer. "I think I want a Sinclair brother," she whined jokingly.

"Take Jared. Please," Emily cajoled, taking another garment from the pile. "Maybe he'll settle down and date a woman more than once."

Randi wrinkled her nose. "Not my type."

Sarah started putting shoes away, dismayed by the designer brands. She might be a doctor, but she was on a strict budget, paying off student loans her first priority. Randi and Emily had arrived at Dante's home with several teenage boys, all of them carrying boxes and bags. Having canceled their get-together at Brew Magic, Emily and Randi decided to just move the location of the party to Sarah, bringing along a new wardrobe Dante had asked Emily to select, and lattes from Brew Magic. Sarah had wanted to go meet Randi and Emily, but Dante had refused. Adamantly. Even though they hadn't seen any signs of John still being in the area in the last several days, he was being cautious.

"Do I even want to know how much he allotted for the clothing?" Sarah asked hesitantly. She was going to have to pay him back. They'd stopped at a discount store the day after the incident—one of the few places Dante had allowed her to be in public—and she'd picked up some essentials and a few outfits before he'd hurried her out the door. He'd mentioned that he'd have Emily pick her up some more clothing, but this was ridiculous. It looked like her friend had bought out several stores.

"Probably not," Emily replied with a mischievous smile. "He's clueless, and threw me the same kind of budget Grady would. In fact, I'm wondering if the two of them consulted."

Sarah's head started to spin, knowing exactly how generous Grady Sinclair could be. If Emily wanted anything, Grady was likely to give her a small fortune for a new pair of shoes. "Was it a lot?" Sarah squeaked, not quite certain that her friend wasn't drunk or on latte overload. How much could it cost for some new clothes? Her knees got weak, and she sat down in the chair beside the dresser. "Please tell me you didn't spend everything he gave you. I'll have a hard time paying it back."

"You're not paying it back. Dante didn't even want me to tell you how much I spent. It's a gift from him. He wanted to do it. And believe me, he's loaded. He won't even miss the money," Emily said conspiratorially.

"Oh, God," Sarah groaned. "Tell me you didn't spend everything he gave you."

"I didn't."

Sarah released a sigh of relief.

"She had enough left to buy the coffees tonight. It was Dante's treat," Randi added chirpily.

"You spent a small fortune on clothes?" Sarah was having palpitations. How anyone could spend that much on something to cover their body, she definitely didn't understand.

"I told you it was nice stuff," Emily replied, the grin on her face growing larger. "Sarah, stop stressing. Dante and his brothers are incredibly rich. I didn't live in that kind of world, either, but I'm getting used to it. I still don't go out buying anything I want, but after what happened to you, you deserve this." Emily put her hands on her hips and stared at Sarah. "He insisted that I spend every penny, and I did. The only other thing he insisted on was that there is at least one beautiful red dress in the wardrobe. I didn't quite get that. But I got a lot of red. I know you like it, and it will look gorgeous on you."

"He knows red is my favorite color," Sarah answered shakily. "God, he's driving me insane. I suppose you two didn't even notice the piano."

Emily and Randi shook their heads silently.

"Well, he decided that he might want to learn to play someday, so he bought one of the most expensive grand pianos on the market. It's in the far corner of his living room. And of course I can play it anytime I want." Sarah expelled a frustrated breath. "He has no intention of learning to play. He bought it so *I* could play. His excuse was totally contrived just so I didn't miss being able to play."

"Oh . . . that's so sweet," Randi gushed.

"It's very pricey," Sarah retorted, but she thought it was pretty damn sweet, too. Unfortunately, that wasn't the point. "And it doesn't make any sense. What is he going to do with the piano when I go back home? I think he's trying to make up for the fact that I had an atypical childhood. And now this . . ." Sarah motioned to the monster pile of clothing and accessories. "He has to stop. I can't ever pay him back for all of this." Sarah was feeling almost distraught. She appreciated Dante and his kindness. But she was an independent woman who wasn't used to getting gifts of any kind. She really felt like she needed to pay him back, regardless of how much money he had. Just looking at the new wardrobe almost made her nauseous. How much had he spent, and how many decades was it going to take her to repay him?

"He doesn't expect you to pay him back," Emily answered, her voice now low and comforting. "The Sinclair brothers were raised with wealth. I know Dante hasn't really spent much money because he was so involved in his job, but he has it just like the rest of the Sinclairs. I think giving gifts is in their DNA. Grady is the same way." Emily waded through a pile of clothing to kneel at Sarah's feet. "Don't chastise him, Sarah. Dante is trying to right something he perceives as wrong. All of the Sinclair men are that way, even Jared. It's one of the wonderful traits every one of them has. They're protective and giving with people they care about."

"It's . . . overwhelming," Sarah answered honestly. "Nobody has ever done anything like this for me."

"I understand," Emily said knowingly. "Grady gave me a brand-new truck and he didn't even know me. He also didn't ask. I was furious when he replaced my old clunker without asking me first."

"What did you do?" Sarah asked curiously.

"I caved eventually because the gift was coming from a place of love, because he was worried about the condition of my vehicle, and Grady can be . . . persuasive," Emily confided.

"Bossy, you mean?" Sarah corrected.

Emily nodded her head. "Sometimes he is. But I know it's coming from the heart, because he wants me to be safe and happy. I let him know when he steps over the line."

"And you don't think Dante is stepping over the line? He's not my husband, or even my boyfriend."

He just made me have a few spectacular orgasms.

"It's pretty obvious that he has a thing for you. The Sinclair men can be astoundingly possessive when they've finally met the right woman."

"He doesn't want that with me, Emily. He's not even going to be here for much longer," Sarah denied.

"We'll see," Emily said knowingly, rising to get back to her task of putting away clothes. "I recognize the look and the behavior."

"So you think I should take all of this in stride? I don't know if I can. I feel like I'm taking advantage. Dante has done so much for me already." Sarah got up and started putting away more shoes. "Just the fact that he's let me stay in his home, putting himself at risk, means a lot to me."

"Here," Randi chimed in as she tossed Sarah a shimmery garment. "Wear this for him and he'll think it was worth every penny."

Sarah caught the red teddy as it flew over her head. The top was fitted with spaghetti straps to hold it up. It was marbled red and black on the top and very fitted, designed to plump up her cleavage. The bottom was solid red silk and lace, and so short it would stop at her upper thigh. She stroked the soft material of the barely there nightgown absently. "We don't . . . do that." Well, they pretty much didn't. After he'd cuffed her to his bed and made her scream with ecstasy, he hadn't touched her except to cradle her by his side every night or kiss her. He'd obviously taken her seriously when she'd refused to let him injure himself.

"Then you should start doing it," Randi teased her. "Dante is seriously hot, and completely devoted to protecting you."

"He's injured," Sarah argued.

"Then you have something to look forward to when he heals," Emily retorted, winking at Sarah. "Admit it. You like him, and you have the hots for him."

Oh, Sarah had no problem admitting that. It was the truth. "I do."

"Then go after what you want. Your childhood seriously sucked. You were nearly killed by a madman just because you were doing your job, and you never do anything just for fun or because you want it. If you want him, take him. I don't think he's going to resist," Emily chortled. "You don't need to analyze it or rationalize the attraction. It's never going to make any sense. Take my word on that."

There was no doubt that Sarah wanted Dante, and that her desire for him was illogical. "He's a good man. But we come from totally different worlds."

"Does that matter if you really care about him?" Emily asked solemnly.

Did it matter? Sarah was wondering the same thing herself. The more she got to know Dante, the less it seemed to matter that they were so different. The only time she was really reminded of his wealth and status was when he did something crazy—like buying her a fortune in clothing. "He does take it well when I beat him at chess," Sarah joked, but honestly, she was touched by what a good sport he was, and how little his ego played into his actions sometimes. Dante never wanted her to give the game anything but her best, and she did, trouncing him repeatedly. But Dante said it made him think, challenged him to get better. He wasn't intimidated by her, and it didn't hurt his male ego to get beat at an intellectual game by a woman. That just made her like him that much more. Of course, he could destroy her at video games, something she'd recently been learning from him. He did crow over every win, which made her determined to get better at the games.

Strange. Maybe he was on to something.

Still, Dante constantly amazed her. For a man who seemed to have an overabundance of testosterone, he was secure in his masculinity all the time. Even when she bested him, he looked at her with pride rather than annoyance.

"You have to appreciate a man who is secure enough to not care if you're better at something than he is," Randi commented candidly.

"I appreciate a lot of things about him," Sarah admitted to both women. In fact, Dante fascinated her.

"Then give him a break and try on some of these clothes. He'll never miss the money, and he'll be ecstatic if he thinks they made you happy." Emily tossed her several outfits, and Sarah caught them reflexively.

Sarah stopped trying to reason out anything that involved her feelings for Dante. He was a good man, and really, that was all that mattered. He was an enigma, so she was trusting feminine instincts that she hadn't realized even existed until Dante. The last thing she wanted to do was hurt his feelings, and she knew instinctively that rejecting a gift from him *would* hurt him.

With a deep sigh of resignation, she reached for a pretty coral-colored ensemble and tried it on.

Downstairs, Dante was having a hard time controlling his frustration. "Joe and I haven't turned up anything significant. It's like the asshole just disappeared," he told Jared and Grady as they all sat in the living room having a drink.

Right now he was having a hard time even having Sarah out of his sight. But he wanted her to have her privacy with her friends. He knew she was going stir-crazy, and that she'd been disappointed when he hadn't wanted her to go out in public to meet her friends at Brew Magic. Dammit, he didn't want to stifle a growing process that had started before he'd ever met her. But he didn't want her to be a target, either.

"He'll turn up," Jared commented, taking a gulp from his bottle of beer before setting it on the table beside his chair. "He's obviously not going to just go away."

Jared was right. Dante knew that someone who had so much rage inside of him was not going to just slip away. He would surface eventually. The only question was . . . when and where?

"How's Sarah handling all of this?" Grady asked quietly.

"She hates not being able to walk and be outdoors. Otherwise, she's dealing with it incredibly well." Dante knew Sarah was scared, but she tried not to show it, doing what she had to do to stay safe. As smart as she was, he knew she'd weighed everything out in her mind and had come to the conclusion that she'd have to live with the situation until her attacker was caught.

"Are you screwing her?" Grady asked bluntly.

Dante turned his furious expression toward his brother. "That's none of your business, Grady."

"It is my business. She's a friend," Grady answered calmly. "I don't want to see her get hurt."

"Her? What about me?" Neither of his brothers seemed to get the fact that he was losing his mind over Sarah's safety right now.

"I appreciate that you want to protect her, and you're definitely the best qualified to do that right now, but Sarah is . . . different," Grady replied.

"Fuck! Do you think I don't know that? She's lived a life that most people can't understand. She was never a child; she was a curiosity to be examined by the scientific community. Not one single person has ever cared that she's a kindhearted, warm woman who wants the same things that other women want. They hear the way she speaks, the way she tries to reason everything out. Or they listen to her talk about something that goes right over their head, and they ignore her, shut her out. Nobody has ever tried to get to know *her*. They were too goddamn insecure and intimidated to want to befriend her." Grady raised an eyebrow at Dante and he added, "She's made friends here, and I know Emily and Randi care about her, but that's new to her. She's happy here. She might be a genius, but she's also still naive and innocent in a lot of ways. She never had a chance to learn normal things. But underneath, there's a woman who just wants someone to care about her. And dammit, she deserves that."

"You are fucking her," Grady stated with a small grin. "You care about her."

"Hell, yes, I care. I wouldn't be protecting her if I didn't. And I haven't been in shape to get that physical. I have to heal so I can protect her if necessary. But do I want to? Fuck, yeah. I want her more than I've ever wanted a woman before." Dante's body was tense, and he glared at Grady. "I'm so damn possessive and protective that I can hardly stand myself. She drives me crazy, but she also makes me feel like I can fly. How screwed up is that?"

Jared shook his head as he said gravely, "You have it bad. I don't think there's any woman in the world worth getting this worked up about."

Dante looked at Jared, but his younger brother wouldn't meet his eyes. What the hell had happened to him? When they were boys, Jared had been the more sensitive, artistic brother. Now he was jaded, almost like he was bored with life. Okay, maybe he wasn't bored, but he was definitely cynical. Dante wondered if there was more to Jared acting like a man-whore than just apathy. He seemed almost bitter, and he hadn't always been that way.

From his seat on the couch, Dante could see Coco waiting patiently at his feet. The damn dog actually liked him. He wasn't sure why, but he had a feeling it had to do with the fact that he snuck Coco human food occasionally, when Sarah wasn't looking. The dog really was kind of pathetic, and Dante hated seeing that expectant look on the mutt's face. He patted his thigh, and Coco sprang onto his lap almost immediately. She circled twice and then settled into his lap, laying her head on his thigh with a contented sigh like she belonged there. "Damn dog," he grumbled, but his statement had very little conviction. He stroked her silky head as he looked over at Grady.

"I have to agree. You do have it bad. But I obviously disagree that no woman is worth it," Grady stated flatly. "Emily was worth it. She changed my entire life, accepted me exactly as I was. I realized that the world hadn't shut me out; I had shut out life. It took meeting Emily to make me realize there was so much more than just work, and that not everybody was like our father."

At that moment, Dante hated himself for not staying closer to his brothers and his sister, Hope. He didn't know what had happened to Jared, and he hadn't realized that Grady had isolated himself so much. "What happened to us?" Dante asked in a harsh, loud whisper. "We were all close as kids. What happened? I can count on one hand the times we've actually all been together since we left for college."

"We were all self-involved assholes?" Jared suggested. "Well . . . except for Hope."

"We were all involved in our careers. But we still could have been there for each other," Dante responded angrily.

"We're here now, Dante," Grady mentioned soberly. "I think that you almost getting yourself killed was a slap in the face to all of us. Hope and Evan call me almost every single day."

"They call me, too," Dante answered.

"And Jared has no business here in Amesport, but he's still around," Grady added, looking over at Jared and holding up a silencing hand. "Don't give me your crap about not having anything else to do. You have a business to run. You were worried and you still are."

Jared shrugged. "Nothing that needs my immediate attention. Now that Dante's playing the hero again, I just want to make sure he doesn't get himself killed."

Dante smirked, knowing Jared was completely full of shit. "I think I can handle myself if you need to go."

"I'm staying," Jared grunted, grabbing his beer and taking a large gulp.

"I could tell you not to mess with Sarah, but I don't think it will sink into your thick head right now," Grady told Dante. "I think you're too far gone."

"What do you mean?" Dante frowned at Grady.

"How would you feel if another man took Sarah out on a date?" Grady questioned sedately.

"I'd kill the bastard. She's mine," Dante growled. "Who is he?"

Grady grinned. "It was a hypothetical question. I haven't seen her date anyone since she got to Amesport. And I just got my answer."

Dante's body had gone rigid and the little dog on his lap looked up at him in alarm, as though sensing he was pissed off. The tension in his body drained away, but he glared at Grady. "That wasn't amusing."

"I thought it was hilarious," Jared drawled.

"You would," Dante snarled at Jared.

"So what is Joe doing about catching Sarah's attacker?" Grady asked, changing the subject.

"He's done everything he can do," Dante explained. "Nobody has sighted him." Dante had made damn sure that the police were doing everything they could, but they couldn't produce a suspect who was hiding out. "We just have to wait. I don't think for a minute that he's left the area. He's biding his time, waiting for an opportunity."

"Eventually, you may have to give him one or you'll never catch him," Jared said thoughtfully.

"No," Dante said emphatically. "I'm not putting Sarah out there as bait." He couldn't stand the thought of her being in harm's way. Joe had suggested the same thing, but Dante couldn't stomach it.

"Is that what we need to do? I'll do it." Sarah's voice was close. "I'd rather take the risk than live afraid forever."

Dante's head jerked to the right to look at her standing at the bottom of the stairs. "Not happening," he insisted as his eyes devoured her. He gaped as he took in the minuscule dress she was wearing. It was a nautical blue-and-white-striped dress with a halter top and was fitted to her body like a glove. Her long, slender legs were revealed to her upper thighs. "New dress?" he croaked, his eyes narrowing as he realized she wasn't wearing a bra. In that dress, the halter bodice made it impossible for Sarah to wear one.

"Yes." She smiled at him, turning in a circle so he could see the dress. "I love it. It's so comfortable."

Holy shit! "Where is the back of it?" Dante's eyes almost popped out of his head as he noticed the dress was nearly backless, and it showed a large expanse of her creamy skin because it was cut clear down to the small of her back.

"It's a summer dress. Emily said she really couldn't notice my shoulder scars. Are they showing?" she asked nervously.

"No." It wasn't her scars he was worried about; it was exposing that slender, shapely body for every other man to ogle.

"Isn't it cute?" Emily exclaimed as she and Randi came down the stairs and stood next to Sarah.

Dante broke out in a sweat and his cock came to immediate attention as Sarah slowly walked into the room. God, she was beautiful. He was hard-pressed not to grab the blanket from the back of the couch and cover her up, but the last thing he wanted to do was squelch her newfound confidence with uncovering her scars.

"Are all of the clothes like this?" Dante looked at Emily desperately as he spoke.

Emily smiled brightly. "A lot of them. The styles this year look fantastic on her. She's so tall and elegant."

"Oh, fuck, I'm screwed," Dante blurted out, his voice pained.

He heard the sound of Grady's laughter as he closed his eyes and leaned his head back on the couch with a tortured groan.

CHAPTER 11

"Honey, Beatrice and I are both feeling so much better. I guess we didn't have food poisoning after all." Elsie Renfrew looked Sarah right in the eyes and lied to her.

Sarah looked at the two gray-haired women sitting in her exam room and bit her lip to keep from laughing. Beatrice and Elsie had made an emergency appointment, the so-called emergency obviously being that their curiosity was killing them.

She'd realized it was a sham almost from the moment the two of them had come into her exam room together with guilty expressions. Both of them looked rosy from the afternoon heat, but neither one of them looked the least bit under the weather.

"No more stomach pains?" Sarah asked calmly.

The two ladies shook their gray heads at the same time.

"No more nausea?"

They kept shaking their heads as they shot beaming smiles at Sarah.

Sarah closed their patient charts and put them on the cupboard. "Okay, ladies . . . what are your questions? You two are horrible charlatans. I was worried when I heard that both of you were sick." She gave them what she hoped was an admonishing look, but it was difficult when they were smiling up at her so innocently. Sarah knew better, but it was hard to lecture two elderly women.

"We heard about what happened to your house. We were worried," Beatrice confessed contritely. "We haven't seen you around town, and you didn't play for senior bingo. You're always there." Beatrice sounded genuinely concerned, her eyes wide and troubled.

Sarah's heart melted. These two might be trouble, but their concern touched her. Not even Elsie could fake the alarm Sarah could see in her sharp eyes. "I'm fine. I've just been busy taking care of things for the house. I'm staying with a friend." She couldn't tell them the truth. It was best if nobody else learned about her stalker and started talking.

"I don't understand why someone would do something like that. Amesport is usually a safe town," Elsie commented, her tone almost frightened.

Sarah put her arm around the elderly woman. "It is safe here, Elsie. Nothing else has happened. It was probably just a drunk tourist." The last thing Sarah wanted was for either of these women to be afraid. They both lived alone, and she didn't want them to be scared in their own homes. The attacker was after her and her alone.

"I'm not worried," Beatrice said ferociously. "If I knew who did it, I'd knee him in the balls for what he did to you, just like they taught us at that self-defense class at the center."

"Beatrice, the correct term is 'testicles,'" Elsie corrected her friend. "Sarah's a sweet girl. Let's not be crude."

It had been a while since Sarah had been called a girl, and she found it amusing that Elsie actually thought using the term "balls" was vulgar. She'd worked in a big-city hospital with a lot of gang-related incidents. There probably weren't any really crude words that she hadn't heard at least hundreds of times. "I appreciate that you were both concerned, but you can see that I'm fine. Next time, don't make up a story to see me. Just stop in." Sarah opened the exam room door, and the two women rose to leave.

"I heard you weren't doctoring that Dante Sinclair anymore. Too bad.

He's one hot tamale," Beatrice informed Sarah as she walked out the door. "You could have burned up the sheets with him."

"After they get married, Beatrice," Elsie said adamantly.

"Really, Elsie, you need to become a modern woman. Nobody waits until they're married anymore," Beatrice muttered informatively.

Sarah watched the interplay between the two women and almost burst into laughter.

"I thought he was the one," Beatrice remarked, disgruntled, as she stepped into the hallway. "I was so certain. But there's always that nice Jared Sinclair. He always stops and chats with us when we see him. I really like that boy."

That surprised Sarah, and she wondered if Jared just couldn't manage to get away from them when he saw them and didn't want to be impolite. She was really wondering how he'd react to being called a boy. "I'm—"

"She's already with me," Dante's low voice sounded from the doorway of the exam room across the hall. "I had to stop seeing her as a doctor."

Sarah gawked at Dante as he joined them in the hallway and proceeded to charm the two elderly women.

"So you understand that I couldn't see her anymore as a doctor because we're together," Dante told the two women, grinning charismatically at both of them.

"I knew I was right," Beatrice chattered. "I knew you two would end up together. I told Sarah that before you even got here."

"Did you?" Dante turned his head and raised an eyebrow at Sarah.

Sarah knew her face was flushed, and she wasn't sure if she was flustered or angry. She'd asked Dante to stay hidden in the exam room across the hall so he didn't make the patients uncomfortable. That had become their daily routine. She saw her patients while Dante sat across the hall with a gun and his computer to kill time.

Most of Dante's superficial wounds were nearly healed, but his ribs had to still be tender—not that he ever complained. She might not be his physician, but at least he was in a doctor's office in case he had any problems.

Sarah sighed as she watched Dante charm his way into the two venerable women's hearts. She could tell by the way Beatrice and Elsie were looking at Dante that he was finagling his way into their good graces. She knew he wasn't doing it intentionally. Not really. He was just being the Dante who was used to working in public service, and he actually chatted with them naturally and appeared to be genuinely interested in Elsie's work at the paper and Beatrice's self-proclaimed talent of matchmaking.

Another reason to like him! He spoils my dog and is nice to old ladies.

"Are you the friend that Sarah's staying with?" Elsie asked stealthily, obviously hoping to get even more of a scoop.

Sarah wanted to laugh at the pseudo-affronted look on Dante's face. "Of course not," he answered, trying to sound insulted. "That would be highly inappropriate, and I respect Sarah," he said emphatically.

Elsie tittered happily. "You're such a gentleman."

Sarah had a hard time not giggling. He'd said exactly what the ladies wanted to hear and made sure they knew he'd be offended if they even suggested she was staying with him. Obviously, he wanted people to know she had a protector, but he didn't want anyone to know her exact location.

The ladies chattered to Dante all the way out to the reception area, where he brilliantly ushered them out the door without making them feel unwanted.

Sarah waved at the two women as they disappeared around the corner and Dante pulled the door closed.

"You realize that you just let the whole town think that we're an item," Sarah told Dante reproachfully.

"Good," Dante replied with a grin. "I was hoping they'd tell everyone. That way, every man in town will know that you're not available. It will keep me from having to beat the crap out of any guy who touches you."

She wasn't available? It had been ten days since Dante had shackled her to his bed and made her lose her mind. "You're being rather presumptuous, aren't you?"

"Not at all," Dante answered arrogantly. "I was the man who caused your first screaming orgasm, the first man to taste your—"

Sarah slapped a hand over his mouth to stop his flow of naughty words. "Stop." They were in the reception area of her office, for God's sake, and her office manager was still here. Kristin had needed to be privy to some of the information regarding Sarah's attack and knew why Dante was there. But she certainly didn't know that Sarah slept with Dante every single night, and dreamed up all kinds of dirty fantasies both awake and asleep. Sarah couldn't think about that night ten days ago without her panties getting moist.

Who am I kidding? Just looking at him or hearing his voice makes me melt.

Dante's hazel eyes were pinning her with a sinfully playful look, one that she was fairly certain no woman on earth could possibly resist. Unfortunately, Sarah knew that Dante was aware of exactly how his dirty mouth affected her. He lifted her hand from his mouth slowly, kissing her palm before letting it go. "They were your last patients. Let's go."

Sarah turned and went into the storage closet to grab her purse and hang up her white coat and stethoscope before joining Dante by the door. For once, she didn't argue with him about wanting to take a walk. She'd worn a new pair of shoes from the wardrobe Emily had picked out for her, and her feet were killing her. Three-inch heels? What had Emily been thinking? Sarah loved the professional skirt and blouse, but her feet were aching from standing all day in very cute but very uncomfortable shoes. Thankfully, they were the only pair of heels Emily had bought that were quite this high.

She hopped into Dante's truck and kicked off the heels with a moan of relief.

"What's the matter?" Dante asked, hesitating before closing the passenger door.

"Shoe torture," she answered with a frown. "My feet hurt."

Dante closed the passenger door quickly and jogged around to seat himself in the driver's seat. "You don't like the shoes?" Dante asked with a scowl as he started the engine. "We'll get different ones."

"No," Sarah answered hastily. "I like them. I just don't think three-inch heels are designed for a working physician. I think they're supposed to be worn for leisure occasions."

Dante chuckled as he pulled onto Main Street and headed toward the peninsula. "Why would you want to wear painful shoes when you're supposed to be doing something pleasant?"

"You know what I mean." Sarah shot him a small smile. "They're for going out to dinner, or to a wedding. They aren't made to work in all day."

They drove in a companionable silence for a while, Sarah rubbing each of her feet to get rid of the cramping.

Finally, she approached a subject that she knew he wasn't going to like, but something they needed to discuss. "Dante?"

"Yeah?"

"You know that we can't live like this forever. I need to start living a normal life again. Joe says that John might not surface until he sees me going about my normal routine."

"Not happening," Dante snarled. "I'm not leaving you vulnerable."

"You can't stay here forever. And I've lived most of my life isolated. I'm grateful that you're protecting me, but I have to move on from this. If putting myself back into a normal routine will help flush John out, I'll do it."

Dante accelerated through the gate of the peninsula so hard that his tires burned rubber. He didn't speak as he drove into his driveway and parked the truck. Sarah waited, as usual, in the truck while Dante checked out the surroundings. He jerked open the passenger door.

"Get out," he ordered, unfastening her seat belt with one smooth motion of his hand.

"You're not being rational," Sarah told him calmly as she slid out of the seat. Honestly, he'd never levelheadedly discussed the possibility of her going about her normal life again to get John to come out of hiding, but she needed him to understand. "I can't hide forever. I need to give him an opportunity to show himself if he's going to."

"You go to work every day," Dante argued irritably.

"Yes . . . with an armed guard. No offense, but you're pretty intimidating even if he doesn't know you carry a weapon."

Dante unlocked the door and let her in after he'd entered first to shut down the alarm system, closing the door with more force than necessary behind her.

"I'm not putting you at risk, Sarah," he answered, giving her an angry stare that would have scared the bejesus out of most people.

Sarah wasn't intimidated. She knew his facial expressions, and she'd seen every one of them, from playful to homicidal. She might not have him totally figured out, but she knew he'd never hurt her, no matter how angry he might be. "It's my choice to make," she informed him sedately, dropping her purse on the dining room table and heading up the stairs to take a shower.

Her heart was aching as she stripped off her work clothes and tossed them into the laundry basket in the guest bathroom. Sarah usually enjoyed using Dante's fancy shower, but she stepped into the enormous tile enclosure distracted. Water hit her from both sides and above her head, the pulsating multiple jets relaxing her as she shampooed her hair.

He's never going to agree. I'm going to have to make this choice on my own.

Showing herself in public again would have to be her decision, and after all Dante had done for her, making that decision when he was so adamantly against it was going to hurt him. That was the last thing she wanted to do. The way he cared about her safety and protected her touched her more than she wanted to admit. Nobody had ever looked out for her the way Dante did. Lately, she'd stopped trying to analyze why he did it, and why they had the connection that they had together. She just enjoyed being with him. Still, reality was reality. He wouldn't be here in Amesport much longer—he was nearly healed—and she'd have to deal with making the decision of how to end her isolation herself.

She rinsed conditioner from her hair as she thought about how painful it was going to be to see him go back to Los Angeles, back to a job that had nearly gotten him killed. Everything inside her rebelled at the thought, and she understood how he felt about her being in danger. She feared the same with him.

Sarah squeaked, startled as Dante entered the shower, completely nude. Before she had a chance to form a single thought, he pinned her against the tile, crowding her with his massive, muscular body, her wrists held captive over her head. Desire flowed through her body like liquid fire as she looked up at his face. His expression was volatile and feral, like a hungry predator on the prowl. His fierceness beckoned to her like a mating call, her nipples hard, her pussy flooding with wet heat, and the rest of her body trembling with need.

"First of all, I'm not leaving until that asshole is either in jail or dead. Do you understand?" His voice was grating and harsh.

"How can you—"

"Don't talk. Don't even try to reason with me. I'm not in a rational mood. Just tell me you understand," he demanded, his chest rising and falling with every labored breath.

Sarah could tell he was fighting for control, but she didn't need him to hold back. She liked him like this: dominant and urgent. Although she really didn't understand how he could keep his promise if the situation dragged on forever, she knew that he would.

She simply nodded, not knowing exactly how he planned to stay. However, she'd learned that when Dante made a vow, he meant it.

"Second, I don't want to risk anything happening to you. When I lost Patrick, I wanted to be dead. Then you came along and brought me back to life again. You're mine, Sarah. I think I knew that almost from the moment I saw you. I know *you're* willing to take the risk of putting yourself out there, but don't you know losing you would kill me?"

Tears started to flow down Sarah's cheeks as she nodded again. The intensity of his emotions was flowing from him to her, waking the same response that had been inside her for a while now. She hadn't acknowledged it because she was afraid of getting hurt, but she knew if she lost Dante, her entire world would go dark. Her defenses shattered as the tears flowed. She wasn't thinking analytically. Dante treated her like a woman, and she was reacting with her heart. When it came to him, it was as though her brain totally disconnected and her heart took over her thinking for her.

"Third, I need to fuck you so desperately that I can't get myself off one more time. It's a damn poor substitute. I need you. Lying in bed every single night and not being able to touch you has been torture. I'm healed. The only reason I didn't fuck you was because I knew I needed to be in condition to protect you, and I needed to heal fast. I also didn't want to do a half-assed job of satisfying you. Understand?"

Like that could really happen. Dante could satisfy her with just his touch. But she nodded anyway, her tears escaping from her eyes unchecked, the water from the shower mingling with her teardrops.

"Fourth?" she prompted after he was silent for moment, his intense stare making her squirm with carnal longing. She felt like she'd waited forever to be with this man, and she couldn't wait a moment longer.

"There is no goddamn fourth," he growled as his mouth covered hers.

Sarah yanked at her restrained hands as she met his tongue with a muffled cry. Dante held her spellbound, oblivious to anything happening around her except the heat of his mouth on hers, his tongue branding her. Her need to touch him was so intense that she was whimpering into his mouth again, and she jerked furiously at her wrists, unable to escape his iron hold.

"What's wrong?" Dante demanded as he pulled his mouth from hers, panting.

"I have to touch you, Dante. Please," she begged, needing him to release her hands so she could explore his body now that he was healed. That desire was so intense that it was actually physically painful.

"I won't last if you do," he warned, but he released her hands and slid his hands down her back and finally cupped the cheeks of her ass. "But I still want you to. Touch me, Sarah."

Sarah didn't waste any time spearing her hands through his wet hair, luxuriating in the feel of his body as she pulled his mouth to hers again. She moaned against his mouth as he nipped at her bottom lip and then licked it soothingly. Sarah shivered with pleasure as she ran her hands over his shoulders and explored the sculpted muscles of his back. His tight ass was pure perfection, and when her hands landed there, she squeezed him tightly.

"Jesus, sweetheart. You're killing me," Dante rasped as Sarah buried her face in his neck and nipped at his skin.

"Fuck me, Dante. I need you," she pleaded in a husky voice next to his ear.

His big body shuddered as he pulled her into the full jets of the shower, turning her around in his arms and cradling her back against his chest. "Soon. I have to make you come first." His voice was deep and demanding, vibrating along the sensitive flesh of her ear. "Let me show you how many ways your body can be pleasured. Have you ever touched yourself in the shower?"

Sarah shook her head fiercely, his blunt questions not even embarrassing her anymore. Her body was too heated, too desperate for Dante.

"I love seeing you like this," Dante crooned in her ear as he cupped her breasts and pinched her nipples just hard enough for Sarah to feel a jolt of electricity shoot straight to her core. "So hot and so needy for me to make you come."

"Yes," she moaned, carnal desire coiled so tightly in her body that she had to find relief or die of frustration.

Dante ran a hand down her abdomen and toyed with her pussy, slowly penetrating her folds with his finger. "Touch your breasts. Do whatever feels good," he instructed, running a fingertip up and down the slit in her folds, not quite going where she needed him.

Cupping her own breasts, Sarah pinched and stroked her nipples, still needing more. "Please," she implored, feeling like she was going to self-destruct.

"I like watching you pleasing yourself, sweetheart. I've got you. Just enjoy this," he said in a soothing voice as his fingers invaded her heat. "Christ. You're so hot. Do you know what it does to me knowing that I'm the only man who has ever seen you like this?"

Sarah knew her core was slick, warm, and pulsating beneath his fingers. She could feel the drumming of her accelerated heartbeat in her ears as she leaned back, letting his muscular body support her. "Only you," she agreed with a whimper.

I need more. I need more.

Dante gave her exactly what she needed as he opened her folds and exposed her throbbing clit to the jetting water, moving her body until she was a prisoner to the pounding against the vulnerable bundle of nerves.

"Oh, God," Sarah cried out, pinching her nipples harder as the coil in her belly started to unfurl.

Dante invaded her channel with his fingers, pumping them in and out like a lover's cock.

"Too much. Too much," she whimpered as she squirmed against him, but he gave her no quarter.

Dante explored her sheath with every thrust, finding and curling his fingers around a G-spot she hadn't realized she even had, caressing the area with every stroke. Sarah's head dropped against his shoulder as her back arched slightly, unconsciously, the pleasure nearly unbearable.

"It's too much," she keened. The overwhelming feel of his fingers, the hard pulsation on her clit, and the sensation of her own hands caressing her breasts was making her body writhe, desperate for relief.

"Come for me, sweetheart," he ordered harshly.

Sarah had no choice. She unraveled, screaming Dante's name as her body detonated, and she flew to pieces, trusting Dante to catch her as she fell.

CHAPTER 12

Dante held her trembling body as Sarah panted, her heart beating so fast that she was lightheaded. He shut the water off and picked her up in his arms as he stepped out of the shower. After sitting her gently on the bathroom counter, he grabbed huge, fluffy towels and started to dry her body and hair with slow, careful motions. Once she was dry, he dried himself roughly and grabbed a brush, running it through her hair carefully as she sat in almost a stupor of postorgasmic bliss.

This is another way he's taking care of me.

"I still need you inside me," Sarah told him shakily, her body and mind needing, craving that ultimate connection.

"I will be," Dante told her huskily as he picked her up and carried her to his bedroom. "The first time I fuck you has to be in my bed, where you belong."

Sarah wrapped her arms around his neck and inhaled his scent, getting intoxicated from the combination of musk and male. Dante exuded testosterone, and she almost felt like she could smell it, get drunk on the scent. He was claiming her in the most primordial way by wanting to take her the first time in his bed. Maybe it was a little like a caveman wanting to drag a woman off to his lair to have his way with her. It was a possessive action, and that just ramped up Sarah's need even more. Something inside her responded to Dante's dominance like a match to dry tinder, making her burn for him more with every possessive command or action, every claiming word he uttered. Her reaction was elemental, and she couldn't stop it, even with logic.

He yanked back the covers on the bed and placed her in the middle, standing back and staring at her with a look so hot that it scorched her.

"I need you, Dante," Sarah admitted honestly, heat pooling in the pit of her stomach and radiating to every fiber of her being.

He crawled onto the bed and wrapped his arms around her, holding her tightly as he lowered his head to her shoulder. "I need you, too, sweetheart. I'll always be here when you need me."

Ferocious longing pulsated through Sarah's body, even though she knew he *wouldn't* always be here. She wanted Dante more than she'd ever wanted anything in her entire life, and she knew his admission wasn't purely physical.

"Be with me," Sarah pleaded, holding him tightly against her. Dante's emotional wounds of losing his best friend were still fresh, and she wanted to hold him tightly like this for as long as he needed her, in whatever way he needed her.

"Sarah," he uttered roughly, intensely, as though she was everything to him, and all of those yearnings were encompassed in just her name.

At that moment, they were locked together in a place where only the two of them existed, and Sarah could feel Dante all the way to her soul.

Dante rolled her onto her back and rose up on his elbows, staring down at her with eyes like liquid fire.

She reached up and stroked his jaw and cheek, both rough and whiskered as they always were at the end of the day.

"Condom," he grumbled.

"No!" Sarah exclaimed. "I've been on birth control for years." What was happening between her and Dante was raw and elemental, and she wanted to experience it that way.

"You didn't tell me. Do you trust me?" Dante asked, his eyes burning even hotter. "You'll be the first woman I've had bare. The only one I've ever wanted that way."

"Yes." She didn't need to remind him right now that she'd seen his medical records. She wanted to be a first to him in that way. "I'm safe, too."

"Sweetheart, you're nowhere near safe right now," Dante rumbled dangerously.

Sarah shuddered in anticipation. She'd waited for this moment for what seemed like forever. "Fuck me, Dante. No mercy."

"No mercy for either of us," Dante rasped, grasping her feet and urging her to put her legs around him.

She complied immediately, flexing her hips up only to feel his engorged cock sliding through her moist heat.

"Please. No more waiting." Her core clenched tight, needing to be filled by him.

"No more," he agreed, positioning his cock at the entrance to her channel and driving himself home. "Holy Christ," he hissed. "You're so damn tight, hot . . . wet."

Sarah felt stretched, filled to capacity by Dante. He was built big, and there was some pain as he buried himself all the way inside her, but the ecstasy of having him completely immersed inside her was worth the discomfort that was already fading away. It wasn't a bad kind of pain; it was a possession, a stretching that reinforced the fact that Dante was finally filling her. "Yes," she murmured, tightening her legs around him to pull him as deeply as he could get. "Fuck me," she demanded mindlessly.

Dante's forehead was already beaded with sweat as he pulled back and thrust into her again. "Mine," he groaned, almost as though the word was a vow as he stroked back out and into her again.

Sarah moaned and tightened her arms around Dante's shoulders, lost in the rhythm of his intense, powerful thrusts. This was what she needed, this cataclysmic, forceful connection with Dante.

Her world tilted as he pounded into her, his hand sliding under her ass to pull her up to meet the volatile strokes of his cock. Her body felt sensitized; every brush of skin against hers as he moved was like a caress. Sarah could feel perspiration trickle down her face as she moved with him, letting him claim her with every thrust of his cock.

Her hands were everywhere, stroking up his back and over his ass, trying to make him go even deeper.

"Harder," she urged him, wanting everything he could give.

Dante responded, hammering into her until she was panting and breathless. "Tell me you're mine," he demanded ruthlessly. "Tell me you need this as much as I do."

"Yes." There was no reason to deny it. If he stopped now, she wouldn't be able to bear it.

Dante shifted, bringing one of her feet up over his shoulder and changing angles until his cock stimulated her clit every time he entered and retreated. His mouth crashed down over hers, his tongue matching the rhythm of his cock as Sarah finally gave in to her impending climax. Her nails bit into the skin of his back, and she felt the vibration of Dante's groans as he continued to kiss her exactly like he was fucking her: hot, hard, and fast.

Sarah's back arched and her legs tightened around Dante's waist while wave after wave shuddered through her body as she rode the powerful orgasm.

Dante lifted his lips from hers and groaned as she milked him, the strong spasms of her channel clenching his cock tightly. He wrapped his arms around her and held her tightly as his warm release flooded her womb, both of them left shaking in the aftermath.

He rolled, letting her rest on top of his body so she could catch her breath. Sarah felt limp and spent, her heart racing out of control as she laid her head on Dante's chest and slid most of her weight off him and to the side. He might be almost healed, but she didn't want to hurt him.

Neither one of them spoke as they came slowly back to earth again.

Finally, Dante said hoarsely, "Do you understand now why I can't risk anything happening to you?"

"Yes." Sarah did understand. She would probably feel the same way if the positions were reversed. It wasn't a rational thought, but for the first time, she didn't care. Her heart was involved now, and caring about someone the way she cared about Dante was never going to make sense. It just . . . was. "I just want to be normal," Sarah responded with a sigh.

"You're never going to be normal, sweetheart," Dante replied bluntly. "You're always going to be special, but there's nothing wrong with that. I think it's fantastic. But you should have been allowed to be a child, and experience things that all normal women do. Being gifted should have opened even more opportunity for you, not kept you isolated." He kissed her gently on the forehead.

"I suppose one of those normal things would be sex?" she questioned, slightly amused, but amazed at how well he could read her, knew her needs almost better than she did right now.

"Especially that. Awesome, mind-blowing sex," he said with an arrogant grin. "And lots of it to make up for lost time."

God, when he throws me that cocky smile of his, I want to jump him all over again.

"And I suppose you can help me with that?" she asked teasingly.

He rolled her under him and trapped her hands above her head. "I'll be the only man helping you," he said greedily.

His expression went from cocky to grim in an instant, his body tensed above her.

"You don't hear me arguing," she answered in a sultry tone. Sarah was taken aback when she felt his hard erection brushing her thigh. "Impossible. You're over the age of thirty and it takes the average man longer to get another erection." *Especially one that's rock hard.*

Dante's lips started to curve slowly into a wicked, wicked grin. "Baby, I'm far from average when it comes to you."

Sarah highly doubted whether Dante could ever be considered average, even when he *wasn't* with her. He was . . . "extraordinary," she murmured aloud.

Dante threw his head back and let out a bark of laughter, and then lowered his head to her shoulder with a groan. "Only you could make that word sound so damn sexy when you're referring to my dick."

"Exceptional?" she tried again with a small smile, knowing that he hadn't realized that she was actually referring to the man and not just his man parts.

"Major turn-on," he agreed, letting his tongue trail along the sensitive spot right beneath her jaw.

"Amazing," she sighed, tilting her head so he could have better access to her neck.

"You're about to find out if you keep talking dirty to me this way," he warned her in a muffled, deep, passionate voice as he bit down gently on the lobe of her ear.

Sarah moaned, knowing just about anything she said to him made him horny. Crazy man. So when he finally impaled her, sinking himself deeply inside her, she moaned, "Phenomenal."

"Dirty girl," Dante answered gruffly.

"Fuck me, Dante," she begged, most of her vocabulary now evaporated along with her common sense.

"Very dirty girl," he said with a husky groan as he did exactly that.

Sarah woke the next day deliciously sore, glad it was Saturday, and wrapped in a pair of strong, muscular arms that had held her tightly and protectively while she'd slept most of the day away. Of course, that was *after* she'd experienced Dante's "phenomenal" several more times, and it had already been daylight when they'd both fallen into an exhausted sleep.

As she stretched her arms over her head and sat up, she noticed it was already four o'clock in the afternoon. "When have I ever slept the whole afternoon away?" she whispered to herself, astonished. She hadn't had that luxury even when she'd worked all day and all night when she was in med school.

"Your fault," Dante said groggily, sitting up and stretching just like she had just done. "You shouldn't have started all of that dirty talk."

Sarah's body reacted just from watching him stretch, his broad shoulders flexing, his biceps rippling as he moved. Her eyes scanned over his sculpted chest and ripped abs, following his happy trail of dark hair that disappeared underneath the tented sheet.

Scrambling out of bed before he could catch her, she laughed as he stalked her, on his hands and knees on the mattress. Her body responded immediately, her nipples hardening as she watched his eyes grow dark and needy. She wanted to let him catch her, but she knew if she experienced Mr. Exceptional one more time she might not be able to walk. "Oh, no you don't, mister. Keep that thing away from me. I'm sore."

Dante flopped onto his back with a groan of defeat that made Sarah giggle. "If you aren't going to let me fuck you, at least feed me," he bellowed tragically, trying to make her laugh. "You're a demanding woman and you worked me over hard. I'm famished."

She did chortle. Sarah couldn't help herself. When Dante was in a playful mood, he could certainly bring on the drama. Oh, she knew very well that he was playing her by trying to look pathetic. There wasn't one feeble bone in his body. But she adored the fact that he was doing this for her entertainment.

Honestly, she probably did need to feed him. He'd expended so much energy, and it certainly wasn't *her* who wore *him* out. Dante was . . . insatiable.

It had come as no surprise to her that Dante couldn't cook well, and she'd found out from day one that she either needed to cook or they'd end up getting pizza or Chinese delivered every single day. She'd gotten into the habit of cooking here, a task she actually enjoyed but rarely fussed with at home because it didn't seem worth the effort just to feed herself. But watching Dante consume multiple plates of food she'd prepared made her happy, like she was actually doing something useful for him. No one appreciated food more than Dante.

"Eggs, bacon, and pancakes as soon as I shower," she informed him as she walked toward the bedroom door, feeling self-conscious about walking around as naked as the day she was born.

"I'll be ready in ten," Dante called cheerfully, rolling quickly to his feet and practically jogging to the shower.

Five eggs, half a pound of bacon, and five pancakes later, Dante was cleaning up the kitchen as Sarah sat at his piano in the living room. He was a big guy, but where the hell did he put that much food?

She'd just finished a concerto, and she cringed as she heard dishes crashing together as he loaded them into the dishwasher. It was his bargain. When she cooked, he cleaned up.

Thank God he doesn't use real china.

Dante cleaned up the same way he did everything else: fast and furious.

She watched him emerge from the kitchen, dressed in a forest-green button-down shirt and a pair of faded jeans, looking good enough to eat.

He came toward her in purposeful strides, his expression stoic as he stopped behind the piano bench and held out his hand. "Okay. Let's go. I have a surprise for you."

His expression was unreadable. "What are you up to?" Sarah asked cautiously.

He grasped her hand impatiently and pulled her gently to her feet. "You better move before I change my mind. Go put on a pair of jeans and a long-sleeved shirt for protection."

What for? She was already dressed in shorts and a tank top. Intrigued, Sarah scampered upstairs to her room to find some clothes. It was probably still hovering around the high seventies in temperature outside, and it was almost always humid. However, she wasn't going to argue about wearing a long-sleeved shirt. Dante was definitely up to something, and she couldn't wait to see what he had planned.

Apprehension seized him as Dante led Sarah outside. He'd put her present together several nights ago when he couldn't sleep, haunted by the warmth and the temptation of her warm body next to his. He'd gotten up and come out to the garage, desperate for something to occupy his time and his dirty mind. He hadn't planned on helping her learn to ride anything but him anytime soon when he'd purchased it. He didn't want her outside or exposed unless it was absolutely necessary. But now his instincts to protect and his desire to make her happy were at war within his aching gut.

I just want to be normal.

That plea, that simply uttered need, had almost brought him to his knees last night. What he'd told her was true . . . she'd always be much better than normal. But she did deserve to do normal things. If he had his way, she'd stay safely tucked away until her attacker was finally caught. But honestly, there was a possibility that the guy had skipped town and he was keeping her sequestered for nothing. He could be vigilant. Still, bringing her outside in the open was nearly killing him. Sure, it was on the peninsula, and chances were that her location hadn't even been discovered yet. But even a small risk with Sarah's safety made him antsy.

Happy or safe?

Why in the hell did it have to come down to one or the other? He wanted Sarah to be happy *and* safe. Was that too damn much to ask?

His Glock was tucked into his waistband at his back and covered by the tail of his shirt. Dante silently scoped out his surroundings before dragging Sarah to the open area of the driveway. Releasing her hand, he went into the garage and rolled out her new bike, watching her face as she saw what he was doing.

"Oh my God. Is that mine? It's beautiful," Sarah exclaimed, her face glowing as she moved forward and reverently ran a hand over the black leather seat.

The bike he was rolling out was a metallic red with black accessories, and the look on her face was priceless, well worth the few hours it had taken to put it together. "This is a beach cruiser and it only has one speed. Perfect for this area and easy to learn to ride. It's good for a starter."

"It's good forever. I can't believe you got this just for me," Sarah whispered softly, her hand moving over the shiny red paint. "It's the best gift ever."

"Better than the piano?" Dante said, amused. Only Sarah would think a starter cruiser bike was the best gift ever from a billionaire. However, he had no doubt that she was more excited about this silly bicycle than she would be about getting high-priced jewelry or anything else he could easily buy for her.

She lifted a brow at him. "You said the piano was for you."

Damn. Busted!

The piano was never meant for him, but he knew he'd needed to make some excuse to suddenly have a grand piano show up in his living room. Yeah, his excuse had been lame. Still, he'd just stuck his big foot in his mouth. "It was," he lied shamefully. He knew that she probably had never bought his excuse, but he wasn't admitting it outright. More than likely, she'd want him to get rid of it.

"Hmm . . . yeah," Sarah answered dubiously, but she didn't push the issue. "Did you put this bike together yourself?" she asked curiously.

"Yep. I wanted to. I wanted to make sure it was safe." He released a silent sigh of relief that she'd dropped the piano subject. Unfortunately, he knew he'd been nailed, but she'd let him off the hook.

Sarah stopped staring at the bike and lifted her gaze to his face. Dante froze as he saw the tears in her eyes, and felt his heart speed up as she curled one hand behind his neck and pulled him down for the gentlest, most tender kiss he'd ever experienced.

"That makes it even more special," she told him softly. "Thank you." Gripping the handlebars, she asked excitedly, "Can I try it?"

"Wait a minute," he ordered, pulling out the safety equipment he'd purchased with the bike. He adjusted the lightweight helmet on her head, laughing as it squashed her curls and sent them protruding out of the sides of the helmet. He made her hold out her arms and legs as he put on knee and elbow pads. "Okay," he said warily, allowing her to swing her leg over, wondering if there was any other protective gear he could have gotten her.

He showed her how to brake the bike, the most important skill as far as he was concerned, and how to balance herself. Honestly, he'd wanted to put training wheels on the bicycle, but he thought that was a little overkill. Now he almost wished he had included them. He was having visions of Sarah battered and bloody on the ground from a nasty fall, even though he knew he was being ridiculous.

"I'm staying with you, so don't pedal too fast. And don't hit the brakes too hard or you could go flying right over the handlebars," he warned anxiously.

"Doesn't it make more sense to go faster? It's simple physics, really. If I'm moving at a higher rate of speed, the bike should become more stable," she said thoughtfully.

Dante watched the concentration on Sarah's face and grinned. He should have known she'd be calculating some mathematical formula for staying balanced. "Not too fast," he instructed. "Mount up."

Sarah used the pedals to slip onto the seat, finding a comfortable position for her hands on the handlebars as he held her steady.

"Okay, start pedaling," Dante coached, keeping a grip underneath the seat and next to the handlebars.

She was a fast learner, and started out a little wobbly, but Dante found himself running along with her after a few false starts. He had her get used to the brakes, letting her bring the bike to a stop every time they reached the end of the driveway.

"I think I can do it," Sarah told him confidently, her face glowing with excitement as they stopped at the end of the driveway after several trips back and forth. "You can let go this time."

I can let go?

That thought rankled, even though Dante was pretty certain Sarah would stay upright. "We'll see." Her face was still shining with excitement, glowing like a child's who was learning to ride for the first time. Dante had never seen her look more beautiful.

She pushed off and got herself seated, and Dante ran along with her for a short distance before letting go. "Don't forget to brake," he bellowed, running alongside of her now.

A startled look appeared briefly on her face as she realized he wasn't holding on anymore, but then she whooped, "I'm doing it myself!"

She was, although Dante stayed close enough to react if she started to go down. He watched as she pedaled faster, and then started to ease on the brake to stop near the garage.

"I did it," Sarah said breathlessly as she lowered her feet to the ground. Clambering off the cycle, she engaged the kickstand and threw herself into Dante's arms, peppering his face with kisses as she bounced around in his arms jubilantly. "That was incredible."

Worth every damn moment I've been sweating out her safety.

Dante was still watching their surroundings, but her happiness had been worth his stress, and having her delectable body bouncing against his was a definite bonus.

"I'm making you the best dinner ever later tonight," Sarah told him excitedly.

Dante wanted to tell her that any time he ate at the same table with her was an incredible dinner, but he wouldn't argue. His skills in the kitchen sucked, and Sarah was an incredible cook. The very best part of having dinner with Sarah was seeing her beautiful face as she sat next to him at the table. It was weird how fast he'd gotten used to not eating alone, to having her there every evening. Probably because he loved having her near him so damn much.

"It's starting to get dark. You ready to head inside?" he asked her reluctantly, wishing he could capture her joy and hold on to it forever. *This* was the way he wanted to see her every single day.

"Yes," she agreed readily, elevating the stand on her bike carefully and pushing it into the garage as though it were one of her most prized possessions.

Dante watched as she carefully removed her gear and stored it in the pouch on the back of the bike.

"Thank you," she told him sincerely, reaching for his hand and entwining their fingers together when she joined him outside again.

He had to swallow a lump in his throat the size of Alaska. He'd never had a whole lot of tenderness in his life, but this woman was making him crave it from her.

Dante shrugged. "It was just a bike ride."

"It was a whole lot more than just you teaching me how to ride a bike and you know it," she replied quietly.

She knew that stepping outside in the open had been difficult for him. She was telling him that she appreciated the fact that he'd compromised for her. It should have surprised him that she understood, but it didn't. Sarah could read him in ways that nobody else ever had.

Hell, there was almost nothing he wouldn't do for her, but he didn't know how to tell her that, so he kissed her instead, giving Sarah the same type of warm embrace that she'd given him earlier, before he wrapped an arm around her waist and took her back into the house.

CHAPTER 13

During the next week, Sarah was relieved that Dante had actually started to loosen the reins a bit on letting her be seen occasionally outside. Yesterday, he'd walked her to Brew Magic so they could get a latte. Of course, he had her shackled to his side with a powerful, muscular arm around her waist, and she knew he was well armed. Still, it was progress. And for the last several days, he'd let her take a few more laps up and down the driveway on her bike, teaching her how to make turns and improving her skills. And then, of course, there were the nights.

Sarah sighed happily as she thought about those incredible nights, with another one on its way. Neither of them could wait beyond five minutes before they were naked and in the shower together after work, each of them ravenous for the other. They usually woke up aroused and ready in the morning, too. Sarah thought her desire would settle down at least a little after she'd been with Dante. It didn't. If anything, it made her need even more acute, more urgent.

Her cell phone rang just as she was exiting Dante's truck after work that day, and she cringed as she dug into her purse and saw her mother's number.

"Who is it?" Dante asked curiously.

"My mother," she replied unhappily. It had been over a month since she'd heard from Elaine Baxter, and although some part of her wanted to talk to her mother because she was her only family, she knew how the conversation would go, how it always went.

Sarah answered it before she could decide to ignore the call. She knew that once her mother had decided she wanted to talk to her, she'd keep calling back.

"Hello," she said apprehensively.

"Sarah?" her mother asked abruptly.

"Yes, Mom. It's me."

"I've found the ideal man for you," Elaine said without preamble. "I met him in one of my Mensa meetings. He's perfect. His IQ is similar, and he's a brilliant neurosurgeon, so you'd have a lot in common. He's older, and ready to settle down now. I need you to come back to Chicago."

Nothing had changed a bit. "I can't," she replied, not mentioning that she had no plans to leave Amesport, a place where she'd never been happier in her life.

"Are you still not working in the hospital?"

"No, Mother, I'm not," Sarah replied flatly as she followed Dante into the house.

"You're going to have to conquer those fears. They aren't rational," her mother scolded. "You don't belong in a small office, working in some town that's hardly on the map. How are you going to keep advancing? You need to meet the man I found for you. Being older, he'll be more stable. But I'm not sure he'll understand your phobias."

Sarah was pretty certain that he wouldn't. If he was a friend of her mother's and she liked this man, he didn't deal in anything that couldn't be proved with scientific evidence or mathematical formulas. "I'd prefer to pick my own husband, Mom," she answered flatly.

Dante swung his head around at Sarah's comment, frowning at the cell phone in her hand like it was an actual person.

Sarah continued. "And there was an incident here that indicates that the man who attacked me might be coming after me. I'm working with the police to try to apprehend him now." Sarah desperately hoped her mother would show just an iota of concern.

"That's all the more reason to get on a plane and come back here. Chicago has a much better police force to protect you," her mother said with a sniff of disgust.

And John Thompson would have a big city to hide in. Just for once, Mom, ask me if I'm doing okay. Ask me what happened and if I'm safe. Ask me if I'm scared. Be a mom instead of a teacher.

"You're wasting your potential there, Sarah. I want you on a plane and home by the end of the week, young lady," her mother added.

Deflated, Sarah sat down in one of the dining room chairs. Dante moved a chair beside her and sat, taking her hand as though he knew she was upset.

Who am I kidding? I'm wishing for a relationship that never has and never will exist.

Her mother was more of a disciplinarian, an instructor whom Sarah could never please and never had, no matter how hard she tried. "I'm twenty-seven years old. I can make my own decisions now. And I'm never going back there. Ever," she told her mother emphatically.

For Sarah, the words meant so much more than just location. She was starting to live, finding friendships after going so long without anybody, and she had a man who was right beside her, lending her support when she needed it. Dante might not be in her life forever, but she was going to appreciate what she had right now. No . . . she was never going back to the sterile, lifeless existence she'd known in Chicago. Not now that she was learning that life could be so much . . . more.

"After all I've done to promote your education, you're just going to throw that away?" her mother asked angrily. "You're horribly scarred, Sarah. Have you forgotten about that? But an intellectual man who can see beyond sex won't mind as much about your scars."

"I'm happy," Sarah replied quietly, wishing it didn't seem like she and her mother were on two different planets. She'd been a very obedient child, constantly trying to keep her mother happy, make her proud. If she had succeeded, her mother had never shown it. Now it was time for Sarah to live her own life and stop hoping to somehow get her only parent's approval. It was never going to happen, so she might as well make herself happy.

"Happiness means nothing to a woman like you," her mother retorted. "You're gifted."

Sarah's body jerked as though she'd been slapped. "I'm also human," she told her parent sadly. "I want more than marrying the right man because of our genes. I want to manage my own life now."

"Fine. I suppose I don't have any choice but to let you waste your life and your talent," Elaine relented haughtily.

"No. You really don't," Sarah agreed, then disconnected the phone with a beleaguered sigh.

Dante immediately pulled her onto his lap and cradled her body against his. "I take it that didn't go well," he queried curiously. "Was she really expecting you to marry somebody you've never met?" His voice got angry, rougher.

Sarah shrugged. "I'm expected to marry a man with a genius gene pool so we can make tons of little Mensa babies for the scientific community to marvel over."

"Jesus, that woman is cold," Dante retorted vehemently. "Not that I didn't know that already." He hesitated before adding, "How do you feel about going out to Tony's tonight? I still owe you that dinner we talked about."

He's actually willing to go out? He thinks I'm unhappy, so he's trying to do something to make me feel better.

"I'd love to go out, but if you're doing this because you think I'm sad, I'm not. I've been dealing with my mother for twenty-seven years," Sarah stated blandly, turning to look at his face.

"Bullshit," Dante said gruffly. "I know what it feels like to wish for a parent who actually gives a crap. I've been there."

Sarah's eyes softened as her gaze met Dante's. She knew his father had been a mean, abusive alcoholic before he died, and his mother had left them all just as soon as Hope was out of the house. Dante and his siblings almost never heard from their mother. It was obvious he really did know exactly how she felt. "It hurts. But I won't let her ruin my chance to be happy."

"Don't," Dante agreed as he stood up, lowering Sarah's feet to the floor. "Go get ready. I'm doing this because I owe you dinner. And it's still daylight. We need to be back before dark."

He didn't owe her anything. It was just the opposite. But he was using that excuse to make her happy. Sarah grinned at him. "I'll be like Cinderella."

"We need to be home way before midnight, and I'm no Prince Charming, woman," he said gruffly.

"No, you're not," she agreed, giving him a lingering kiss on the lips. "You're even better. And I'm almost certain you're better endowed," she answered in a sultry voice as she teased his large erection through the denim of his jeans with her palm and fingers. Sexually, she was getting bolder and bolder, and she loved feeling her own feminine power.

A low, reverberating sound came out of his throat, and Sarah scampered off before he could catch her. She squealed happily, the sound echoing through the house as she sprinted up the stairs with Dante hot on her heels.

"I can't believe I actually let you walk out of the house in this dress. Every man who sees you will be fantasizing about fucking you," Dante complained as he opened the passenger side of the truck, his eyes roaming over the long expanse of the bare legs exiting the vehicle.

"You wanted me to have a red dress," Sarah reminded him. "Emily thought it was hot. You don't think so?" She loved the dress, but she had to admit that it was meant to be sexy. It had a halter neck that made it impossible to wear a bra, and it was backless, the material starting at the top of her buttocks. The skirt was short and fitted, and it cupped her ass and the tops of her legs lovingly, ending at the middle of her thighs. It was revealing, but elegant enough not to make her look like a slut or a woman on the prowl.

"Too damn hot," Dante griped. "My dick will be hard all through dinner just like it is now, and I'll want to kill the first guy who shows the same appreciation I have for that particular dress."

Sarah smiled at his unhappy tone. He'd already told her how beautiful she looked, and she felt beautiful. She'd put her hair up, letting some of the curls frame her face, and she'd used a heavier hand with her makeup than she usually did. Every time Dante glanced her way she felt like he wanted to devour her whole. She'd worn her torturous three-inch heels, but Dante still towered above her, his broad shoulders encased in a suit jacket that just emphasized his mammoth size. In jeans, Dante Sinclair was mesmerizing. In a suit and tie, he was so devastatingly handsome that he took her breath away.

They were shown to their table by the window. When she went to sit down, Dante gently grasped her upper arm and guided her to the seat across from him.

"I like to face the door," he told her gruffly, pulling the chair out for her and seating her before he seated himself.

Sarah knew he was carrying a gun, and she assumed he wanted to be able to see who was coming and going from the restaurant. "A cop thing?" she guessed.

"Yep," he answered with a grin. "I always face the door."

They ordered drinks while they looked over the menu. The restaurant might be touristy, but Sarah loved the nautical decor that was appealing without being tacky. They both decided on the turf and surf, steak and lobster, and Sarah leaned back in her chair and sipped her wine, the novelty of sitting in a restaurant like she was on a real date delighting her.

"What are you smiling about?" Dante looked at her quizzically.

"I feel so young—like I'm out on a date with the hottest guy on the college campus."

"If I were still in college and I were dating you, all I'd be thinking about was whether or not I'd be getting laid afterward," Dante commented with a wicked smile.

Sarah leaned forward and whispered conspiratorially, "I think you most definitely *will* get lucky this time." She was already hot for him, and looking at his handsome image across from her, she wanted to crawl over the table and have *him* for dinner.

"You think?" Dante answered, his voice husky.

He shot her a heated, warning look across the table that made her heart skip a beat. She nodded slowly. "I even wore some hot new panties for you to check out later. They're very scandalous and almost transparent." Okay, now she knew she was poking at the beast, but she loved Dante's feral wildness, so she continued. "And the matching silk garter and stockings are lovely."

"You didn't show me those," he growled.

"I wanted to eat," she told him laughingly. "I was afraid we'd never leave the house." That was definitely the truth. Had she modeled the underwear for him before they left, they'd still be in bed. Although she still didn't understand Dante's insatiable desire for her scarred body, she accepted it as truth. He proved it over and over, every single day, and she was getting used to the fact that he really did want her.

"We wouldn't have left," Dante confirmed harshly. "Jesus Christ. How am I supposed to sit here now? My dick is already hard," he grumbled unhappily.

God, it felt good to tease him. Sarah had never in her life felt comfortable enough to flirt with a man. Maybe this conversation with Dante was a little beyond flirting, because they were already in a sexual relationship, but she loved seeing the intense look of desire on his face and the twin flames of his eyes burning into her as he watched her intently.

"You'll pay for this later, woman," Dante told her roughly.

Sarah shivered in anticipation. "I hope so," she answered teasingly. She was definitely prodding his dominant instincts, and maybe it was dangerous to do so since Dante was already plenty alpha. He was sexually bossy and authoritative, but she couldn't resist pushing him even more. Dante encouraged her to explore her deepest desires, and she was definitely delving into them right now.

His eyes turned to molten fire. "Is that what you want? Punishment?"

Sarah shuddered at the thought. Dante would never hurt her, and she knew the only thing he'd really dish out was pleasure. Judging by his heated look, the thought of making her pay for teasing him enflamed him just as much as it did her. Opening her eyes wide, she gave him an innocent look as she replied, "Only if you think I deserve it." She slipped her foot out of her high heel and brushed her toes gently against his engorged erection, hoping she'd get herself into even more trouble, wondering just how far Dante would take this.

"Right now I'm ready to paddle your ass until you beg for mercy," he warned ominously.

Her pussy flooded. Maybe she was kinky, but the thought of Dante being that bold made her body incinerate. She had no doubt he'd do it. He wasn't the type of guy who didn't back up his words with action. If this didn't stop, she'd be nothing but a pile of ashes in the chair of a fancy restaurant.

The waiter appeared with their food, and Sarah removed her foot, slipping it back into her shoe. The tablecloth was long and covered their laps, but she didn't want to be discovered. This was all too new for her, too surreal. Dante really wanted her to the point of desperation, the same way she needed him.

Their conversation turned to more bland topics as they ate, but she could feel Dante's gaze boring into her as she consumed an excellent steak and succulent Maine lobster.

Eventually, they talked about his brothers.

"Evan is almost always traveling. He needs to slow down or he'll burn himself out by the time he's thirty-five," Dante told her as he finished his steak and placed his utensils on the plate.

"He must be lonely," Sarah commented, wondering what it would be like to travel the world with nobody to share it with.

"I guess I never thought about it that way. But yeah, he probably is. He's surrounded by people all the time in his business, but I don't think any of them really give a shit about him. Most of them are just kissing his ass to improve their own financial interests. Evan works himself into the ground, and he doesn't have to anymore. He never really did. It's almost like he's out to prove something, maybe that he can do a better job running the company than my father did," Dante mused.

"And does he?" Sarah asked curiously, finishing her own dinner and placing her napkin on her plate, declining dessert when it was offered politely by the waiter taking their plates. She had already eaten until her stomach was completely full.

"Definitely. He's made the corporation more successful than any of us could have ever imagined. The company was already worth billions of dollars, but Evan has probably tripled its value since my father died. I just wish he'd give it a break for a while." Dante frowned as he slipped his credit card into the folder for the waiter, who picked it up immediately.

"And Jared?" Sarah prompted. She already knew Grady and much of his history from Emily. But Jared was still a mystery to her.

"Jared's changed. Something happened to him, but I don't know what. He blows it off if I try to ask him about what changed him, but he never used to be this way. Is his business successful? Very. But he's not the same person he used to be growing up."

"What was he like when he was younger?"

"Creative. Smart. He was always drawing something. He was a talented artist, and he went after architecture because he loved creating things, or rebuilding them. I think he's bored with commercial real estate, but that's what's made him even richer. I don't know. He just seems . . . lost." Dante paused before saying, "He's acting like an asshole, but he was always the first one to notice when Grady or one of our other siblings needed us, even though he was younger. He used to be curious about the world, kind to everyone. Now he's just a jackass."

"He's still nice to old ladies," Sarah pointed out, remembering what Elsie and Beatrice had said about Jared.

"I guess that's something," Dante said dubiously.

"What about Hope?" Sarah asked, wondering what it must have been like to be the only female among the Sinclair siblings.

"She's happy now. She's married to a childhood friend of the family, Jason Sutherland. He actually handles portfolios for Grady and me. He's an incredible investor, one of the sharpest in the world."

"I've heard of him. He's a genius with mathematics and numbers, too, besides being a brilliant investor," Sarah commented with awe.

"I'm sure your mother would love him, but he's already married to my sister," Dante replied morosely.

He looked irritated and possibly . . . jealous? "If my mother would like him, then I probably wouldn't," she told him adamantly.

"Every woman pants over Jason," Dante grumbled.

"Not me," she denied matter-of-factly. "I've seen his picture and my tongue definitely did not leave my mouth."

"Good. I'd hate to have to hurt him. He's my brother-in-law now," Dante grunted, obviously satisfied. "He and Hope are back in New York at the moment, but I know they don't plan on living there full-time anymore." Dante signed the receipt for their dinner, which had been dropped off by their efficient waiter, and stuffed his copy in his wallet. "Ready?"

"Yes," Sarah sighed, feeling relaxed from the wine she'd consumed. "It will be getting dark soon. Cinderella needs to return from the ball."

"There's only one problem with that," Dante observed.

"What?"

Dante took her hand in his and pulled her gracefully to her feet. "We haven't had our dance." He tilted his head toward the small dance floor in the bar. "Dance with me, Sarah."

She looked at the dancing area, and only a few other couples were on the floor. The music was slow and romantic, and the couples were gliding around the floor elegantly. "Dante, you know I've never—"

"Just follow me. I happen to be an excellent dancer. You're musical, sweetheart. You'll have no problem. It will be another first for you." He tugged her toward the small floor, weaving between tables until they reached the bar.

Sarah took a deep breath and blew it out again. She might make a fool of herself, but she'd do it in Dante's arms. He held one of her hands and circled her waist with his other arm. Ordinarily, she'd be running away from making a spectacle of herself, but Dante's confidence in her sometimes made her feel like she could fly.

I can do this.

"Follow me, mimic my movements. Trust me to guide you," he instructed as he started moving smoothly around the small floor.

Sarah concentrated and stepped on Dante's foot several times before she finally just let herself go on instinct, matching her body to his. "You *are* an incredible dancer."

"I'm a Sinclair. I think dancing was mandatory almost from birth," Dante whispered huskily in her ear. "I don't remember a time when I wasn't required to know how to dance."

Sarah relaxed as her body learned Dante's lead, losing herself in the music. Sometimes she forgot that Dante had been raised in a very wealthy, socially prominent family. Brought up as part of the very rich elite, of course he knew how to socialize, how to charm, how to dance.

As the tempo slowed, so did Dante, and she leaned her head on his shoulder as he tightened his arm around her waist and brought her closer to him. "I don't think you're going to step on my toes anymore," he teased gently. "You're a natural."

She lost track of time as they swayed around the floor. Inhaling against his neck, she got drunk on the smell of him, the way his body moved, and the novelty of her first experience actually dancing.

Finally, the musicians stopped for a break, and Dante kissed her on the forehead. "Are you ready to go home, Cinderella?"

They turned and walked toward the front entrance together. It was starting to get dark as they stepped outside.

Sarah wanted to tell him how much all of this meant to her, how much she'd enjoyed her first dance, but she couldn't find the words. "Thank you" was what came out of her mouth. Very inadequate, but Dante seemed satisfied as he opened the passenger door of the truck and lifted her into the seat.

"You're welcome," he answered back, slipping his hand beneath her skirt to lift it slightly, using his body to block hers. "Holy shit, you weren't just teasing." He gaped as he got a brief glimpse of her sexy lingerie.

She smiled. "I never joke about lingerie." She meant serious business with the ensemble she was wearing.

He dropped the skirt and ran around the truck, starting the vehicle and putting it into motion so fast that Sarah barely had time to fasten her seat belt. Knowing exactly what was motivating his haste, she laughed.

CHAPTER 14

Sarah was giggling by the time she raced inside the front door, Dante following close behind.

"Wait," he told her sternly.

Sarah stopped and stood by the door until Dante had looked around the house and switched off the alarm system. When he came back, he snatched her by the hand and pulled her into the living room. "Show me."

"Here?" she squeaked innocently.

"Here. Right now," he said demandingly.

She knew exactly what he was waiting expectantly to see. After kicking off her shoes, she shimmied the fitted skirt over her ass and up to her waist, her breath hitching as she heard Dante's low-pitched groan.

She turned around slowly, revealing her bare ass cheeks to him. The minuscule panties were a thong—not her usual underwear of choice, but she'd worn them for him.

"Perfect for what I'm going to do to you," he threatened as he stepped toward her, eyes blazing. "Sometimes I like it rough, Sarah. I think you want that, too, or you wouldn't have asked for it."

"I do," she breathed softly, her pussy clenching with need. She wanted this man's hands all over her, and she wanted his intensity right now. "But you'll have to catch me first," she called over her shoulder as she sprinted to the kitchen. After exiting through the sliding glass doors, she headed for their one safe area, a place Dante had allowed them to go: the dock on the small private beach behind his house. It was long and narrow until it fanned out at the very end with a sitting area. Dante could see anyone approaching, so they'd started sitting outside at the end of the dock when she needed some fresh air. Sarah sprinted across the short expanse of sand, her feet hitting the wooden dock at a mad dash. She ran full speed until she reached the end of the dock, panting.

Dante was right behind her, his long legs eating up the distance down the dock. He stopped before he reached her. "You shouldn't have run outside like that. Nowhere to go. What are you going to do now? You can't get past me, and I don't think you're planning to jump into the water."

Sarah's heart was racing, her pussy flooding as she watched Dante stalk her. "I can swim," she informed him, stepping closer to the edge of a dock she had no intention of using to leap into the ocean. The dress she was wearing had been one of Emily's picks and probably was quite pricey, and really, she had no desire to run very far from Dante. There was no way she was swinging her leg over the waist-high slatted fence around the end of the dock and plunging into the Atlantic Ocean.

Dante prowled closer, removing his suit jacket as he moved slowly forward, and then started unknotting his tie. "You aren't jumping."

He knew her all too well, but Sarah stepped closer to the edge, so close that her ass bumped into the wooden railing. Grasping on to it, she said confidently, "I might." *Not!*

"Take the dress off, Sarah," Dante demanded sternly. "Now." He hit the switch on the tiny lamp at the end of the dock, flooding it with dim light. He pulled the gun out from the small of his back and set it carefully on the wooden dock in an area that wouldn't get wet, within reach but out of the way.

Her nipples hardened at the sound of his harsh order, but she wasn't ready to give up yet. "Make me," she challenged him, sending him a defiant look.

His expression turned stormy as he lunged forward and trapped her body between the railing and his muscular form. He grasped both sides of the halter and jerked, the dress splitting completely down the front. "I just did." He pulled roughly at the halter tie, making the bow come loose and the garment slide from her body to the dock floor. "I can make you do anything I want right now," he informed her gutturally, pulling the pins from her hair and letting the curls fall to her shoulders.

Sarah hardly noticed the dress. She was too busy being mesmerized by his unyielding gaze. Her body quaked as she suddenly felt her wrists being restrained. She glanced down and saw he'd used his tie to wrap both of her wrists together, the ends of the tie flapping in the light breeze. Tugging against the restraint, she found herself bound tightly enough so she couldn't separate her wrists. "Can you?" she asked in a sultry, low voice that she couldn't control.

Dante slowly dropped the zipper on his pants and let them fall, stepping out of them to leave him only in a pair of black silk boxers. "I want you to get down on your hands and knees on the blanket, and I want you to do it willingly."

There was a blanket spread out in the corner of the dock, one that they always left there to sit on as they felt the spray of the waves on their faces and the light, cooling breeze of the ocean through the open slats of the fencing.

Sarah hesitated, but somehow she knew he wanted her to do this without him forcing her into it. He wanted to know if she wanted to continue to play or stop. "Punishment time?" she asked, her nipples hardening to painful peaks.

"Pleasure time," he answered gruffly.

With her hands still tied, she walked to the blanket and went down to her knees, excitement making every nerve ending in her body come alive. "What now?" In her heightened state of arousal, she was ready to give him anything, everything.

Dante lowered himself onto the blanket beside her and demanded, "Bend over." He made a pad for her elbows by wadding the blanket up to protect her skin.

Sarah went down with Dante guiding her. She squirmed, her body more than ready for him. The anticipation was nearly killing her.

"Spread your legs," he insisted hoarsely.

Sarah could hear the need vibrating in his voice, and she knew that her sexual obedience turned him on even more than her defiance. She parted her legs, her heart pounding as she trembled with need. "Please," she begged, not even knowing what she wanted.

His hand moved to the cheeks of her ass, stroking the bare skin. Sarah could feel the gentle rocking of the dock and the light mist of the waves that was starting to make her body slightly damp. Every crashing wave just seemed to increase the wildness in her soul.

She moaned loudly as Dante's fingers delved underneath her panties and stroked through her folds.

"Jesus, you're wet. Does this make you burn, Sarah? Do you want me?"

Oh, dear God. "Yes," she panted, her ass wriggling high in the air as she tried to manipulate his fingers where she wanted them.

"Should we talk about your teasing now?" he asked her, his voice heated with arousal and passion, as he stroked his fingers through her folds. "Or should we discuss the fact that you ran out of the house tonight without even looking around first?" He finally gripped the flimsy panties and yanked them from her body in one strong pull.

He had complete access and he took advantage of it, stroking her clit lightly, sending waves of pleasure through her body before he firmly smacked her ass. "Oh . . ." she moaned, the sting on her butt cheeks making her even wetter.

Smack.

Smack.

Smack.

Smack.

Her body jerked with every connection of his palm to her ass cheeks. He wasn't gentle, and the firm strokes stung. Sarah let her head fall forward as she felt him delve between her thighs again, the combination of pleasure and pain about to drive her mad. His palm stroked her heated rear gently as he asked, "Are you sorry for teasing me?" His finger slid over her clit again, applying even more pleasure.

"No," she moaned, knowing her denial would get her more of his irresistible dominance. She was giving him permission to take this as far as he wanted to take it.

The strokes to her ass came swift and heavy, and it stung so good. This time, when his fingers teased her clit, stroking through her wet heat, she heard him groan. He slid two fingers into her channel and pumped hard. "Are you sorry now?" he grunted.

Sarah moved her hips back to meet the deep strokes of his fingers, needing him to fill her now. "Yes. Just fuck me, Dante. Please."

He didn't. Instead, he lay down on his back and pulled her hips back until she was straddling his mouth and he squeezed her fiery ass, devouring her pussy at the same time.

Sarah's scream rang out into the dark night, mingling with the sound of the waves crashing to the shore. Dante squeezed and lowered her pussy flush with his face, using his whole mouth, nose, and tongue to consume her, to feast on her as she moaned with ecstasy, her body trembling from the intensity of her pleasure. The combination of the pain of his grip on her blazing ass and his fierce hunger for her pussy were pushing her way over the edge of desire and into insanity.

"Oh, God. Dante!" She shuddered and let go of a hoarse cry as her climax seized her body and wouldn't let go. Riding the waves of pleasure, she gripped the wadded-up blanket, trying to hang on to anything that would keep her from flying off into the stratosphere.

Moving urgently, he plunged his cock into her from behind as her channel was still clenched from her orgasm. Sarah heard him groan harshly as he buried himself balls-deep inside her. A corresponding moan escaped her lips as he stretched her, making her take every single inch of his cock so deeply that the satisfaction was almost too much to bear. In this position, he went deeper, filled her harder, and he grasped her hips and pounded into her, slapping her ass with every forceful stroke.

"Come for me," he commanded, his deep, graveled voice full of uncontrolled arousal.

Sarah shook her head, her body so aroused, so sensitized that she didn't think she could come again without losing her mind. "I can't."

Dante grasped a lock of her hair and pulled her head up. "You can, and you will."

He insisted that she climax again with every deep thrust of his cock, his groin slapping against her ass with every strong entry. One of his hands left her hip and slid between her thighs, brushing over her clit with rough fingers. Gathering the bud between his thumb and index finger, he pinched her clit lightly, exerting pressure as he slammed into her channel over and over, frenzied.

Sarah imploded. Her body shuddered hard, her climax pounding through her body, almost in sync with the roaring of the waves hitting the shore. She heard Dante's coarse, guttural cry as he found his own release, pulling her hips hard against his and burying himself deeply as he growled, "Mine!"

Her chest heaving, Sarah relished the word, feeling like she'd just been thoroughly claimed.

Leaning against her back, Dante quickly slipped the knot that was holding her hands and then collapsed on his back, rolling and turning her with his muscular arms around her waist until she was sprawled over his body.

Sarah could hear Dante's heart pounding in the same rapid rhythm as hers as she laid her head on his chest. The swaying of the dock and the gentle mist that cooled their heated bodies lulled Sarah slowly back into reality. Dante lifted her chin and kissed her gently, wrapping his arms around her body as they both lay there on the dock, completely sated.

Finally he spoke huskily, "Sweetheart, you aren't going to be able to sit down comfortably tomorrow." He ran his hand gently down her back and caressed her bottom.

"Your fault for getting so kinky," she told him with a sigh.

"I think you have a kinky streak yourself," he said with a hint of amusement.

She had to admit, "I think I do, actually. But you said you'd teach me everything. I'm a fast learner."

Dante chuckled. "So now you know what happens when you tease me."

Sarah smiled. "I think I'll do it again fairly soon. I think I like it when you go all crazy dominant on me, sexually. Just don't try going that far outside of our sexual relationship or I'll knee you in the balls."

Dante's booming laughter rang out in the humid night air, a sound that made Sarah's heart squeeze tightly in her chest. "I wouldn't dream of it," Dante choked out while he was still laughing.

"Good." Sarah knew Dante was an alpha male, but he respected her. However, she wasn't going to complain if he decided he wanted to go completely controlling dominant again in the bedroom someday. He stirred a wildness in her that she had never known existed.

"Are you cold?" Dante asked, concerned.

She was damp and had just noticed she was shivering. "A little," she admitted.

Dante slipped out from under her and started picking up his clothing, holding up the remnants of her red dress and tattered panties as he muttered, "I think you'll need a large supply of these."

"I don't usually wear thong underwear. They annoy me," she mentioned casually.

"Then why wear them?" he asked with a frown.

"Because I wanted to turn you on," she admitted.

"Here's a news flash for you, sweetheart: you turn me on no matter what you're wearing." He grinned at her sinfully as he offered her a hand and pulled her to her feet. "Hold these." He handed her his pile of clothes with his Glock sitting on top of them.

She looked at the gun and took the pile gingerly. She squealed as he lifted her up in his arms, her body clad in only the garter and stockings. "Careful. I have your gun," she said nervously.

"Sorry. I don't exactly have any place to put it at the moment," he replied mischievously.

Sarah laughed as she wrapped one arm around his muscular shoulders and held his bundle with the other. "In that case, I think I'd better hang on to it."

Dante strode down the dock, his long legs eating up the distance. Sarah opened the slider and Dante walked in, looking around the house and deactivating the alarm again to give himself time to turn Sarah around so she could lock the door.

After resetting the security system, they sprinted up the stairs, and he took the pile of clothing from her before lowering her gently to the bed. Then he set his Glock on the nightstand before he knelt and rolled the damp stockings down her legs. He stripped off the wet garter belt and wrapped her in a blanket from the closet. "Better?" he asked anxiously.

"Better," Sarah agreed, smiling at him as she wrapped the blanket around her body. Dante was amazing, and had so many beguiling facets to his personality. He had been giving her a rough, screaming orgasm just a short while ago, and now he was showing his nurturing side. There were so many others that it astounded her: dominant, demanding, bossy, tender, sweet, protective, and totally possessive. Each one touched her in a different way.

She watched as he rummaged through the drawer, pulling out a pair of flannel pajama bottoms and putting them on. Sighing, she mourned as he covered his powerful legs and tight ass. But she still ogled his six-pack abs and muscular chest.

He's so damn perfect.

His bruises had faded, and his other wounds were nearly healed. He'd always have the scar on his cheek, but even that would eventually fade until it was barely noticeable. Dante grew facial hair fast and had a five o'clock shadow well before it was actually five o'clock. Once his face was covered in stubble, the scar wasn't noticeable at all. Even when it was visible, it just made him more rugged. Men definitely wore their scars better than women.

"Are my scars really as bad as I see them sometimes?" she asked Dante quietly.

He sat on the bed beside her, frowning. "How do you see them?"

"Ugly. Sometimes I don't think they're really that bad, and that they healed pretty well. Some of the cuts were jagged, so I know they show. But I guess I see them as glaringly hideous and deforming at times. Emily always swears she can hardly notice them, and only if she's really looking for them very closely," she confided.

"I thought you were over that. I thought you realized that nobody notices them," Dante rasped. "What changed?"

"Something my mother said today. It's not really important. I just wondered." Sarah wished she hadn't even mentioned it. For the most part, she *was* over feeling unattractive because of some of her scars. Dante had helped her considerably not to be self-conscious. Unfortunately, her mother had hit a vulnerable spot today.

"What did she say?" Dante asked angrily. "Talk to me."

"She said that I need an intellectual man to see past my scars, someone who isn't as interested in sex," she admitted in a rush.

"No, you don't. All you need is me. And I'm very interested in fucking you on a daily basis, more if possible." He paused before asking, "Do you want the honest truth?"

Sarah took a deep breath and nodded.

"I don't see your scars. I never really have. I thought you were beautiful from the first time I saw you, and that's never changed and never will. I crave you like a goddamn addiction, and it wouldn't matter what kind of scars you had," he finished solemnly.

Sarah looked at his earnest, stubborn expression and sighed. "That's because you're crazy. The scars are there." Her heart melted, belying her words. Dante was special, and he already saw past her scars. He always had.

"Emily's right. If I try to look at you without a raging hard-on—which almost never happens, by the way—they're not noticeable." He tipped her chin up and Sarah looked into the depths of his eyes. He was telling her the truth, his truth. "We all have scars, sweetheart. Some are on the outside, and some are so deep inside us that they never heal. Yours did heal, and they're a symbol of just how brave and resilient you are. Never be ashamed of them. They're part of who you are."

Dante's words were so eloquent that it made her want to cry. "Are you forever scarred inside because Patrick died?" Sarah asked gravely, wondering if he'd ever get over the death of his partner.

"No," Dante answered honestly. "I still hurt, and I'll always miss him, but I think he would have wanted me to live my life the best way I can because he can't anymore. He was a good man who didn't deserve to die. But I'll keep taking care of his wife and son the best way I can. I think that's the best way to honor him."

Sarah nodded. "I think so, too. How are they doing?" Sarah knew that Dante called Karen and Ben almost every day.

"Surviving," Dante said regretfully. "Karen's strong for Ben. And Ben's an exceptional kid. Every day will get easier for them. They have each other."

"Did they know you're a billionaire Sinclair? Did anyone?" She'd wanted to ask him that since the outpouring of pleas had come in through her answering service. Now she understood why everyone had called. Dante Sinclair was an extraordinary man.

Dante shook his head. "I never wanted anyone to know, and after a while, it wasn't important. I didn't want to be judged worthy because of the family I was born into. I wanted to be judged on my own merit."

God, he was amazing. Sarah couldn't imagine any other guy who wouldn't want to flaunt the fact that he was incredibly rich and born of one of the most prestigious families in the country. "Why do I have a feeling you somehow made sure Karen and Ben were going to be fine for the rest of their lives?"

"I did. I donated some money to them anonymously. I know Karen. She'll invest the money, and she'll have money from the police department. She'll be fine financially, and Ben will be able to go to any college he wants, pursue his own dreams. Karen's educated, and she wants to go back to work now that Ben is almost grown."

"You're amazing," she told him reverently. "Do you miss your job? I know you can't stay here forever."

"I'm staying until this asshole is caught. I'll be on leave from the department as long as necessary."

The thought of Dante leaving ripped her heart to pieces. "It could take forever," she told him sadly.

"Then I guess you'll have to put up with my ornery ass for a very long time," Dante grumbled.

She smiled as he wrapped his arms around her and pulled her against him. Sarah decided to let tomorrow take care of itself. Dante was a gift to her, and she'd enjoy him while he was still here. She'd never regret being with him or the time she'd spent with him, because Dante had taught her so much, awakened her soul. She would always be grateful to him, even if it meant she'd suffer the pain of disconnecting from him later. Whatever the future outcome, she knew Dante had changed the way she looked at herself and life. Her brain told her that what they had experienced together would have to be enough, even though her heart was telling her something completely different.

CHAPTER 15

How the fuck did I let her talk me into this?

Dante had gotten used to doing some small things in public again with Sarah, but having her go back to teaching her piano classes and playing for the seniors at the youth center was way out of his comfort zone. The center was too damn open, and there were too many places to hide. It was also busy, especially on senior bingo night, and it was always open to the public.

His arms crossed in front of him, he sat in the fourth row of chairs set up in the music room, his emotions already raw from hearing and watching Sarah play. He'd locked the door after all the seniors had filed in, but he didn't like having the door at his back. Also, he didn't care for the fact that he wasn't closer to Sarah. The eager seniors had arrived early, leaving him farther away than he wanted to be from his woman.

Glancing at his watch, he knew the impromptu concert would only last about five more minutes, but it was going to feel like a goddamn lifetime for him. Granted, almost everyone in the room was over the age of seventy-five except for Grady, Emily, Jared, and Randi, but he wasn't worried about who was already in the room. His gut instinct was screaming at him to scoop Sarah up and take her away to a place where he could protect her. If her asshole attacker knew her routine, he knew that she taught classes here and was connected to the center. Dante was pissed off at himself that one look at her pleading violet eyes had made him agree to let her move on with her life. She was right in some ways. It had been a while, the perp still hadn't been spotted, and she needed a normal life. Unfortunately, reason wasn't his friend right now. He wanted Sarah to be safe.

Four more minutes.

Would he ever get used to Sarah exposing herself in public if Thompson was *never* captured or killed? He'd spend every single moment of the rest of his life with that niggling, fucking irritating worry, terrified that one small slipup could get her killed. The longer it took to catch the asshole, the more willing Sarah would be to go on with her life. It was exactly what she'd done after the attack, moving to Amesport and starting a new beginning.

Three more minutes.

Dante cringed as Sarah moved on her piano seat, causing the garment she was wearing to inch up on her thighs. What the hell was she wearing, anyway? She'd called it a tube dress, but all Dante knew was that she was showing way too much skin and the dress hugged every delectable curve of her body. Starting at the tops of her breasts, the striped one-piece outfit *was* like a tube that clung to everything from her chest to the middle of her thighs. It wasn't like he didn't appreciate the garment, especially the length of time it would take him to get her out of it. One tug and it would slide down to her hips. One more would bring it down to her legs and sliding to the floor. He was good with that. However, he wasn't crazy about the fact that he could see the outline of her nipples at certain angles, or the fact that he was sitting here rock hard just from hearing her play in that *fuck-me* dress.

Two more minutes.

As usual, Dante was fighting an inner war between his desire to protect Sarah and his desire to make her happy. One look into those fathomless violet eyes of hers had nailed him. Oh yeah, they were really dark blue, but they damn well looked violet to him, and they'd been pleading with him to give her some space to get back to a normal life. When she gave him *that look* he was completely destroyed. He wondered if she knew that. Probably not. Still, it made him want to give her anything and everything she wanted to make her happy. Problem was, he needed to protect her, too, and he was discovering that it was damn difficult to make her happy and keep her safe at the same time.

One more minute.

God, she was beautiful. Dante's eyes caressed her lovingly as she continued to play like an angel, her face almost glowing with pleasure. Truth was, he already knew he was all-in with this woman and probably had been soon after they'd met. He was looking at his future, and he was surprisingly serene about that fact. This complex, amazingly intelligent, beautiful, sexy female had turned his life and his emotions upside down, but she belonged with him. There was no way in hell he could live without her anymore, and he didn't plan to.

Time's up. Thank fuck!

Right on time, the concert ended so all of the silver-haired ladies could scurry off to senior bingo. There were choruses of appreciative words called to Sarah as they filed out, the room emptying quickly. Dante breathed a sigh of relief as he stood by the door, watching to make sure nobody entered. Emily and Randi went to join Sarah, while Grady and Jared stepped out the door to talk about a new project Grady was working on.

Everything changed in an instant.

One moment Dante was caught by Elsie Renfrew to say hello, and the next he turned back to Sarah to see a sight he'd only ever envisioned in his nightmares: John Thompson using Sarah as a shield, the barrel of a 9 mm pistol to her head. It had happened in a split second. Where in the hell had the bastard come from? He was guarding the door, and he'd searched every inch of the room before Sarah's performance.

"One wrong move from anybody, and she's dead, her brains splattered all over this room, along with the rest of her friends," Thompson screeched hysterically.

Dante froze, taking in the situation in seconds. Emily and Randi were flanking Sarah and the gunman, neither of them moving, both afraid the asshole would kill Sarah. Dante's Glock was within reach, so close, but he didn't have a clear shot, and he couldn't be sure he wouldn't hit one of the women if he shot in haste. They were all too close, and Sarah was being used as human armor. Dante was damn fast with a gun, but not so fast that a psychotic gunman with a twitchy trigger finger couldn't kill Sarah before he could get a shot off. And even if he did kill the bastard, the gun in Thompson's hand might still discharge.

"Get out and close the fucking door. Lock it or she dies," Thompson demanded in a high-pitched, frantic voice.

Dante could see the fear in every one of the women's eyes, but not one of them moved. His heart thundering against his chest wall, he stepped back as he saw the slight tightening of the man's grip on the pistol. He met Sarah's eyes and she subtly nodded, silently telling him to do what Thompson demanded.

There was nothing Dante wanted more than to pull his gun and shoot the bastard right between his beady, crazed eyes, but he didn't. He took in every detail he could about the man holding Sarah hostage while he was slowly closing the door: his skinny frame, the wild-eyed look on his face, the scruffy brown beard he was growing, the shoulder-length greasy hair, and the orange T-shirt and torn jeans that were littered with stains.

Then, he trained his eyes on Sarah as long as he could until the metal door slammed closed, locked. He wasn't worried about the lock. Someone had keys. His biggest concern was the fact that there were no windows in the door, no windows in the music room, no way to know what was happening inside.

"Fuck! Call nine-one-one and get ahold of Chief Landon. Now!" Dante bellowed, the desperate sound bringing Jared and Grady to his side.

"What are we reporting?" Elsie asked as she pulled a pink cell phone from her large purse and dialed.

"Hostage situation. Three women with a psychotic lunatic. He has a nine-millimeter Smith and Wesson seventeen-round pistol. Tell them we need a hostage negotiator and a SWAT team." Turning to Jared, he instructed, "Evacuate the building as fast and as quietly as possible. Have the seniors use the side door to exit the building. Jared, can you handle getting everybody out?"

"Done," Jared replied, already in motion to get people out of the building.

"I have to find Emily," Grady said desperately.

"Grady!" Dante grabbed his brother by the arm. "She's in there with Sarah. So is Randi."

Grady broke away from him and charged toward the door. Dante had to put his own brother in a headlock to stop him. "You can't go in there. It's locked, and doing anything to agitate him could get Emily killed. Think, goddammit! And screw your head on straight. Do you want her to die?" Dante held on to Grady until he stopped fighting against him. "I know exactly how you feel, but you have to pull it together for Emily."

"I love her," Grady said, panicked. "She's my whole life."

"Sarah has become my whole fucking life, too, and I know how you're feeling. But you gotta think right now, Grady. Emily is being brave. She isn't doing anything stupid. Calm the fuck down, and remember that his main target is Sarah." Dante needed Grady to stop losing his mind. They didn't have much time. He knew what John Thompson's objective was—he wanted Sarah dead.

"Okay," Grady answered in a husky voice. "I got it. Let go."

Dante released Grady and they faced each other.

"What do we do?" Grady asked in a calmer voice, but his eyes were still wild with worry.

"We get our women back," Dante replied, his voice filled with harsh determination. He was going to rescue Sarah, Randi, and Emily no matter what it took to get them out of there alive.

He could see Jared herding people out the side door, and police officers came streaming in the main entrance, Joe Landon at the front of the pack.

Everything was happening in his peripheral vision, but Dante was staring at the wall on the other side of the room to clear his mind, racking his brain for a plan that wouldn't get the three women killed.

Sarah shoved aside her panic, trying to think of a way to get Emily and Randi out of John's control. After the door had closed, John had shoved the three of them into one of the far corners of the room, his body between them and escape. The pistol was still trained on her, but he moved it when he gestured, which was a whole lot when he was talking.

"You have no idea what my life has been like since you sent the fucking police after me," John whined. "Before you, I could use women and dispose of them, and nobody ever knew."

Dear God . . . is he saying what I think he's saying?

"Women back in Chicago?" Sarah questioned carefully.

"It was just Chicago until you made me leave the city. Now it's been Chicago, Boston, New York . . . I find the bitches, use them, and then get rid of them so they can't talk. Nobody even suspected me, nobody ever knew. I was a family man with a wife and kid. I had a respectable job, and I was smarter than the cops. I made sure not a single one of those women stayed alive to talk," John answered angrily, staring murderously at Sarah. "Until you," he finished furiously.

If a man or woman has the capability to murder, it's already there.

Dante had been right when he'd told her that. Trey had always told her that his father had a bad temper, but Sarah feared it was much more than that. John Thompson had killed while his wife and son were alive? They were his cover? That meant the murders had gone unsolved for quite some time. All of the victims had been women. Used?—probably meant raped *and* murdered. Suspicion crept into her brain and wouldn't leave. She knew there hadn't been another similar murder in Chicago since John had attacked her.

Dear God, it can't be him.

She felt Emily squeeze her hand, and Sarah knew her friends were trying to suppress their own horror. John Thompson was a serial rapist and murderer, and had been way before she'd ever met his son, Trey. Sarah squeezed back, trying to encourage her friend to keep quiet. Emily was sitting in the middle, and Sarah knew Emily and Randi were probably having the same silent exchange.

"You're the Windy City Carver?" Sarah asked blandly, her stomach rolling as she realized exactly who was standing in front of her. The serial killer who had raped and killed so many women in Chicago had never been caught, and it had always been assumed that he was an opportunistic killer. He'd trolled for stranded female motorists or women walking alone at night.

"That's me," John answered proudly. "I never left the cops any evidence that would identify me. I was smart. I used a condom when I used the bitches and always cut them up in my truck inside a plastic liner. Then I tossed the pieces into the water. Even if they had been able to find some kind of fiber evidence, I was a family man with no criminal record. They had nothing to match it with. I was never a suspect. And I never struck twice in the same area." He pointed the gun in her direction. "You. Ruined. Everything. I didn't have time to use you before I almost killed you, and I didn't have my favorite carving knife. I had to use a worthless pocketknife because I hadn't planned on wasting you that day. I saw you, and I wanted you dead for taking away my last bit of cover. You fucking deserved it. A guy with a wife and son was better, but I needed Trey because my bitch of a wife was already dead. Hiding in the stairwell was a last-minute decision, but all I had was a pocketknife. I knew it wasn't going to be very satisfying, but seeing you bleed to death had to be enough. I could always find another bitch to carve after you were dead." He reached into the pocket of his jeans and pulled out a knife, unsheathing the blade from its protective cover with a flick of his thumb, his face becoming that of a demonic killer.

Pure evil.

Sarah shuddered as she saw the lethal carving knife that had at least a seven-inch blade with jagged edges. The sight struck terror in her heart, but she tried not to show it, even when he waved the knife close to her throat.

Think, Sarah, think. You can't give in to fear right now.

Somehow, she had to find a way to free Emily and Randi. If she had to use herself as bait and a victim, so be it. But she wasn't watching her two friends die because of a situation she had created by moving here to Amesport. She'd brought trouble to them, and now she had to get them away from it. She hadn't known just how deranged John Thompson really was, but she knew it now. He was a cold-blooded killer and always had been. She was a medical doctor, a woman used to seeing blood and gore. Still, the stories about how he'd carved some of his victims had made her stomach roll, imagining the terror those women had gone through before they died.

"John, let Emily and Randi go," she said calmly. "If you're planning on raping me, you'll have a difficult time of it with them here. I'll do whatever you want."

"I could just shoot them now," John mused manically.

"The police would break down the door if you shoot them, and if you try to attack one of us with a knife, the other two will fight you. Do you really want to risk losing the opportunity to kill me the way you've wanted to do for over a year? Think about it. You've waited a long time for this." Sarah held her breath, praying he wouldn't shoot her friends, but she didn't think he would risk having the police rush in after the gunshots. He'd lose everything he had planned. Her heart palpitated wildly while she waited for his decision. Bile rose in her throat from discussing her own rape and death, but she swallowed hard, knowing she had to do this for her friends. She'd deal with John and her own fate once Emily and Randi were safe.

"If they go, they'll open the door," John said, starting to appear confused and hesitant.

"Hold the gun to my head. The door will get closed and locked again." Sarah couldn't believe she'd just said that, but she was desperate to get her friends out of harm's way. She'd offer her life up for her two innocent friends without hesitation if necessary.

"Is this a trick? You're a smart bitch," John asked defensively.

"No tricks. Just let them leave and we'll be all alone." The thought made Sarah's skin crawl, but she kept her expression blank.

John took the tip of the knife and ran it along her upper arm. "I can still see my work here."

"I have plenty of scars," Sarah admitted.

"They're faded," he commented unhappily. "Shitty knife."

"Let them go and you can do the job the way you want to this time," Sarah urged calmly.

Emily squeezed her hand again, this time in alarm. Sarah shot a sideways glance at Emily and Randi, and she saw a look of horror that neither one of them could hide.

No fear. Don't show him fear. Just get Randi and Emily out.

Emily's cell phone started to ring, startling all of them. The musical tone echoed through the room, and Emily turned frightened eyes to the killer. Sarah looked at John and observed, "It's probably the police."

"Gimme the phone," John told Emily nervously.

Sarah watched as Emily dug into her front pocket, her hands shaking as she looked at the caller ID. "It's Joe Landon, the chief of police."

John ripped the phone from Emily's hand and pushed the "On" button. "Make one move and these women are all dead," John yelled into the phone, agitated.

Sarah didn't know what Chief Landon was saying, but John wasn't buying it. "Tell him you're sending the other two women out," Sarah suggested quietly.

John hesitated, appearing to consider her suggestion before saying into the phone, "Two women are coming out. Try anything and I kill the fucking genius doctor. Got it, asshole?"

Emily leaned against Sarah's shoulder and whispered furiously, "We can't leave you here, Sarah. He'll kill you. We have to do something."

"No," Sarah hissed, watching John as he engaged in a pointless rant with Joe over the phone. "Do this for Grady. Do it for Randi. It will be easier for them to attempt a rescue if it's just me," Sarah whispered quietly but fiercely. Honestly, she wasn't sure if anyone would be able to rescue her, but it *would* be easier if the police only had to deal with one victim instead of three.

Turning her head, Sarah noticed that Emily and Randi were both crying, silent tears streaming down both of their faces.

"I can't," Emily said, keeping her voice soft. "It's like leaving you for slaughter."

"No. You have to do this to help me," Sarah replied in a hushed voice. "Please go and let the police handle the rest. It's my best chance." Really, Sarah didn't think she was going to make it out of this room alive, but at least she'd know Emily and Randi were safe. "Let Dante know that I'll keep him talking as long as possible. Tell him that John Thompson is the Windy City Carver, and that he's killed in other cities after he attacked me and left Chicago. He'll know the case." The Windy City Carver case was probably one of the most famous murder cases in recent history, especially since there had never even been a suspect.

Emily nodded reluctantly. "I'll tell him."

"Move, bitches," John screamed, frenzied. He hung up the phone and waved the gun toward Emily and Randi. "Move slowly toward the door and get your asses out. Make sure the door stays locked after you leave."

Breathing a sigh of relief, Sarah grasped Emily's shirt and urged her up. Emily stumbled to her feet awkwardly, her eyes glued to Sarah as Randi got to her feet.

"Go," Sarah mouthed silently at Emily, who was momentarily blocking John's view of her.

John waved the gun at them. "Get the hell out."

Sarah's expression remained blank as she watched Emily and Randi slowly walk to the door, both of them glancing back at Sarah with terror in their eyes. She'd be damned if she'd break now. Emily and Randi were almost out of the room.

She watched her friends, silently urging them to move faster, eager to see them exit the room.

Finally, Randi opened the door slowly and slipped out with a final distressed look at Sarah. Emily followed, her expression a silent apology as she met Sarah's eyes. Sarah looked away as Emily hesitated, wanting her friend out the door. Emily had nothing to be sorry about; it was Sarah who had brought this filthy murderer to their town.

A moment later, the door clicked shut, the ominous sound actually a comfort to Sarah.

They're safe. They're out of danger.

Her body relaxed as she accepted the inevitable for herself. She'd fight to the death now that Emily and Randi were safe, but even if she was fighting to stay alive for Dante, she wasn't sure it would be enough. John Thompson was a madman, crazier than anyone had ever imagined.

Think, Sarah, think. What good is being a damn genius if you can't save yourself now?

She turned back to John and started talking.

CHAPTER 16

The two women came out the door hesitantly, Emily spotting Grady almost immediately and throwing herself into his arms. Randi was caught up by a uniformed police officer and comforted as he spirited her away from the door.

Joe Landon stood next to Dante. He wiped his sweaty brow as he said, "Thank God. Two of them are safe. Hostage negotiators and the SWAT team are en route now. It's going to take another fifteen minutes or so. There's nobody local. I can act as the negotiator, but the bastard doesn't seem to want anything other than for us to back off. He's not making any demands."

Emily pulled herself from Grady's fierce embrace and grasped Dante's arm, still panicked. "She doesn't have fifteen minutes. He's going to rape her and then kill her with a huge knife. He's not who you think. There's some Windy City Carver who raped and killed women in Chicago, and then he killed more women while he was on the run. He's not an enraged father or husband like we thought. He's a psychotic rapist and murderer. He's angry because Sarah blew his cover when he tried to kill her after his son died. He isn't just holding her hostage. He wants her to die."

The Windy City Carver? Impossible.

Hell, there wasn't a police officer in the country who didn't know about the Carver. Still an unsolved mystery in Chicago, the bastard had been responsible for the rape and murder of over a dozen women in the past decade. "Are you sure?" Dante asked Emily urgently, not wanting to believe that Sarah was the prisoner of an insane sociopath like the Carver. But strangely, gut instinct was screaming at him that Emily was speaking the truth. There hadn't been a Carver victim in Chicago for quite some time, and the intervals between killings were usually pretty much the same. Once he'd stopped killing for much longer than he usually did, many had assumed that he'd died or fled.

"Yes, I'm sure," Emily sobbed. "When Sarah confronted him, he admitted it. Dante, she set herself up as bait, telling John Thompson he could rape and kill her easier if we were let go. She knows she'll never get out of there alive. We have to do something. She said to tell you that she'd keep him talking as long as possible. But he's not going to wait very long. He's too nervous."

"We have to wait for backup," Joe said firmly.

Wait for backup. Wait for backup. Wait for backup.

In a perfect scenario, waiting for backup was protocol. But this wasn't really a hostage situation, and Sarah had no time. Waiting for backup was exactly what Dante and Patrick had been doing when his best friend had been killed, and waiting for backup hadn't worked out well for his partner. Dante had been trying to formulate a plan, but Joe had told him that they had to wait for SWAT to arrive. Granted, they had heavier armor, but it wasn't going to do Sarah any good if she was already dead. Thompson was the goddamn Carver, and unstable as hell. If Emily said they were out of time, she meant it.

Fuck that! I'll go it alone. Sarah's not dying because we're waiting for backup.

He shook off Emily's hold and walked out the main entrance without looking back. There was no way he was waiting another goddamn minute. If Joe felt he needed to wait for backup, then Dante was on his own.

The Windy City Carver.

A cold chill flooded Dante's body as he moved around to the side of the building. The Carver was one sick bastard and left his victims in nothing but pieces. Dante couldn't stand the thought of anyone touching Sarah, much less her being in the same room as that sick, twisted bastard.

A cloud of red was starting to form over his vision, but he pushed it back. Right now he needed to be as cold and calculating as the killer inside the building with Sarah.

He and Joe had assumed that John had been lying in wait somewhere, but Dante had checked the room before he brought Sarah in. Granted, maybe somehow he could have missed some small hiding place, but his gut instinct was telling him something different, that there was a point of access they didn't know about. He'd checked every damn inch of that area.

He drew his Glock as he approached the area outside where Sarah was being held, immediately noticing the high window with broken glass, a space that would be damn hard to get his big body through. That window had been the point of entry. It was high, and the window was small, but the asshole had somehow managed to break the window and gain entry to the tiny bathroom attached to the room where Sarah had been playing. Most likely, Sarah's music had drowned out the sound of breaking glass, and after that it had just been a matter of waiting for his opportunity.

There was no window on the inside.

Dante remembered checking the bathroom, and the window hadn't been visible from the interior. The entire small bathroom had been wallpapered. The building was old, and obviously someone had done the cheapest job possible to make the bathroom look better before Grady had taken over refurbishing the center. Grady hadn't gotten to the music room yet.

Why bother working around the tiny window when it could just be covered with a board and some wallpaper?

"Fuck," he whispered harshly. Dante shoved the Glock back into his waistband and reached up for the windowsill. Just as he was about to pull himself up, he was yanked back down midjump.

"What the fuck are you doing?" Jared asked furiously, pulling Dante's arms away from the window.

"Back the hell off. I don't have time. I'm going in," Dante growled at his brother.

"Backup is coming," Jared reminded him heatedly.

"Too late. I need to take this guy down now." Dante yanked his arms from Jared's grip and turned to face his brother, ready to coldcock him if he needed to. "This bathroom is attached to the room where he's holding Sarah. He came in through this hidden window in the bathroom. You can either help me or get the fuck out of here. We're out of time."

Jared gave him a stormy look, but answered, "You're going to end up getting yourself killed."

"I don't give a shit. If something happens to Sarah, I might as well be dead. If she dies, I die with her." He'd never be a functional human being again. They'd have to put him in a straitjacket and haul him away.

"Shit! Fine. What do you want me to do?" Jared answered, sounding frustrated. "I can follow you in."

"No," Dante answered harshly. "Go back inside. Find somebody with a key to the door and see if you can unlock it without making a lot of noise. I might need backup if I have to go hand-to-hand with this asshole. Listen at the door. You'll know it's time once you hear a scuffle or gunshots. Before you do anything else, get Sarah the hell away from him. Promise me."

"Done. Be careful," Jared responded hoarsely. "Don't get dead."

"I'm not planning on it," Dante replied, hoisting himself onto the windowsill without looking back. Jared might be a pain in the ass, but Dante knew he could count on him when he really needed him.

As Dante started to force his large body through the small space, he could hear Sarah's eerily calm voice and the replies from the murderer.

That's it, sweetheart. Keep him talking. Smart woman.

When he heard John starting to talk about Sarah's scars and how much he was looking forward to doing a better job at carving her to pieces, Dante almost lost it. The moment the asshole mentioned slicing off Sarah's nipples, Dante stopped thinking like a cop and reacted like a man.

I'll kill the fucking bastard.

By the time he dropped quietly to the floor of the bathroom, he was running on purely primal instincts, and he knew the Windy City Carver wasn't leaving the room alive.

I can't let him see that I'm afraid. I need to stall for more time.

Sarah was waiting for the right time, and it wasn't now. He had the gun pointed directly at her head and John wasn't close enough for her to get a shot at his groin. Since she didn't have a weapon of any kind, her best bet was to maneuver him close enough, with the weapon pointed away from her vital organs, for her to take her chance at immobilizing him. If she could disable him for even a few moments, she could get out.

Just wait to make your move. He'll have to change position eventually.

She talked to him steadily to buy herself time, but he was getting tired of talking about himself. He had her on her feet and he'd jerked her tube dress down to her waist. Right at the moment, he was tracing every one of her old scars with the mammoth knife in his right hand, letting her know exactly how he was going to carve her up this time, while the gun remained steadily at her temple in his left hand.

"I'll take your nipples for a reminder of how much I enjoyed slicing you up," John told her, now sounding crazed.

Sarah flinched as the knife blade scraped over her nipples. It was sharp, and she was bleeding from a few nicks he had left when he was assessing her old scars with the point of the knife.

"I think I'll slice your throat just enough to watch you bleed to death while I'm using you," he decided, lifting the knife to her throat.

Sarah had just decided that she would rather die from a gunshot wound than let him defile her body while she was bleeding to death when a furious blur passed by her face.

"Like hell you will," a homicidal Dante roared as he flew through the air, putting his body between her and John, grasping the murderer's wrist that was holding the gun, taking John down with him.

Sarah watched in horror as both men flew through the air and hit the floor. She swore she heard the crack of Dante's skull as it connected with the hardwood platform for the piano as he fell.

"Get the fuck out of here, Sarah!" Dante said furiously.

She didn't. She couldn't. Instead, she froze in place, watching in horror as John escaped Dante's hold and rose. He ran for the bathroom, minus his gun and blade, which had been knocked to the floor.

Dante was slow to rise, and Sarah reacted on instinct as John staggered toward the bathroom, obviously to escape.

Here's my chance.

Sarah blocked his path and lifted her knee hard into his balls. John stopped and cursed, his voice a furious, angry snarl. She'd stopped him, but she wasn't sure for how long.

"Move," Dante demanded angrily.

Sarah moved instinctively to Dante's command, stepping sideways and dropping to the floor. She looked at Dante, blood pouring down his face, as he lifted his gun without hesitation and shot the Windy City Carver straight through the heart before he fell backward and collapsed.

The police burst through the door, swarming the room, but Sarah's mind was on nothing but getting to Dante. Not even sparing a glance for the dead man on the floor, she crawled across the room until she reached her savior, and cradled his bleeding head in her lap.

"Dante," she cried frantically. "Open your eyes." She sought and found the laceration on his head, feeling a hematoma also starting to form on his scalp.

"Pull your dress up." Dante's voice was weak and muddled.

His eyes were barely open, but Sarah was relieved to see him responding. Of course, Dante's first concern was her pulling up her dress to cover her breasts. EMTs came up beside her to help. "Do you have some sterile gauze?" she asked the female technician closest to her anxiously, yanking her dress up and over her breasts.

"We can take over from here," the EMT said in a soothing voice as she handed Sarah some gauze.

"I'm a doctor," Sarah informed her, gently placing the gauze over Dante's laceration and putting pressure on the wound. It was bleeding profusely, as most head wounds did, but she didn't like his sluggishness or the forming hematoma. "Dante?"

"Am I going to die?" he asked incoherently. "If I am, the last thing I want to see is your face. Don't leave."

"You're not dying," Sarah told him sharply. "And I'm not going anywhere. Stay awake with me."

"What kind of injury is it, Doc?" the EMT questioned.

Since Sarah didn't go into the hospital, she wasn't familiar with most of the hospital staff. "Head injury. Blunt trauma from a fall. He has a hematoma forming, and a laceration. I'm worried about his mentation." She held the gauze in place and stroked his cheek. He'd risked his life for her, obviously without permission from the local police. Had Joe been planning a rescue attempt at that moment, it would have been the local police who entered the building, and there would have been a lot of them.

"We need to do spinal precautions, Doc," the EMT reminded Sarah.

"Yes," she agreed with a nod of her head.

Moving back, she made room for the EMTs to get Dante on a backboard and apply a neck brace, strapping him to the board to prevent him from moving until he was X-rayed. She knew she was in no frame of mind to take care of him medically right now, and she let the EMTs handle it.

"Dante?" she called from her place near his head. This time he didn't respond. Dante was out cold.

"Sarah?" a male voice called gently from behind her.

She turned to see Jared behind her, and he put an arm around her waist and pulled her to her feet.

"Are you hurt? What happened to Dante?" Jared asked, his expression troubled.

"He saved my life. He jumped between John and me, and they both went down. He hit his head pretty hard. He's unconscious." She was babbling and she knew it, but she was trying to relay information to Jared as quickly as possible.

"He must have killed the bastard first. I promised him the first thing I'd do was rescue you, but he obviously took care of that himself before he passed out. You okay? The bastard didn't . . ." Jared's voice trailed off, and he actually looked disconcerted.

"He didn't rape me. And I'm okay, Jared. I'm just worried about Dante," Sarah said tearfully, her body trembling with reaction now that her adrenaline level was down.

"His vitals are stable," the EMT informed Sarah. "We're going to load him up now. Do you want to ride with him to the hospital?"

"Yes," Sarah said anxiously, looking at Dante's face. She saw his lids flicker open and then closed again. "He's starting to wake up."

Jared put an arm around Sarah's shoulders and told her supportively, "He'll be okay. He's got a hard head." He hugged her tightly and used the hem of his shirt to dry the tears from her eyes. "You sure you're okay? You're covered in blood."

"It's Dante's," she told him as she hugged him back, knowing Jared was worried. She could see it on his face. "Head wounds bleed a lot."

The EMTs put Dante on a gurney. "We're ready to go, Doc."

"It's Sarah," she told the EMT with a weak smile. "Let's go." She was anxious to get Dante to the hospital as soon as possible.

"We'll follow you," Jared told her huskily.

Sarah walked with the gurney to the main door, watching Dante's face. He opened his eyes occasionally, so she knew he was semiconscious.

"Sarah, we have questions," Joe Landon told her as he caught her arm by the main door.

"Catch me at the hospital. I'm going with Dante," she told him firmly. Questions could wait. John was dead, and the investigation could be conducted after she made sure Dante was going to be okay. That was her only concern right now.

"He wasn't authorized to enter the building," Joe told her as he shook his head, his voice more awed than reproving. "He killed the Windy City Carver. I should be pissed off that he acted on his own, but the man has some balls. We didn't even think to check the outside of the building because neither room is supposed to have any windows. We figured the killer was already here by the time you entered. He's one hell of a cop, even if we were supposed to be waiting for backup from SWAT."

"Yes, he is. And if he hadn't acted exactly when he did, I'd be dead," Sarah answered, wanting to tell Chief Landon that Dante was one hell of a man in general, but she hurried after the rolling gurney, not wanting Dante out of her sight.

She clambered into the back of the ambulance, and sat at Dante's head. His eyes were open again. "Dante? Can you hear me?" Sarah left the exam to the EMTs, knowing she was too emotionally involved to be taking care of Dante medically. Right now she wasn't a doctor. She was a woman who was tormenting herself about whether or not the man she loved was going to be okay.

"I hear you. Are you okay?" Dante pulled at the restraints on his body that kept him from moving around. His voice was suddenly frantic. "Did the bastard hurt you?"

Sarah put a hand on his shoulder. "Stop fighting. I'm fine. He wasn't able to do anything other than touch me. You can't move around right now until you get some X-rays."

"Thank fuck," Dante muttered, sounding relieved as he stopped fighting the constraints on his body. "Is the asshole dead?"

"Yes. You killed him," Sarah replied, knowing it was Dante's pure stubborn determination that had allowed him to shoot before he succumbed to the blow to his head.

Dante's brows drew together in concentration. "I remember. I told you to get the fuck away from him. You stopped him with a kick to the nuts. Goddammit, you were supposed to run."

"I had to do it," Sarah confessed. "My anger at what he'd done took over, and I wasn't going to let him get away and live in fear again. I didn't want him to ever take another woman's life. I already knew you were injured, and I was pissed." It felt good to actually say that. She'd acted totally on emotion, something she had never done before she met Dante.

"It worked. But don't ever do that again," Dante said grudgingly. "Jesus, he was even more sick and twisted than I thought. Did he really admit to being the Windy City Carver?"

"Yes. When he was talking about the women he raped and killed in Chicago, I figured it out before he even told me. You were right. If a man has the capability to murder, it's already there. His attack on me didn't just happen because his wife and Trey died. He was furious because he didn't have the cover of being a working family man anymore. He didn't really care about either of them at all." Sarah's heart grew heavier when she thought about poor Trey and his mother.

"Completely sociopathic," Dante replied angrily.

"He was," Sarah admitted. "He wanted me dead when he caught me in the stairwell. If not for a couple of coincidences, I would have been. If not for you, I would have ended up dead this time. He was ready to cut my throat. I'd just decided I'd rather fight and die by a gunshot wound than let him rape me as I was dying."

"Fuck. That thought will haunt me forever," Dante answered savagely.

"No, Dante. It wasn't meant to torment you. I wanted you to know that you're the bravest man alive, and you saved my life. It's just killing me that you were hurt while you were doing it. Again. You just healed."

"My head hurts like a son of a bitch," Dante admitted. "I must have hit something."

"You did. You cracked your head on the stage platform when you grabbed John. I'm worried," she admitted, running a hand down his cheek lightly. "You were unconscious. I don't even understand how you stayed coherent enough to shoot him." Really, she shouldn't be surprised. Just weeks before, after taking several bullets himself, he'd managed to accurately shoot the man who had killed his partner. Dante was an extraordinarily stubborn man, and she'd never complain about that again. That sheer bullheadedness had saved her life.

He grinned up at her. "Don't worry. I'm hardheaded," he answered, amusement in his voice.

"That's what Jared said." Sarah smiled weakly back at him. She was still worried, but her heart was lighter from seeing him coherent.

"Bastard," Dante mumbled.

Sarah's smile grew larger. Obviously it was okay for Dante to be self-deprecating, but he didn't like hearing it from his brothers. "He was trying to be supportive. I was freaking out a little."

"You? What happened to my logical and rational woman?"

Sarah wanted to tell him that she hadn't been sensible since the moment he'd come crashing into her life, and she'd gotten more emotional every day since then. "I think you ruined me."

"I was scared, too. I was afraid I was never going to see your beautiful face again. I need to touch you," Dante told her in a husky voice, his eyes tracking over her face.

Still stroking his hair and touching his face, she understood his need, but she replied, "You can't move right now."

"Then kiss me," he demanded grumpily.

Sarah glanced at the EMT and the woman smiled. "I'd kiss him," she informed Sarah with a wink and a shrug.

Leaning over, making certain she didn't touch anything except his lips, Sarah fitted her mouth to his in a gentle embrace. Her heart squeezed inside her chest as he kissed her back like she was the most coveted woman on earth.

Pulling back, Sarah watched Dante as he closed his eyes and fell asleep with a satisfied smirk still on his face.

"We're here," the EMT told Sarah as the ambulance came to a stop. The woman jumped out at the emergency entrance, the driver joining her so they could pull Dante from the vehicle.

Sarah followed Dante without a thought, never leaving his side as they wheeled him into a room in the emergency department.

CHAPTER 17

"Dante's tests all came back negative, but he's going to have to stay for a day or two for observation," Sarah announced to a waiting room that had pretty much been taken over by the Sinclairs and friends. "He lost consciousness and they need to watch him for complications of the concussion."

"How is he? Is he talking?" Grady asked anxiously.

Sarah smiled. "He's talking a little too much, and I think the ER staff would like to gag him. He's . . . um . . . not too happy about his hospital stay, and he's let everyone from Dr. Samuels to his transporter know all about it with some very colorful language."

"Then he's back to his usual ornery self?" Jared questioned, sounding more relieved than cynical.

"He'll be okay," she reassured the people in the waiting room. "Staying is a precaution. A *smart* precaution." No amount of curse words would get Dante out of the hospital until they made sure he wasn't going to have any adverse effects from the concussion.

Sarah looked around the room. Grady was holding Emily in his lap, looking like he was afraid to ever let her go. Jared, Randi, Elsie, Beatrice, and Joe Landon were all occupying some of the other available seats. Even her medical assistant, Kristin, was here, a worried look on her face.

"If he has the energy to bitch, he must be doing okay," Grady said hesitantly. "I'll stay with him tonight. He's likely to get up and leave."

Sarah held up her hand. "I'll stay until he's discharged. I'll just need some clean clothes tomorrow, if you wouldn't mind." She gave Emily a pleading look. Sarah had already showered and quickly thrown on a pair of light blue scrubs, but she wanted some clean clothing.

"Of course I'll bring them," Emily agreed readily. "I'll even pick you up a latte at Brew Magic."

"We'll bring food," Beatrice said firmly. "I had to stay in a hospital once, and all I wanted was some decent food to eat while I was there. I had to get my nephew to bring me something edible."

Elsie nodded in agreement.

"Are you sure you can handle him?" Jared said doubtfully.

Sarah smiled at Jared. "He's staying, even if I have to wrestle with him to keep him down in bed. He'll sleep tonight. He's fighting it now, but he won't be able to keep it up forever."

Emily wriggled out of her husband's lap and threw herself at Sarah, Randi right behind her. Emily started to sob as she clung to Sarah, who savored her friend's loving embrace by wrapping her arms around Emily and hugging her close, bringing Randi into their circle for a group hug. She was so relieved that they were both safe.

"I was so afraid, Sarah," Emily sobbed.

Randi nodded her head. "I was, too. I don't know how you managed to not show your fear when you were basically sacrificing your own life for ours."

The three women hugged each other for several minutes, then Sarah finally stepped back to say, "I brought you both into that situation, and I'm sorrier than I can ever say. Neither of you deserved to be there, to have to experience that. I brought a serial killer to Amesport." Sarah's gut still rolled at the thought.

"You haven't deserved any of this, Sarah. Everything that's happened right from the beginning," Emily said fiercely as she went to take the seat next to Grady, but he pulled her right back into his lap. Randi found her own seat again next to Beatrice, and the elderly woman reached out and took Randi's hand comfortingly.

"Are you ready to talk about it, Sarah?" Chief Landon asked gravely.

Sarah nodded. "I know you want to talk to Dante, too, and we can meet you up in his room if you can wait for them to settle him into his bed."

"No problem," Joe agreed readily. "But we do have an issue." He released a long, frustrated sigh as he added, "We have a real media circus outside already. The Windy City Carver has been a big mystery case for a long time. This is a huge national story. Obviously we aren't going to let them enter the hospital or private property, but they'll be pestering every one of you wherever they can." He looked around at every person in the room in warning.

Sarah looked at Joe, and then turned her gaze to Elsie. "I think that Elsie should break the story. After all, she was there, and she helped get the police there quickly." She knew the elderly woman would be thrilled, and both Elsie and Beatrice looked traumatized. It might help to get their minds on something else.

"I'd get the scoop?" Elsie's face perked up.

Sarah shrugged. "I think it's only fair that Amesport is the first to report it. And you were an eyewitness. Who would do a better job of reporting it?" Besides, if Elsie scooped the story, maybe the media would slowly fade away, using that information to write their own stories when nobody wanted to talk.

Joe caught her eye and winked at her, obviously understanding exactly what she was trying to do.

"Of course. I have the inside scoop, and all of you to give me the information I don't have," Elsie said excitedly.

"I'd say you better get to work as soon as possible and break the story by tomorrow morning," Sarah told Elsie emphatically. *The earlier the better.* Sarah was hoping the craziness would die down by the time Dante was released. "I'm heading back to keep an eye on Dante. He should be headed up to his room in a few minutes," Sarah said purposefully, knowing she needed to get back to Dante and make him behave. The poor nurses were starting to draw straws over who had to take care of him. "Joe, I'll see you shortly in Dante's room."

Joe nodded. "I'll be up."

"Sarah?" Emily called just as Sarah was ready to head back to the ER.

Sarah turned back to her friend. "Yes?"

"Are you okay?" Emily asked nervously.

"I'm holding up," Sarah said, trying to reassure her friend. At the moment, she was functioning on autopilot, trying not to think about anything except Dante's care.

"I hate to mention this, but you're in a hospital. I thought . . . I guess I was worried . . . oh hell, I just wondered if you were doing all right with that," Emily said breathlessly.

Sarah stopped and gave Emily a blank look. And then it dawned on her. Emily was the only one except her mother and Dante who knew the *whole* story about her past and her panic attacks.

I am in a hospital. I'm not freaking out. I'm not having panic attacks. Everything just feels . . . familiar.

She slowly grinned at Emily. "Your brother-in-law has made me so crazy that I didn't even think about it." Sarah shook her head in amazement. "And yeah, I'm doing just fine with it." Strangely, she *was* doing well in a hospital setting. She'd been so worried about Dante that she hadn't had time to be afraid.

Emily gave her a tremulous smile, and Sarah turned around and went back to the ER with an amazed expression on her face.

Dante woke up feeling unnerved and in a place he hadn't wanted to see again for quite some time.

Another fucking hospital.

It was still dark, no light coming through the window blinds.

What the hell time is it?

He leaned forward and squinted at the clock on the wall, barely able to see the hands with only the dim light near the door to illuminate the room.

It's after three a.m.

He'd fallen asleep soon after he and Sarah had spoken with Joe to give him a statement of what had occurred at the center.

Sarah?

He froze up anxiously for a minute until he saw Sarah near him, asleep in the recliner next to the bed.

Thank fuck!

His eyes caressed her lovingly, damn grateful she was still alive. He collapsed backward again, letting out a small groan as his head hit the skimpy pillow.

"Dante?" Sarah's sleepy voice called out, and she sat up immediately. "What happened?"

Dante grinned at her sheepishly as she hovered over him. "Nothing. I forgot that I hit my head."

Damn! Even exhausted she looks beautiful.

Close up, he could see the dark circles under her eyes, and her hair was tousled, but at the moment she was the sweetest sight he'd ever seen. She was here. She was breathing. And she was breathtaking.

"Are you okay?" she murmured quietly, running a hand lightly though his hair, avoiding the injured areas on his scalp.

The anxious look on her face floored him because he knew it was all for him. She'd been through hell in the last sixteen or so hours, but her every thought was about him. She hadn't shed a tear over what had happened, or talked about almost dying. Every thought, every action, had been for him. She had surrounded herself with a veneer of calm to take care of him, just like she'd done to protect Emily and Randi.

"I'm lonely." He flipped back the covers and scooted to the left, making room for her in the small bed. "Come sleep with me."

He was wearing a pair of what almost looked like surgical scrub pants. He'd gotten rid of the annoying patient gown and just kept the drawstring pants on to cover his junk. They'd disconnected him from his intravenous fluids, so he didn't have any lines going into him—just an irritating port in the top of his left hand. Probably the only reason he'd slept for a while was because they'd stopped pumping him full of the fluids that had sent him to the bathroom to piss every five minutes.

Dante watched Sarah's face as a moment of indecision passed over her features. He took her hand and pulled her forward. "Don't analyze it. Just crawl in here." He was afraid if she thought about it for too long, she'd scurry back to the recliner, and he desperately needed her close to him. She'd been so busy taking care of him that she hadn't dealt with her own trauma. She needed comfort, and he wanted to give it to her. She'd been strong for long enough.

"Okay," she whispered, crawling gingerly into the space he'd made for her.

He covered them both with the blankets, and then brought her head to rest on his chest, trying to make her comfortable. "You put on a brave face all evening. Do you want to talk about it?" he asked quietly, knowing she'd eventually have to break in order to heal.

Sarah shook her head, but her arm curled around his abdomen and she clenched him tightly.

Dante's heart swelled as he held the vulnerable Sarah in his arms, the side of this woman that few people ever saw. "Do you want me to tell you how I feel?"

She nodded jerkily.

"I feel like I never want to let you out of my sight again. Not for any damn reason. I think every time I close my eyes for a long fucking time all I'm going to see is the sight of you with a gun to your head. I think I'm going to hear Thompson's voice in my head, talking about how he wants to carve you up, until I can finally clear it away and fill my mind with other memories. I think you have to be the bravest and smartest woman in the world to have kept him talking for so long, and manage to get your two friends out of that room." He paused for a moment. "And I think I'm the luckiest bastard in the world to actually be holding you in my arms right now."

"I'm not that brave," Sarah whispered in a rush. "I was scared. I was afraid for Emily and Randi, petrified that I'd brought them into the situation and I was going to get them killed. Then, once they were out, I was hoping I didn't literally get sick and vomit just from the thought of him touching me. All of that fear was there, Dante. I just couldn't let it out. He wanted me to be frightened, and I couldn't let him see it. When I saw you get hurt, my fear turned into rage, and I wanted to hurt him somehow. That's why I kneed him in the balls. I didn't want him to get away. I was glad you shot him. I was relieved that he was dead. If I had had a gun, I would have done it myself. After that, I was in a panic that you were injured, so afraid that you wouldn't be okay." She started to cry, her voice tearful. "So I'm not very brave at all. I was scared, so very scared the entire time," she cried in a distressed voice, the dam breaking as she sobbed into his chest, her arm clutching him even tighter.

Dante wrapped both of his arms around her shuddering body, rocking her as she cried, the sound of her fear and pain nearly splitting his heart in half. He'd never seen her sob like this, and if he never heard it again, it would be too soon. But she needed this, she needed to let everything out, and his heart swelled because she was doing it with him. "I know, baby. I know. I was scared, too. I was afraid he'd hurt you," he said soothingly, running his hands over her hair and back, holding her until the storm of tears had finally ceased. Finally, he said, "You're here in the hospital. Christ! I forgot how you react to hospitals." Dante was angry at himself. He'd been so wrapped up in everything else that he'd forgotten about her panic attacks.

"I'm okay. I was so worried about you I didn't think about it. And then, it didn't seem to matter. I actually feel comfortable being back. I missed it. I guess I just needed to get myself back through the doors. Or maybe it's because my attacker is dead. Either way, I'm doing good."

Dante breathed a sigh of relief. "Jesus. You really have been through hell, sweetheart." No matter how much she denied it, she was the bravest woman he'd ever know. And she was his.

"I can't believe he was really the Windy City Carver." She sniffed wearily.

Dante couldn't believe it either. "Even in Los Angeles, law enforcement talked about that case."

"The media is everywhere. You're a hero," Sarah sighed.

"I don't want to be a hero. I just wanted you alive. But I'm glad he's dead. The women he killed needed some kind of justice. It used to bug the hell out of every homicide detective in the country that he wasn't caught and didn't pay for those murders," Dante told her thoughtfully. "I hope the media doesn't become a pain in the ass." He'd worked a lot of high-profile cases, and dealing with the media wasn't exactly one of his favorite parts of his job.

"They're all about to be scooped," Sarah told him, her voice slightly amused. "Elsie is breaking the story in the morning. I'm sure it will all die down."

Dante chuckled, the thought of the curious elderly woman finally getting her big news article amusing him. "Your idea?" It was actually brilliant. If Elsie scooped the story, the media *would* die down.

Sarah shrugged. "It's big news. Elsie will be talking about it forever. I'm sure it will go syndicated."

"Media or not, I'm going home in the morning," Dante grumbled.

"You'll go home when Dr. Samuels says you can go home," Sarah retorted sharply.

"Bossy woman," Dante replied grumpily.

Sarah lifted her head to look at him. "I can actually go back to my cottage now. I didn't think about that."

"No. Not yet." Dante couldn't stand the thought of Sarah not being with him, and he tightened his grip around her reflexively. Hell, he was even getting fond of her pathetic little dog. "Coco?" He hated the thought that the dog might be at his house with no food and no way to get outside.

"She's with Emily. No doubt she's spoiling her with human food as badly as you do."

"Stay with me for a while," Dante demanded. It was going to take him a long damn time to reassure himself that she was okay.

"I have to go home eventually."

No, you don't.

Dante had a hard time keeping that thought to himself. As far as he was concerned, she belonged with him. He stayed mute but was determined she wasn't going anywhere. She needed to be someplace safe, somewhere that she could get over the trauma that she'd been through. And that place was with him. "Not now," he settled for saying. They hadn't talked about the future because they'd been too busy trying to survive in the present. But they would be talking about it. Soon. There was no way he was going to live without her.

Dante heard her sigh softly. "Not now," she agreed sleepily.

He held her, satisfied for the moment, still running calming strokes over her back and hair until she finally slept.

CHAPTER 18

Dante was discharged the following afternoon, much to the relief of every person working on his unit. It hadn't been long enough for the town to settle down, and much of the media still remained, hoping for an interview. But Jared and Grady managed to get him home without incident, and the gates to the peninsula were locked and guarded by some of the local police force. After dropping Dante and Sarah off, the men headed back to the gate to make sure no one could enter, and to let the press know they weren't doing any interviews. They were going to make an official and brief statement, hoping it would satisfy the reporters enough to just use Elsie's account for their story.

Sarah and Dante were greeted at the door by an excited Coco, Emily having returned the dog earlier in the afternoon.

"Damn dog," Dante grumbled as he reached down and scooped the canine up and held her gently in his beefy arms, giving the pup more than a token amount of affection. He stroked Coco's quivering body and scratched the top of her head.

Sarah tried not to smirk as she watched the exchange between dog and man. Coco had made Dante's home and its owner part of her territory. Coco adored Dante, and Sarah knew her big, tough guy loved the little dog, no matter how much he tried to deny it.

She's going to miss him so much when he's gone.

Her little dog had gotten as attached to Dante as Sarah had. Now they were both going to pay the price for loving a man who didn't belong in Amesport.

I love him. I really do love him.

Although she'd probably fallen for Dante way before today, admitting it to herself made her feel shot through the heart. She couldn't go on denying it. She'd fallen completely and irrevocably in love with this strong, dominant man who was also capable of such gentle tenderness that it made her want to weep.

He's going back to Los Angeles. I knew he wouldn't be here forever.

She *had* known. Still, it hadn't kept her heart safe. Dante Sinclair had been an irresistible temptation for a woman like her, a man who made her feel safe and adored after a lifetime of being alone. He'd held her tightly while the dam had broken and her emotions had overwhelmed her last night, something that had never happened to her quite like that before. Now that everything had escaped, she was fairly certain she'd never be able to put every feeling she had back in a safe place again, buried beneath logic and reason. But honestly, she didn't really want to. Living a life without emotion might be easier, but it would never make her happy.

I'm going to be alone again.

That thought made her want to run back to her own little cottage, where she could nurse her broken heart in private.

It isn't going to help.

Sarah sighed as she walked to the kitchen and leaned back against the counter, needing a minute to sort out her emotions. Even though seeing him go was going to be unbearably painful, it wouldn't make it any less painful if she parted from him now, or a week from now. Right now Dante didn't seem to want to discuss anything, preferring to live in the moment.

I've never really done that before.

Except for the few times she'd lost herself in Dante, she'd never done anything spontaneous or without thinking of the future consequences.

"Walk with me," Dante's husky voice demanded from the kitchen entrance.

Sarah turned and looked at him, his outstretched hand waiting for her to grab it.

Take this time with him. Live in the moment and take whatever happiness you can get.

Looking into his turbulent gaze, Sarah knew he wanted to go out for a walk simply because they could. John was dead; the threat was over. They could go walk out on his private beach without worrying about constantly looking over their shoulders.

She didn't debate the right and wrong of what she was doing, thinking only with her heart as she took his hand.

They walked out onto the beach with Coco following behind, talking about absolutely nothing important. Both of them laughed as Coco approached the lapping waves warily, as though they were the enemy, and then watched them retreat with a brave bark every time the water moved backward, as though the canine had scared the enemy away. Dante helped Sarah make a sand castle, a first for her, which ended up looking more like just a big pile of mud than anything resembling a fortress, but Sarah was proud of it anyway . . . until Coco decided to run across the top of the pile, throwing both her and Dante into a fit of laughter.

Sarah's heart ached every time Dante gave her a lingering kiss. Some of his caresses were meant to brand her, and some were just cherishing strokes of his lips against hers, as though he was still trying to assure himself that she was beside him. Sarah saved up every one of those embraces, fixing them in her memory and keeping them close to her heart.

Dante shared some of his more amusing stories about growing up with his siblings, tales that didn't include his abusive father or emotionally vacant mother.

They all protected each other.

Every story concluded with one sibling bailing another one out of trouble. They might have teased the hell out of each other, but they'd always come to the rescue in the end.

"I always wished that I had a brother or sister," Sarah told him wistfully as they stumbled back into the house, wet and caked with sand.

"Your mother never came close to getting married again?" Dante asked curiously.

"No," Sarah replied thoughtfully. "She never even dated. Everything was about my education."

She and Dante stepped back outside the door, deciding to shed their jeans to keep from dropping mud through the house.

They ran upstairs to shower, Dante grumbling when Sarah sent him to his own bathroom. "No stress today," she told him sternly as she walked toward the guest bathroom. "That includes any type of exertion," she called back over her shoulder, knowing he'd understand that "exertion" equaled sex.

He didn't follow, but she felt his eyes on her as she went to the guest room and closed the door.

The window of Dante's bedroom was open, but the soothing sounds of the ocean weren't helping him tonight. Sleep was eluding him, and he knew exactly why.

I can't sleep without her.

Dante rolled over onto his back with an annoyed grunt. Knowing Sarah was sleeping in the guest room right down the hall was making him nearly insane.

There's nothing worse than being obsessed with a female who's a damn doctor!

She'd insisted, lecturing him about the need for sleep and recovery time because of his head injury.

I have a head as hard as a damn bowling ball. I don't need to sleep alone and I don't want to sleep alone.

Granted, he probably could have seduced her, made her want to come to his bed, but he hadn't done it. She'd threatened to leave his ass and go back home if he didn't behave.

Like hell she will.

However, just the thought of not having her close to him was enough to make him back off. After dinner, they'd spent a lazy evening together, Sarah eventually wandering to the piano to play. Dante wasn't that familiar with classical music, but he didn't need to be. He picked up on her emotions immediately: everything she played was broody and dark. Something was bothering her and he didn't know how to fix it. She'd nearly killed him with her open sobs of fear and pain last night in the hospital, and he'd tried to absorb every bit of it as she wept, hoping he'd never see her that upset again. But it was something different this time. She didn't appear frightened, but Dante couldn't seem to put a finger on what exactly was causing her to appear so unusually fragile. He didn't like it.

She seemed . . . almost sad, melancholy. He shouldn't have left her alone, but he'd been afraid that she would bolt, and he couldn't really object to her leaving anymore because her life wasn't in danger.

She's free to do whatever she wants.

While that fact should make him happy, it actually scared the shit out of him. Yeah. Okay. He was glad that she was out of danger and wasn't stuck indoors anymore because it made her unhappy. But the thought of her actually leaving, going back to a life without him, made him completely crazy.

So, here he was, staring up at the ceiling while a woman he wanted more than anything else in the world was sleeping in the guest room down the hall. Dante figured having her close was better than having her gone completely.

It's bullshit.

He'd never been the type of guy to settle for anything, and it was irritating the shit out of him that he was doing it now. Truth was . . . the thought of losing her shook him to the core.

So I'm going to lie here all night and stare at the damn ceiling?

What he really should have done was fuse her to him so completely that she'd never be able to shake him off. When had he ever let fear stop him?

When have I ever had this much to lose?

He hadn't. Not ever. Honestly, he was a hell of a lot more comfortable chasing murderers than dealing with the possibility that Sarah might leave him and never come back.

Not happening!

Dante rolled out of bed with a combination of apprehension and determination. His stubbornness and persistence weren't going to allow him to just lie here anymore. If necessary, he'd be the biggest pain in the ass Sarah Baxter had ever dealt with before. She wouldn't be able to ignore him.

Dante grinned wickedly as he opened the door and headed down the hall to Sarah's room, where he grasped the handle and let himself into the bedroom. After closing her door quietly, he leaned back against it. Her bedroom windows were open, illuminating the figure on the bed with a dim glow. What he saw made him freeze instantly in place, unable to tear his eyes from the sight in the middle of the mattress.

Sarah was awake, her head thrown back, eyes closed, and her hand between her thighs. Dressed in a short baby doll nightgown, she looked like a fiery seductress in red and black, the minuscule panties that matched the ensemble on the floor beside the bed.

He watched, fists clenched, as she rubbed her clit harder and harder, whimpering his name quietly. Her head tossed on the pillow, sending curling waves of hair over her face.

Jesus Christ!

He held his breath as he watched her reach for her climax, desperate to get there.

She's fantasizing about me, thinking about me making her come.

Dante was torn between seeing if she found fulfillment and helping her. Part of him wanted to be an observer, to watch the carnal, erotic sight right in front of him until she shattered. But his cock was a demanding little bastard, and he wanted her right now, needed to see her break into little pieces that scattered around him as he buried himself to his balls and they lost themselves to each other.

He let out the breath he'd been holding, making his final decision as she stopped touching herself with a muted cry of frustration and pulled a pillow over her head, unsatisfied.

She's still learning her own body, exploring herself.

And Dante would be damned if he'd let her feel like she had failed.

He crawled onto the bed and uncovered her face. "Try harder," he demanded, grabbing the hem of the sexy nightgown and yanking it up over her head. It landed on the floor before she could ever say a word. "Touch your nipples." He threaded his fingers through hers on the hand next to her pussy and guided their conjoined hands between her thighs.

"Dante, I can't—"

She sounded mortified that he'd seen her trying to make herself come, and Dante wanted to tell her not to be ashamed, that it was the sexiest thing he'd ever seen. Instead, he decided to show her. "You can. Touch yourself," he commanded, saturating their joined fingers between her folds before he started guiding her fingers to circle her clit. She was already hot and wet, and their fingers slid easily together around the pulsating bud, forcing a cry from her lips.

He grasped her other hand and placed it on her breast. "Tease yourself," he instructed firmly, gratified when he saw her hand start plucking and caressing her nipples, moving from one to the other. "You look so beautiful right now, sweetheart. Make yourself come," he said harshly into her ear.

"I tried," she panted. "It felt good, but I couldn't—"

Dante forced her first two fingers to cover her clit, pushing hard to make her put more pressure on the sensitive nub. "Rub harder."

Dante watched her face as his hand helped her pleasure herself. Somehow, this was almost more intimate than fucking her, watching her open and vulnerable as she started to climb higher and higher. Her eyes closed again, and she tossed her head back, her hips starting to rise from the bed to meet the pressure of their fingers rubbing against her clit.

"Imagine my head between your thighs, my tongue devouring your pussy," he croaked into her ear.

Jesus. That was exactly where he wanted to be right now. But now was Sarah's time.

"Yes. That feels so good," she moaned with abandon.

He watched, mesmerized, as her body tensed and her back began to arch, her moans filling the room as their joined fingers moved urgently, roughly over her clit. She was pinching her nipples now, and her body was starting to tremble.

Dante tightened his fingers with hers, looking down to see the erotic vision of their joined hands getting her off.

"Come, Sarah. Let go," he encouraged urgently, waiting.

She climaxed with a strangled moan. "Dante."

His heart swelled as she splintered moaning his name, and he kissed her, trying to capture his name on her lips.

Her body stilled, and her ass and back came down to meet the mattress, the only sound in the room her labored breaths.

At that moment, Dante felt closer to her than he ever had.

Mine.

He was desperate to pull her even tighter to him, mold them together so nothing and no one would ever be able to pull them apart. "I need you," he told her huskily.

She went up on her hands and knees, looking down at him with adoring eyes. "I need you, too. But you can't exert yourself."

"Then make love to me, Sarah." He rolled onto his back, waiting. He watched her for a minute, holding his breath.

"How?" she breathed softly.

He grabbed her thigh and swung it over his body. "Like this." He seated her over his cock. "Ride me. I'll let you set the pace." He ground his teeth as he felt her indecision, and let out a sigh of relief as she grasped his cock and lined it up at her entrance. "Join us," he ground out, feeling like he'd lose his mind if he didn't get inside her wet heat right that second.

Taking him in slowly, Sarah lowered herself onto his cock with a ragged moan.

Dante grasped the sheets beside him, trying to keep from grasping her hips and taking control, but he let her swivel her hips as she seated him inside her, throwing her head back in ecstasy. "Yes. You feel so deep, so hard."

"Fuck me," he groaned in an urgent voice, needing her to move.

She braced her hands on his shoulders and started to move, slowly at first, up and down, grinding her pelvis against him every time she took him deeply inside her. Unable to stop himself, he put a hand around the back of her neck and brought her mouth to his, spearing his tongue into her mouth in a silent demand. She tasted like mint and lust, the combination about to drive him completely out of his mind.

"Help me," Sarah pleaded in a whisper as he released her mouth. "I want this to feel good to you."

Dante groaned as he felt her hard nipples abrading his chest. "Baby, if it felt any better, I'd be dead." He was a dominant in the bedroom, and he didn't usually screw this way, but with Sarah, it felt natural, right. He inhaled her intoxicating scent, let it surround him as she moved slowly up and down on his cock, gloving him in her tight, wet heat.

She sat up, her hands traveling over his chest, her short fingernails biting into his abdomen, and she left her hands there to stay in a completely seated position.

Unable to take the torment any longer, he grasped her hips and thrust himself up inside of her, meeting her every downward stroke.

"Yes," she cried as Dante took control, holding her hips as he stroked upward, trying to get as deep as possible.

Her body tensed, and Dante knew the moment that she imploded, her channel clenching down on his cock as the walls pulsated, milking him. He thrust one more time and released himself deep inside her with a groan, his body shuddering from the intensity of his orgasm.

"Fuck," he rasped, pulling Sarah down on top of him, wrapping his arms around her trembling, perspiration-soaked body.

She's mine, and nobody is ever going to take her away from me.

"So much for you not exerting yourself," Sarah whispered in his ear with a hint of amusement in her voice.

Dante ran a hand through her thick curls. "Way too much temptation," he answered hoarsely.

"I didn't mean for you to see—"

"Don't be embarrassed. There's nothing wrong with what you were doing. Sweetheart, there's a whole lot more to sensual pleasure than just mating for the species," he told her emphatically.

She laughed delightedly. "I think I figured that out from the moment you touched me," she answered, her voice still choked with laughter.

Dante cuddled her body on top of his, smiling. God, how he adored this woman. This warm, courageous, intelligent, beautiful woman who still retained her sense of humor and sweetness after all she'd been through. "Spend time with me. Not because you have to, but because you want to," he said, unable to totally keep a pleading tone from his voice. He and Sarah had been thrown together with him as her protector. Now he wanted her with him by choice.

I want her to choose me.

She was silent for a moment, her head on his shoulder, and Dante almost wondered if she had fallen asleep. "Okay," she finally agreed in a soft whisper.

The tension left Dante's body, and his arms tightened reflexively around her. Maybe her answer wasn't as enthusiastic as he wanted it to be, but just having her agree was enough. For now.

She moved off his body, slowly sliding to his side. He brought her soft, warm body next to his, and they were both asleep moments later.

CHAPTER 19

"What are you looking at?" Dante strolled over to Sarah as he devoured the last of his lobster roll.

Sarah stood outside of the last house on Main Street, looking into the window. "I like this shop."

The monstrous old home at the very end of the street was aged and weathered, the paint peeling on the outside, but every time she stepped into Mara Ross's shop, she could feel the sense of history that clung to the home. Dolls and Things was a lovely, eclectic store, and Sarah adored it.

"Let's go in," Dante suggested, wrapping an arm around her waist.

Sarah shrugged. "I never buy anything. I just like the store." She looked at the dolls in the window, noticing her favorite—a large, blonde Victorian doll with blue eyes and a red velvet dress—still hadn't sold.

Dante pulled open the door and held it for her. Sarah went in, shooting him a broad smile as she passed through the entrance.

She browsed around, examining the art on the walls and the expert craftsmanship of some of the dolls. Mara Ross had taken over the store from her mother when she'd died a year or so ago, keeping the tradition of having a doll maker in the town of Amesport. The skill had been passed down for several generations. Sarah didn't hurry as she looked at the new additions, a habit that she'd developed after spending the last week in Dante's company. It had been the happiest week of her life.

Dante had taught her how to do things just for the fun of doing them, and he'd seemed to enjoy it just as much as she did. They took long walks together and sat out on the beach for hours just to absorb the feel and the sound of the ocean. Dante had gotten himself a bike, and they'd ridden most of the bike trails in the area, stopping whenever they felt like exploring. Unfortunately, Dante still hadn't gotten over his insistence that she wear her protective gear, but at least he'd given up on the jeans and long-sleeved shirts after Sarah had complained about suffocating in them with the weather so warm.

She played his massive piano at night, or they messed around with some children's games that were probably better suited to grade school kids. But Sarah had enjoyed every minute of it. She'd cut her work schedule light so she'd have more time to spend with Dante, knowing all the while that it was going to make saying good-bye to him even harder. Strangely, she wouldn't trade a moment of their time together, though. It had been a magical, relaxing week.

When she'd finished work today, they'd had a latte at Brew Magic and strolled down Main Street like curious tourists. They hadn't rushed, checking out every shop that caught their interest. Dante hadn't been able to resist grabbing a lobster roll—or three. Sarah was pretty sure he was completely addicted.

He's going to miss those when he's gone.

She quickly shook off the thought, determined to not think about tomorrow, to keep living in the moment.

She still hadn't moved back into her cottage, even though it had been refurnished and it was ready. Somehow, she couldn't seem to resist spending every night with Dante. His body was like an addictive drug, and every night with him was different. Sometimes he liked it rough, sometimes it was sensual, and there were moments when it was so tender that it touched her soul. Every single time, it rocked her world.

Sarah made her way back to the front of the store just as Mara was handing Dante a large bag. Apparently, he'd found something he liked.

Mara Ross was a quiet, curvy woman with dark, shoulder-length hair that was currently pulled back in a clip at the nape of her neck. Her glasses covered sharp brown eyes, and she always smiled readily, even though she was a little bit shy.

Sarah came to the front just in time to hear Mara tell Dante, "This house was originally owned by a Sinclair. I'm surprised you never knew."

Mara knew the history of the whole town, her family having been here since the town was founded. "It was?" Sarah asked curiously.

Mara nodded at Sarah. "It belonged to a Sinclair sea captain." She looked at Dante. "How do you think your family acquired the peninsula? The captain purchased the land to build his wife and children an even bigger home, but he died at sea before it was ever built. This house was eventually sold, but the land on the peninsula stayed in the Sinclair family."

"I didn't know," Dante admitted. "My family owns property everywhere. I guess I never looked into the history."

"The peninsula has been in your family for generations, Mr. Sinclair," Mara told him informatively.

"Dante, please," he corrected with a charming smile.

Mara nodded shyly before commenting. "I think your brother, Jared, knows most of the history. He came in asking once, and I sent him to the clerk's office for the old town records. I know the basic history, but I thought some of the records might help answer his specific questions."

"Jared had questions?" Dante asked, looking perplexed.

Mara shrugged and flushed. "He seemed interested in the Sinclair history."

"How did your family end up owning the property?" Dante asked curiously.

"We don't. We've rented the house since my grandmother's day. It's actually owned by another party, someone who doesn't live here anymore." Mara frowned. "I know the house needs some work, and I do whatever I can, but the landlord just doesn't have any interest in the property anymore. He doesn't want to do much as far as repairs."

"It's a beautiful old home," Sarah said thoughtfully.

"It is," Mara agreed with an enthusiastic nod. "I just wish I could do more to fix it."

Dante thanked Mara for her help, and Sarah wandered outside with him, waving at Mara as they departed.

"What the hell is Jared up to?" Dante muttered quietly.

"Maybe he's just interested in the Sinclair history," Sarah suggested, taking Dante's outstretched hand as they walked back up Main Street.

"Doubtful," Dante replied dubiously. "More than likely he's interested in Mara. Did you see her face when she talked about him?"

"She's sweet," Sarah argued. "And that's hardly Jared's type." Somehow, she couldn't see Jared trying to romance a shy, girl-next-door kind of woman like Mara. Jared was more the type to go for style and sophistication.

"Come to think of it, I haven't seen Jared with any woman since he's been here. And you think she's not his type just because she's sweet?" Dante asked meaningfully, pulling her into an alley between shops. He crowded her, pushing her back against the brick wall. "Emily is sweet, and look what happened to Grady. You're sweet, and look what's happening to me. I think sweet women are a Sinclair downfall," he told her gruffly. "We gravitate to sweet because we're all assholes."

Sarah looked up at him, trying to swallow the gigantic lump in her throat. His expression was teasing but vulnerable. "What's happening to you?"

"I'm as pathetic as Grady," he answered, but he sounded far from unhappy. "And I need you to kiss me."

"What happens if I don't?" she asked teasingly, wanting to immediately breach the distance between their lips and devour him whole.

"I'll pass out right here in the dirt from yearning, and you'll have to resuscitate me," he replied with a wicked gleam in his eye, his body starting to sway playfully.

Laughter bubbled up inside her as Dante rolled his eyes, trying unsuccessfully to look weak.

"I'm fading," he told her dramatically.

"Don't worry. I'm a doctor. I think you'll live," she answered, still laughing as she grasped the front of his T-shirt and yanked him toward her, curling her arm around the back of his neck and bringing his mouth down to hers.

Her heart skittered as Dante immediately took control, pinning her against the wall and kissing the breath from her body with an embrace meant to brand her. He swept his tongue into her mouth, pressing his hard body against hers until she could feel his engorged cock against her lower abdomen. He teased, he possessed, and he enticed until she no longer cared who saw them. They were tucked away into an alley, but they still had a view of the entire town. It didn't seem to matter. She was swept away by the power of Dante's possessive embrace, drunk on passion.

Sarah was panting for air by the time he lifted his mouth from hers.

Dante put his head against the wall and scooped her into his arms. "I can't do it. I can't go back to Los Angeles without you, Sarah." His voice sounded tortured. "Come with me. Be with me. I do need to go back, but I can't go without you."

She took a deep breath, letting it out as she laid her head on his shoulder. They had lived for the moment, but the future was catching up with them. "When do you have to go?" she asked quietly.

"Friday," he answered hoarsely. "I have to check back into the department or put myself on leave again. They're shorthanded—"

"I understand." She cut him off, not needing to hear his explanation. Dante had responsibilities, and he was thinking about the good of the department. She didn't expect him to be any other way. Still, he was leaving Friday, and it was only two days away.

"I need you with me. I know I'm asking for a lot. But money will never be an issue. You can take as long as you need to set up your practice there. We can be together." He sounded desperate. "Come live with me, Sarah."

She sighed, trying hard not to cringe over the thought of living in a big city again. She loved living in Amesport, but she loved Dante more. Location wasn't truly going to matter if she didn't have him. "I can't leave Friday," she told him tremulously, still stunned at the fact that he was leaving and he wanted her to go with him. "I'll have to reassign my patients, take care of things here."

"But you'll come," he pushed urgently, pulling back to look down at her, his gaze intense.

"It will take me a month or two at least," she reasoned.

"Two weeks. I'll never make it a month," he insisted.

"A month or two," she repeated breathlessly, his urgency making her heart pound until she could hear the deafening sound ringing in her ears. "Dante, I can't just leave, either. I have a responsibility to my patients."

He groaned. "I know. It's just going to be hard. Literally. All the time."

She laughed and pushed against his chest. "Is that all you ever think about?"

"Since I met you . . . yeah. Pretty much," he answered unhappily.

Sarah pushed harder, getting him to step back. "I'll move as soon as I can." Relief flooded through her body, elated that she wasn't going to have to try to live without Dante.

He wants me with him.

They'd been avoiding any mention of the future, but now they were going to have one together. "Coco has to go," she mentioned casually.

"Damn dog," he muttered, but he was smiling. "I can handle that if you come with the deal."

Sarah knew Dante adored Coco. When it came to her dog, Dante was a total fraud. He fed her human food at every opportunity and spoiled the little dog rotten. "You'd miss her if she didn't come with me." She started to step carefully through the dirt alley to reenter Main Street.

"Sarah?" Dante grasped her upper arm, his voice compelling.

She gave him a questioning look.

"I'd miss more than the sex," he told her gravely. "I'd miss you."

Her heart skipped a beat as she looked at his earnest expression. "I'd miss you, too," she admitted, reaching out to run her palm over the stubble on his cheek. Living without Dante now would be like taking the light he'd lit inside her and putting it out, plunging her back into loneliness. Except now that aloneness would be all the more profound because she knew what it was like to *not* be lonely.

He took her hand from his face and kissed it before leading her back to the pavement. "Here." He handed her the bag he'd gotten at Dolls and Things.

She tilted her head and looked at him. "What is it?"

"Something you should have had a long time ago," he rumbled, waiting.

Sarah opened the bag and pulled out the gorgeous Victorian doll she'd always admired in the window of Mara's shop. "Oh my God. Dante," she breathed reverently. "I love this one." She hugged the doll for just a second, stroking the velvety softness of the dress.

Dante's eyes softened. "Why didn't you buy it?"

"I'm twenty-seven years old. It didn't—"

"Make sense?" Dante finished, grinning at her. "Woman, a lot of really good things in life don't make sense."

Like she hadn't learned that? In reality, she and Dante made no sense at all, yet they fit together perfectly. "She'll be a wonderful memento of Amesport," Sarah said, still in awe that Dante had bought her something so simple that touched her so deeply. "Thank you."

Dante shrugged. "It was nothing."

He was wrong. It was definitely . . . something. It was a gift from the heart, and it touched her soul. It was ironic that the best gifts she'd ever gotten, her bike and this beautiful doll, had come from Dante. How had he ever gotten to know her deepest desires so quickly?

She tucked the doll back into the bag carefully and Dante took it from her to carry. He snatched her other hand possessively as they continued walking back to the other end of the street, where he'd left his truck.

"You're not driving back to California?" Sarah asked curiously, wondering why he wasn't taking his truck.

"Hell, no. I'm letting Evan send it back. I'd cut off my time here if I drove. I'd already have to be on the road."

Friday. The day after tomorrow.

Really, they only had tomorrow if Dante had to leave early enough on Friday to check back into the station before the weekend. "What would you like to do tomorrow?" Sarah asked earnestly. "I'll see if I can clear most of my schedule since it will be your last day here."

"Anything I want?" Dante asked, turning his head toward her and grinning wickedly.

"Yes." Sarah knew that evil grin, and her heart started to beat faster.

"You'll be sorry," he warned her.

Sarah wasn't sorry, but she was sore the next day. Dante got his wish, and they never left the bed the entire day.

The next evening, Jared and Grady left Dante's house after saying goodbye to Dante, both of them a little solemn.

"I guess you'll be headed out pretty soon, too," Grady commented thoughtfully to Jared as he started his truck.

Honestly, Jared could have walked back to his house, but he welcomed Grady's company for a little longer. "In a while," he said noncommittally.

"Was it me, or did those two look like they've been heating up the sheets all day?" Jared had noticed that Dante looked worn out but smug, and Sarah had been more than a little tousled. "Maybe we should have called first."

Grady grinned as he turned out of Dante's driveway. "Naw. It was more fun to watch both of them scrambling and looking guilty as hell. I think we interrupted a very long good-bye." He didn't sound the least bit repentant. "Going there was pretty pointless other than the fun of watching the two of them squirm."

Jared looked at Grady's mischievous expression. And everybody thought *he* was cold? Dante was their brother, he'd almost died, and he was leaving. "We don't know when we'll see him again. I wanted to see him before he took off."

"He'll be back by Saturday," Grady said nonchalantly.

"He's leaving tomorrow," Jared answered, perplexed.

"And he'll be back by the next day. He's in love with Sarah. I don't even know if he realizes it yet, but he isn't going to be able to stay away from her for the month or two it will take her to get her business taken care of here," Grady replied, no hint of doubt in his tone. "Besides, he knows she's happy here, and I think he's been happy here, too."

"What does love have to do with anything? He has a job he needs to get back to, a life in Los Angeles," Jared grumbled, thinking Grady had temporarily lost his mind.

"You'll meet a woman someday, and she'll knock you flat on your ass," Grady commented hopefully. "She'll be a woman who will make you lose all control, make you think about nothing except her until you realize that love is the most important thing in the world."

"You're dreaming," Jared replied caustically, but he squirmed just a little in the seat of the truck, trying not to think about how badly he wanted to go back into Mara Ross's store again just to see her sweet face or listen to her voice.

She's going to hate me.

Considering his plans, his chances of Mara Ross ever speaking to him again were slim to nonexistent.

Grady pulled into Jared's driveway as he said, "Saturday. Want to place a bet?"

Do I? Oh, hell no. I've seen the way Grady is with Emily, and I see the same damn look on Dante's face.

It was highly possible that both of his brothers were lost causes now. "Shit," he mumbled as he opened the door of the truck, his sympathies with Dante if he was going to become as sappy as Grady. "No thanks. I'll pass and see what happens."

"You know I'm right," Grady said knowingly as Jared exited and slammed the door of the truck behind him.

Jared watched as Grady's taillights disappeared after he turned his truck around, seriously wondering if Grady really was right.

Another brother bites the dust?

If Dante was another victim, Jared hoped he ended up as happy as Grady was with Emily. After all Dante had been through, he deserved it. Judging by the look on Dante's face tonight, Grady was probably right. Dante probably wouldn't even last a day without Sarah.

Someday you'll meet a woman . . .

Jared didn't agree with Grady. Happiness and love weren't for guys like him. What he'd done today had solidified the fact that he was a complete and selfish prick, and he knew it. He put his hands in the pockets of his pants, his expression grim, and headed for the front door of his house, knowing that he deserved to be alone, and always would be.

CHAPTER 20

I should have told him. Why didn't I tell him?

Sarah had watched as Dante went through security and disappeared out of sight to board Grady's private jet. Right then, she'd felt the urgency pounding at her, the words stuck inside her by a lump the size of a grapefruit in her throat. She'd been afraid that it was too soon to tell Dante, too soon to let him know. Everything for them was too new, too surreal. She hadn't wanted to spoil what they had by blurting out that she loved him prematurely. Now the words were pounding at her soul.

I should have told him.

She and Dante had never talked about love. Need, want, desire . . . yes . . . but never love. Now that she wanted to tell him, needed to tell him, it was too late.

Tears streaming down her cheeks, she walked outside, making her way to the parking lot, searching absently for her car.

She, of all people, knew how short life could be. At the age of twenty-seven, she'd already had two brushes with death and knew that anything that had to be said should be said when she wanted to say it.

I was afraid.

Sarah readily admitted to herself that she would be shattered if she said those words and Dante didn't respond favorably. Now she realized it shouldn't have mattered. The fact was that she did love him, and he needed to know that, especially if he wanted them to have a life together. He'd either have to accept the way that she felt . . . or not. Admittedly, she wasn't used to loving a man, didn't know what he'd say, but she should have said it out loud. Yesterday, she'd tried to tell him with her body how much she loved him, but she'd clamped down hard on her lips to keep from letting the words escape her mouth.

I should have told him.

Sarah didn't start her vehicle. She leaned her head back against the seat and let the pain of her separation from Dante flow over her like a river. The agony was for the words that had gone unsaid. Had she told Dante that she loved him, maybe it wouldn't hurt quite as badly. But he was leaving not knowing how she felt.

Suddenly, it didn't matter that Dante had never said it, or if it was too soon. *She* needed to say it, and the compulsion was so vital that she started rifling through her purse for her cell phone. Knowing Dante's plane had already left, she sent a text message, relief flooding through her body at the thought that he would know as soon as he switched on his phone in California. It would have to be enough.

She'd say the words out loud as soon as she talked to him, but for now, she'd done everything she could to let him know the minute he was within contact range again.

"I love you," Sarah whispered, wishing she'd been able to tell him before he left.

With a long sigh, she swiped away her tears and started the car to begin her drive back home.

"I apologize for the delay, Mr. Sinclair. We'll be in the air shortly."

Dante nodded at Grady's pilot abruptly before the middle-aged man went into the cockpit, wishing the damn plane would just take off. Now that he couldn't see Sarah anymore, he was antsy and ready to get back to Los Angeles.

For what? So I can see my empty, tiny apartment's white walls without a single picture or decoration to make the place less depressing?

No doubt everything in his refrigerator would be growing mold, which wasn't anything new. He never ate at the apartment unless he brought home fast food, and leftovers eventually became rotten. Usually, he waited for the smell to get so bad that he threw the stuff out. Most times, he came back to his apartment so damn tired that the only thing that really got used there was the bed.

I need to get back to work.

Granted, Dante had liked his job, had lived for it. Now that Patrick wasn't going to be his partner anymore, he wasn't quite sure how to feel. The passion for police work was still there, but he couldn't seem to muster the same enthusiasm that he used to have, and he no longer looked forward to filling every lonely day and night with work.

I have Sarah now.

Frowning, Dante leaned his head back against the seat and closed his eyes, trying to picture a life with Sarah in Los Angeles. But all he could see was her smiling face in Amesport.

She doesn't belong in Los Angeles. She agreed to move because she wants to be with me.

Dante's chest ached as the reality of her sacrifice really sank in.

She's not a city woman. She didn't like her life in Chicago. Amesport is the first place she feels like she really fits in.

Honestly, Dante had been happy here, too. If he left, no more sounds of the ocean lulling him to sleep, no more endless bike trails waiting to be explored, no more friendly small-town folks, and—dammit—no more lobster rolls.

Joe Landon had just offered him a job again yesterday when they'd bumped into each other in town. Dante had blown him off automatically, never stopping to think of the possibilities. Admittedly, he wouldn't be handling a ton of homicides, but it would still be part of his job, and he'd be able to work on a variety of felony cases, adding some diversity and probably less intensity to his job sometimes. But it wouldn't be any less important than what he did in Los Angeles. Hell, he might even enjoy it.

And Sarah could stay here where she belongs. With me.

Really, Dante was pretty sure Amesport was where he belonged, too. Some young, eager detective would happily step into his place in Los Angeles, and Dante could stay here with Sarah. He'd have family again: Sarah, Emily, and Grady. No doubt Jared would eventually leave, but Dante missed his family more than he'd even wanted to admit. Patrick had once taken the edge off that pain, but his best friend was gone.

Dante's eyes flew open as the jet lurched, ready to taxi down the runway.

He was ready to get out of his seat when his cell phone beeped. He pulled it out of his pocket distractedly, his attention immediately diverted to the phone when he saw it was a message from Sarah:

I miss you already. I hope you'll get this message as soon as you land in Los Angeles. I need you to know that I love you. I know you didn't ask for that, and I'm not even sure you want it. Maybe it's too soon, but I need you to know. I love you, Dante.

The message nailed him right in the heart, and the organ was pounding out of his chest as he finished reading the message, tracing the words with his index finger.

She loves me.

Right at that moment there was nothing more urgent than hearing those words coming from her gorgeous lips in person. Jesus. There was nothing more critical than actually hearing her say that.

"She loves me," he rasped, trying to wrap his head around that information. Hell, he loved her, too. Probably had for a long time, although he'd never put it into words. "I should have told her."

Dante felt the plane start to turn so it could execute takeoff, and he punched the button for the cockpit. "Turn the plane around, Captain. I need to get the hell off now," he growled.

A reply came back through the intercom. "Did you forget something, Mr. Sinclair?"

I forgot a lot of damn things. I forgot to tell the woman I love how much I love her. I forgot that I like it here in Amesport. I forgot how much I miss my siblings. But aloud, he simply answered, "Yeah. Yeah, I did."

He breathed a sigh of relief as the plane started to taxi back to the airport, and he traced Sarah's words on his phone as he waited impatiently. Part of him wanted to text her back, tell her how much he loved her, too, but he needed to tell her in person, hear her say it aloud. They would be the sweetest words he'd ever heard.

Dante sprinted down the steps of the aircraft as soon as it stopped.

"What time can I expect you back, Mr. Sinclair?" the captain called after Dante.

"Never," he hollered back with an exhilaration he'd never experienced before, his heart lighter than it had ever been. "I'm already home," he said to himself as he jogged into the airport, looking around in vain for Sarah. He knew she'd already left because his flight had been delayed, but desperation made him hope.

"Need a ride?" an amused male voice asked from behind him.

Dante turned to see his brother Jared lounging casually against the wall. "What the hell are you doing here?"

"I figured you wouldn't make it into the air before you realized you wanted to stay." Jared pushed off the wall and walked the few feet that were separating them.

"How did you know?" Hell, Dante hadn't even known that himself. If he had, he would have stayed home in bed with Sarah. Why had he been such an asshole? Why hadn't he reasoned all of this out before he'd gotten on the plane?

Jared shrugged. "You love her, don't you?"

"More than anything," Dante answered honestly. "I didn't tell her."

"Let's go. I'll take you home," Jared told his brother blandly, but his lips were twitching, partially turned up in a small smile.

Dante fell into step with Jared, who was making his way to the outside entrance, still perplexed as to why his brother was here but grateful that he was. Right now all Dante wanted to do was go home to the woman he loved, and Jared would get him there as quickly as possible.

Sarah halfheartedly packed a few things into a suitcase in Dante's guest room with a sigh. He'd wanted her to stay here in his home, but she didn't really want to be here when he wasn't. It didn't feel right. She decided to put some clothes together and head back to her own cottage. Maybe she wouldn't miss him as much if she wasn't staying in his house. There were just too many memories here.

I have to quit moping. I'll see him in a few months. Missing him already isn't even logical.

Smiling sadly, she dropped a pair of shoes into the suitcase and wandered down the hall to Dante's room, knowing the old, analytical Sarah was gone. Loving Dante hadn't affected her IQ, but it had changed her priorities. Love wasn't at all reasonable. It was a complicated, messy emotion that robbed her of all sensible thought. The problem was, she didn't care, and she didn't even try not to feel it. She'd much rather feel alive and burn in Dante's arms than to go back to being the woman she was before: a woman of reason who felt . . . almost nothing.

She curled up on Dante's bed and pulled his pillow to her face, taking a long, deep, intoxicating breath of his scent until his essence made the sensitive flesh between her thighs start to pulsate with need.

Startling as Coco launched herself onto the bed, Sarah laughed when she saw the little canine and pulled the dog against her chest. "You miss him, too, don't you?" She scratched the top of Coco's head the way that Dante usually did and hugged her warm body, grateful that she wasn't the only one already pining for Dante.

The door slammed downstairs, and Sarah sat up, alarmed. She hadn't locked the door or set the alarm system. She'd only planned on being here for a short time, and the imminent danger was over. Dropping Coco gently to the floor, she rolled out of the bed and cautiously walked into the hall, taking the steps slowly. Maybe it was Jared or Grady. It could also be the lady who cleaned his house once a week, although she usually cleaned on Mondays.

Don't panic. It could be someone Dante knows. It most likely is.

Reaching the bottom of the stairs, she stopped and looked around.

Nobody.

The sliding glass door was ajar, and she wondered if someone had gone out the back. Moving closer to it, she nearly had heart failure as a large body emerged from the kitchen.

"You didn't lock the door," the large form said in an angry, guttural tone.

Dante!

Sarah's heart stuttered for just a second before it kicked in and started beating again. "Dante. Oh my God. You scared me," she told him breathlessly.

"You were here alone and you didn't lock the damn door," he grumbled.

"What are you doing here?" she asked, still stunned.

"I got your message," he said huskily, his intense, hazel eyes like liquid flames as he scanned her face.

He hadn't left yet? "You weren't already gone?"

"Almost. We were delayed, but I was already planning on coming back."

"Why?" Sarah asked, her eyes roaming covetously over the handsome, beloved face that she hadn't expected to see again for quite some time. "Did you forget something?"

"Yeah," he answered gruffly. "You."

Sarah's heart fell. "Dante, I can't leave right now—"

"I don't want you to leave. I want you to stay here with me."

She shook her head. "I don't understand."

"I mean I'm not leaving, Sarah. You belong here, and I belong with you. I want us to stay here. I want you to marry me." Dante continued to watch her expression anxiously.

Sarah tried to clamp down on the elation she felt coursing through her veins. Dante couldn't stay here. She could practice anywhere, but he had a career to worry about in Los Angeles. "Your job—"

"I can take a job here. God knows Joe Landon reminds me about the detective vacancy he has every time I see him. My job won't be the same anymore without Patrick. I think it's a good time to move on with everything, including us. I need you, Sarah. We're happy here. If you'd marry me, I'd be even happier," Dante rumbled, his expression pensive.

"We've never talked about marriage," she replied, dazed and overwhelmed. There was nothing she wanted more than to be with Dante forever, but he'd never mentioned marriage. He hadn't even told her what he'd thought about her declaration of love.

"I don't want you to resent me later, once the thrill of a new relationship wears off and you realize that you gave up a career you worked very hard for." Would he hate her later if he gave up his job in Los Angeles?

"I'm not going to resent you. In fact, you saved me. I don't want to go back," he told her roughly. "Jesus, you're stubborn. Aren't you listening to what I'm saying?"

She was definitely hearing him, but part of her was afraid this was all just a very good dream. He wanted to stay here, marry her, and build a life together? "I am listening. I'm just afraid that this is all too good to be true," she told him quietly. "I never planned on you, Dante."

"I never planned on you, either, sweetheart, but you're the best damn gift I've ever gotten," Dante rasped, holding his arms out to her.

Sarah didn't think, she just leaped, catapulting herself into Dante's strong, capable arms with a squeak of elation. Wrapping her arms around his neck, she closed her eyes, breathing in his masculine, musky smell that always made her feel like she was home, no matter where she was. She felt his arms tighten around her, holding her like he'd never let go.

"Thank fuck," Dante said in a harsh whisper against her ear. "Now tell me," Dante demanded, his voice vibrating against her temple. "I want to hear it in person."

Sarah didn't hesitate. "I love you," she said obligingly. "I don't know why it happened or when. I just do. I can't help it."

"I don't want you to help it," Dante replied in a low roar, moving her forward until her back was against the wall. "I love you, too. I love you so much that I can't think straight. Maybe if I would have actually had a brain cell left in my head, I would have realized that I really didn't want to go anywhere."

Sarah smiled against his shoulder, her heart thundering like a jackhammer. He loved her back.

He pushed slightly away from her and lifted his forest-green shirt over his head and dropped it on the floor. Then he pulled her T-shirt over her head and released the front clasp on her bra, pulling it down her arms until it dropped into the growing pile of clothing at their feet.

"What are you doing?" she asked, bemused.

He unsnapped her jeans and then his own, jerking the denim down her legs and taking her scanty panties with it. "I need to hear you say it while I'm inside you," he said, his breath coming heavily between his lips.

"What if I don't want to say it right at that moment?" she asked him teasingly.

"You will," he grunted, pinning her against the wall with her hands over her head. "Tell me," he demanded arrogantly.

Sarah's body flooded with heat and her channel clenched hard. Looking into Dante's fierce gaze, she knew she wouldn't last long. She would say it. More than likely, she'd be screaming it. "Tell me first," she requested.

"I love you," he said readily, his head lowering so that his warm breath wafted over her temple. "Now say you're going to marry me."

She was. Oh yes, she was. She wanted this delirious pleasure for the rest of her life, and she wanted this demanding but sweet man to be the father of her children someday. But mostly, she wanted him to be hers.

Shivering as his fingers moved down to stroke the wet, sensitive flesh between her thighs, she squeaked, "I want to marry you."

"And you love me," he declared hoarsely. "Tell me." His fingers found and caressed her clit.

Sarah's head fell back against the wall, giving Dante better access to her neck, and his tongue stroked over her skin, leaving a path down her neck that had her squirming. "I love you," she moaned, pulling his head up by his hair to kiss him.

He stopped teasing her and lifted her by the ass until she could feel his stiff cock probing between her legs. Immediately, she wrapped her legs around his waist, and he released her wrists, positioning himself and plunging into her channel at the same time his tongue was invading her mouth. He wasn't gentle as he matched his pummeling thrusts to the thrusts of his tongue, but the last thing she wanted right now was tenderness. Sarah wanted affirmation, proof that this was happening, that he'd really come back because he loved her. Wrapping her arms around his neck, she speared her fingers through his hair, her body clamoring for everything he had to give.

He pulled his mouth from hers, his chest heaving. "Say it," he urged forcefully, pounding his cock into her tight sheath again.

Sarah was on the precipice, ready to tip. "I love you, Dante. I love you so much," she choked out as her channel starting to clench around him. Wrapping her arms around him, she held on tight as her body started to tremble with the force of her climax.

"There'll never be another woman for me but you," Dante groaned, burying himself deep inside her, his hot release flowing out of his body and into hers.

Sarah panted as she went limp in Dante's arms. He walked with her to the couch in the living room and collapsed with a masculine sigh, bringing her down with him. Sarah rolled to his side, her body trapped between his unyielding, muscular body and the back of the couch.

Luxuriating in her warm haven and the feel of Dante against her, she traced the muscles on his sculpted chest, her face glowing with exertion and joy. "I just want you to be happy," she said solemnly, still worried that Dante was giving up a job he loved. "You love your job."

He wrapped a muscular arm around her and rolled to face her. "I am happy. Happier than I ever thought I'd be. And I did like what I did in Los Angeles, but I wasn't happy. I think I was obsessed with it because it was all I had. Patrick used to tell me if I didn't slow down, I was going to burn out by the age of thirty. I'd spend some nights in the office when I didn't need to, going over evidence that I'd already been over a hundred times before. Now I wonder if it wasn't because I had nothing at home to look forward to. I had friends, but I was only ever really close to Patrick."

Sarah's heart ached for this man who had been in a big city, surrounded by close to four million people, and had still felt alone. She could empathize very well. She'd probably been the loneliest woman in Chicago. "I felt empty, too. I guess I was just waiting for you."

"You found me. Now what are you going to do with me?" he asked.

"Love you," she sighed happily.

"Show me?" he requested in a rare, vulnerable voice.

Sarah pulled his mouth to hers and proceeded to do exactly that for the rest of the day.

EPILOGUE

"She's coming to the wedding," Sarah said as she hung up the phone, astonished.

She and Dante had finally come up for air on Sunday, and Sarah had listened to her messages, knowing she had to return her mother's call. Elaine Baxter had called five times. Sarah had finally picked up the phone to call her back, dreading the conversation.

She couldn't say that her mother had actually been ecstatic about the fact that Sarah wasn't marrying a Mensa candidate, but she'd actually agreed to attend her wedding to Dante.

After Sarah had firmly told her mother that she loved Dante, and that she was marrying him, Elaine Baxter had broken down and told Sarah how much she had loved her husband, Sarah's father, and how badly it had hurt to lose him so young. The conversation had still been stilted, but it was the first time her mother had really told Sarah that she'd loved her father.

"Is her coming to the wedding a good or bad thing?" Dante asked carefully, seated on the couch with Coco on his lap.

Sarah explained the phone call to Dante. "It's strange, but she almost sounded . . . happy when she was talking about my father. She's rarely mentioned him over the years. Maybe it was too painful."

"Are you happy she's coming?" Dante dropped Coco gently to the floor and swept Sarah into his lap.

"Yes. She might never change much, but she's my only family. She was never actually abusive. She was just so focused on my education that nothing else ever mattered. I think she thought she was doing the right thing by focusing only on my education." Elaine Baxter was never going to be a warm and fuzzy mother, but she *was* her mom. "At least I won't have to worry about her trying to marry me off anymore."

"Damn right you won't," Dante rasped. "You're mine now. We're going shopping for your ring tomorrow."

Sarah rested her head against Dante's shoulder with a smile. "She wanted to know when we're getting married and what your IQ is."

"Next week," Dante said emphatically. "And I've never been tested. I think you're smart enough for both of us, sweetheart."

Sarah rolled her eyes. "Even a small wedding takes time to arrange." In a more serious voice, she said, "And I think you've taught me a lot more than I've taught you."

"Next month," Dante grumbled unhappily.

Sarah laughed, delighted that Dante was so eager to get married. "I was thinking about next year. I'd have more time to arrange everything."

He dropped her carefully on the couch and came down on top of her, most of his weight resting on his elbows. "Try again, woman. I'm not waiting a year for you to be my wife."

Sarah looked up at his ferocious expression and smiled. "Next year. Early next year," she compromised.

"Not. Happening," Dante answered belligerently.

"I'll talk to Emily and see how quickly we can get it together. But I think she'll agree with me," Sarah answered firmly.

"I'll talk to my siblings and they'll help me get everything together within a month," Dante argued. "And I doubt Emily will agree. Grady married Emily within weeks. We Sinclairs work fast when we decide we really want something," he mentioned arrogantly.

"Do you think all of your siblings will be able to make it?" Sarah asked, concerned. She wanted Dante and his siblings to start connecting again. Obviously, they all needed each other; they just didn't want to admit it.

"I'll make sure I pick a time when they can all come," Dante replied, running a finger down her cheek softly. "I want Hope and Evan to get a chance to meet you."

"And Jared? Do you think he'll stay for a while?" Sarah queried curiously.

"Something's going on with Jared. I just haven't quite been able to figure out what he's up to. Something tells me he'll still be here," Dante answered cagily.

"What? You know something," Sarah accused.

Dante shrugged. "Not really. But I think he must have his eye on a woman who isn't easily persuaded. He's been here for weeks, and I haven't once seen him with a female."

"It hasn't been that long," Sarah argued.

"Long enough," Dante answered mysteriously, leaning down to kiss her into silence.

Sarah forgot everything the moment his lips met hers. She wrapped her arms around Dante's neck and stroked his naked, muscular back. She had gotten dressed again in a pair of jeans and summer shirt, but Dante had just pulled on a pair of jeans to come downstairs.

He pulled back to gaze into her eyes, and his look was unusually vulnerable and pleading as he said huskily, "Marry me, Sarah. Don't make me wait."

Getting married in a month wasn't reasonable, nor was it sensible. It would be a mad dash to get everything done on time, and she'd need to enlist the help of a lot of people in the community, including Emily, Randi, and Dante's siblings. No . . . it wasn't the least bit rational. But when she looked into Dante's hopeful eyes, she saw her future, a future with the man she loved.

As insane as it might be, she didn't want to wait, either, so she murmured, "Yes. We'll find a way."

His eyes lit up with a joy that warmed Sarah's heart, making her fall even further under his spell.

"Yes," he shouted triumphantly, spearing his fingers into her hair to give her a kiss that took her breath away.

Through a haze of passion, Sarah decided that sometimes madness was better than intellect. As Dante carried her back upstairs to the bedroom to show her exactly how happy he was, she was positive that in this situation, foolishness was absolutely divine.

THE END

AUTHOR ACKNOWLEDGMENTS

First and most importantly, I want to thank all of my readers for your patience and your interest in The Sinclairs. I know it took a while to get to the other siblings in The Sinclairs series, and I hope you'll find that *No Ordinary Billionaire* was worth the wait.

A huge thank-you to everyone at Montlake who helped me make it through a whole new-to-me process of editing and publishing. To my editors at Montlake, Kelli and Maria . . . my deepest gratitude for making this transition easier, and for believing in me and my books.

To my street team, Jan's Gems, all I can say is that you ladies rock. Your kindness and support amaze me every single day.

Thank you to my husband, Sri, who is seldom seen, but is always in the background doing the jobs that have to be done so that I can write. I love you and you're amazing.

I hope you all enjoy reading Dante and Sarah's book as much as I loved writing their story.

—Jan (J.S. Scott)

ABOUT THE AUTHOR

Photo © 2013 Carrie Herzog

J.S. "Jan" Scott is a *New York Times* and *USA Today* bestselling romance author. She's an avid reader of all types of books and other forms of literature, but romance has always been her genre of choice. Creating what she loves to read, Jan writes both contemporary and paranormal romances. They are almost always steamy, generally feature an alpha male, and have a happily ever after because she just can't seem to write them any other way!

Jan loves to connect with readers.

You can visit her at:

Website: www.authorjsscott.com

Facebook: facebook.com/authorjsscott

You can also tweet @AuthorJSScott

For updates on new releases, sales, and giveaways, please sign up for Jan's newsletter by going to http://eepurl.com/KhsSD

Printed in Poland
by Amazon Fulfillment
Poland Sp. z o.o., Wrocław